WREAKING VENGEANCE

WREAKING VENGEANCE

A Joe Erickson Mystery

Lynn-Steven Johanson

WREAKING VENGEANCE

A Joe Erickson Mystery

Lynn-Steven Johanson

First published by Level Best Books 2026

This novel is entirely a work of fiction. The names, characters, and incidents portrayed in it are the work of the author's imagination. Any resemblance to actual persons, living or dead, events, or localities is entirely coincidental.

Author Photo Credit: Aaron Johanson

First edition

ISBN: 979-8-89820-227-9

Cover art by Level Best Designs

This book was professionally typeset on Reedsy.
Find out more at reedsy.com

In memory of Rex McGraw, Richard Nichols, and William R. Morgan

Praise for Wreaking Vengeance

"The gruesome murder of a wealthy young widow from Chicago's Gold Coast makes no sense. Who would kill a dog breeder and dog show judge? But when a second and then a third victim turn up, Chicago police detective Joe Erickson and his partner Sam Renaldo race to find a connection. Fans of the Joe Erickson Mysteries will love this fast-paced, tightly plotted police procedural."—Connie Berry, *USA Today* bestselling author of the Kate Hamilton Mysteries

HEADS ARE ROLLING IN THE WINDY CITY! "Chicago is under siege as a killer leaves behind a trail of terror—and severed heads. Detectives Joe Erickson and Sam Renaldo chase one dead end after another until a disturbing truth surfaces. When justice collides with vengeance, the investigation grows personal, forcing the detectives into a desperate race against time to prevent another brutal decapitation. The clock is ticking, and the next name on the list could already be marked. Author Lynn Johanson delivers a gritty, immersive look at police work on Chicago's unforgiving streets, taking readers deep into the details of an investigator's job, and showcasing the relentless pressure of the hunt."—**Kerry Peresta**, author of the Olivia Callahan Suspense series

Chapter One

Like a leopard concealed in tall grass, head low and frozen in an ambush position, he was ready to spring forward and pounce on his prey. Hidden from view by overgrown yew shrubs and boulders adjacent to the bike path, he waited in anticipation. His thoughts were winding him tighter and tighter. Would she be riding today? Was she riding alone? Would there be another rider a short distance behind her and thwart his chances once again? Today marked his third attempt, and by now, the hunter's frustration had grown into anger.

Glancing to his right, he spotted her in the distance. This time, no other riders or joggers were in view. She wore the same distinctive red and white helmet, and her long blonde hair trailed out the back. The pressure was on. Timing was critical. He had to spring from his hiding place at just the right moment.

She drew closer. After pulling the hood of his black sweatshirt over his head and tying the string, he slipped on his gloves and drew his knife from the scabbard on his belt, gripping it tightly with his left hand. Adrenalin pulsed through his body, and he felt rivulets of sweat trickling down from his armpits.

Closer she came. Closer. Closer. And then…he made his move, springing out from behind the yew and knocking her off her bike. She didn't know what hit her and had no chance to respond before he plunged the knife into her chest over and over again.

Slitting the strap to her helmet and ripping it away, he grabbed her by the hair, lifted her head, and began to cut and slice. The knife was razor sharp, and in seconds, it was done. He looked down the bike path in each direction. Clear. Holding her severed head by the hair, he ran to the edge of the lake, scampered fifty yards down the rocky shore, and heaved the head as far as he could out into the water. Splash! "Fucking bitch," he mumbled as he watched her head sink below the surface.

Returning to the bike path, he stopped, looking left and right. Seeing a jogger approaching in the distance, he gasped. Near panic, he began making his escape by running across the path into a small grove of trees that stood a short distance away. Blood covered his clothes and shoes, but by the time he exited the trees, he had already peeled off the sweats covering his t-shirt and jeans. Pulling a garbage bag from his pants pocket, he shoved his sweats, mask, gloves, and knife into it and made his way toward the parking lot. His bloody tennis shoes were the only incriminating evidence now. He slipped into other shoes, placing the bloody ones into the bag before dropping it into his car's trunk.

His hands shook as he tried to insert the key into the ignition. Still breathing heavily from running, he took a few deep breaths before starting the car. Pulling the shifter into reverse, he backed out of the parking space. He needed to avoid thinking about what he had done and concentrate on his getaway. Focus. Be calm. No mistakes. Not now. His plan had worked. He could relive his triumph later.

By the time he had driven several blocks away, the jogger he saw in the distance had come upon the victim. Horrified, he called 9-1-1 and reported the heinous crime. The first officers on the scene were taken aback by the gruesome death and immediately called in the dicks.

* * *

Joe was enjoying the drive to his office on Belmont. The sound of his supercharged Camaro's exhaust was music to his ears as he accelerated down the street. He was returning to work after his two days off. He and Destiny, his life partner, had spent a relaxing time together. But his upbeat mood would not last long. As soon as he sat down at his desk, he received a call about a homicide on a bike trail near the shore of Lake Michigan.

Joe secured the keys to their squad car and met his partner, Sam Renaldo, as he was entering the building.

"We caught one already," said Joe.

"Already?" asked Sam.

"Yeah. Let's go."

Sam made a quick turn and followed Joe out the door. Arriving at the crime scene fifteen minutes later, they saw officers had shut down the bike path in each direction and strung up crime scene tape. They approached a large, middle-aged officer standing outside the taped-off area. His name badge read "Fuller."

"What have we got?" asked Joe.

"Man! I haven't seen anything this bad before," replied Fuller. "The blood…"

"Besides the blood," pressed Sam, impatient that he had not answered Joe's question.

"A woman…she was decapitated."

"Decapitated?" Joe repeated in surprise.

"Yeah. Uh, it's bad. See for yourself," said Fuller as he lifted the crime scene tape for them to duck under.

Joe and Sam approached the body, which was lying partially off the path. Blood was everywhere, and the coppery smell of it hovered in the air. Stopping a short distance away so as not to contaminate the scene, they could see the Spandex-clad body was intact, but the head was missing.

"This is bad," repeated Sam.

"Yeah," acknowledged Joe as he looked around for the victim's head. They walked to the other side of the taped-off area. Another officer, a young guy, looked pale as he approached them. He stopped a short distance away and asked, "You the detectives?"

"Yeah," replied Joe. "Erickson and Renaldo. Who are you?"

"Officer Conlin."

"You look a little green around the gills, Conlin."

"I haven't seen anything like this before."

"Get used to it. You'll eventually see worse."

"You're not gonna puke, are you?" asked Sam.

"Already did."

Joe glanced at Sam and saw him chuckle silently in response.

"Did you look to see if the victim's severed head was around anywhere?" asked Joe.

"We checked. Didn't see it anywhere nearby. Her helmet's lying over there, but what was in it doesn't seem to be around."

"Any witnesses?"

"Yes, sir. One. Over there," he said, indicating a man sitting on a boulder. "His name is Derek Chamberlain."

Joe and Sam approached Chamberlain, who was looking at his cell phone. He was fifty-something and dressed in black and green jogging togs. After identifying themselves, Joe said, "Tell us what you saw, Mr. Chamberlain."

Putting his phone in his pocket, Chamberlain said, "Well…I jog here almost every day, and as I was running, I saw someone near the body. When he saw me, he ran off."

"It was a man?" asked Sam.

"Well, I assume so. But I was too far away to be sure."

"Can you describe him?" asked Joe.

Chamberlain ran his fingers through his salt and pepper hair. "Reminded me of a Ninja."

"A Ninja?"

"Well, yeah."

"What do you mean by that?"

"I'm not saying it was one. But he was wearing all black—black hoodie, sweatpants, and a black ski mask."

"A Ninja, huh?" said Sam.

"Sort of reminded me of one. Yeah."

"Did he have a sword?"

"Not that I saw."

"In what direction did he run?" asked Joe.

"Up there," said Chamberlain, pointing toward the trees on the west side of the bike path. "Like I said, I was pretty far away when I first noticed him. But it stuck with me since he looked like a Ninja. Then I got closer and saw…God! I'll never get this out of my head."

Joe and Sam questioned Chamberlain further, but did not gain any information pertinent to the case. They gave him their cards and told him to contact them if he remembered anything else.

Joe strolled over to check out the bicycle that lay a short distance from the body. Looking it over, he saw it was a Roubaix SL8 Comp model. Never having heard of such a bicycle, he made a quick internet search on his phone and found that this model sold new for over five thousand dollars.

"Holy shit," Joe mumbled to himself, reacting to the price.

Overhearing him, Sam asked, "What is it?"

"This is a five-thousand-dollar bicycle."

"No shit? She a professional cyclist or something?"

"Or something. No beginner, that's for sure."

"I'm surprised the offender didn't take it, given its value."

"Maybe his objective was committing murder, not theft."

"A bike like that one would probably be easy to trace," replied Sam. "I'll bet there's not a lot of them around. Hard to fence."

"Yeah, if he even knew what it was."

Upon closer inspection, Joe saw a white oval sticker from an Owens Cycle Shop near the pedal assembly. He noted it. As he was returning his notebook to his pocket, he turned and saw Kendra Solitsky, the Medical Examiner, walking toward them, pulling a two-wheeled cart containing her equipment. Her auburn hair had been trimmed shorter since the last time he had seen her. Joe and Sam walked back and slipped under the crime scene tape.

"Good morning, gentlemen," she said. "Ruining my morning again?"

"Joe smiled. "Good morning to you, too."

"Well?"

"It's a wonderful day in the neighborhood," remarked Sam.

She looked past the crime scene tape and saw all the blood. "What the hell happened?"

"Someone decapitated a cyclist this morning," replied Joe.

Shaking her head, she said, "It's never a simple heart attack with you guys, is it?"

"The rookies get the easy ones. This calls for the pros."

"Well…no time like the present," she said, removing Tyvek coveralls, booties, and nitrile gloves from her pack. When she was fully suited up, Joe lifted the crime scene tape for her, and Kendra pulled her equipment cart under it. She began by photographing the scene in detail before examining the body. Fifteen minutes later, she walked to the edge of the tape and removed her mask.

Looking at Joe and Sam, she said, "Liver temp indicates death occurred about two hours ago. I'm calling in the Evidence Techs. Given the situation, they'll need to process the scene. Maybe they can locate the victim's head."

"You have an ID for her?" asked Sam.

"Here," replied Kendra, handing him a plastic sleeve containing a driver's license. "Found this in her fanny pack. Jennifer Anne Logan. Nice looking woman, according to her photo."

Seeing her address, Sam looked at Joe and said, "Near North Side address. Gold Coast resident."

"Great," replied Joe. Chicago's Gold Coast is one of the most affluent neighborhoods in the country, second only to Manhattan's Upper East Side. They did not like dealing with its wealthy residents since many did not like talking to the police and often referred them to their attorneys. Hopefully, this would not be the case.

"Looks to me like she might've been ambushed by the offender," said Joe. "Let's look around."

While Kendra waited for Evidence Techs to arrive, Joe and Sam split up, with Sam taking the area leading to the lake and Joe taking the area west of the path. Joe looked around the shrubs bordering the bike path and saw a yew with broken branches. Behind one of them, he noticed a partial shoeprint in the dirt. The area was directly across from where the victim's body lay. Casting the shoeprint fell under the purview of the Evidence Techs.

They scoured the area around the crime scene and found a blood trail leading to the lake. They notified Kendra. Half an hour later, Evidence

Technicians Art Casey and Jerry Bristow arrived to process the scene. They worked in conjunction with Kendra, collecting evidence. Two hours later, they released the body, and Kendra rolled the gurney with the black body bag to the medical examiner's van, which was parked about fifty yards away.

Joe followed her to the van. "You'll let me know about the autopsy, right?"

"I'll do that," replied Kendra as she pushed the gurney into the van. She loaded her equipment and closed the van's back doors. Turning to Joe, she continued, "It will be hard to complete an autopsy without the head. I'm going to hold off a day or two to see if it's been found."

"I think there's a good chance it was thrown into the lake, given the blood trail," said Joe.

"Art mentioned calling in a diver to search the shore area. One can hope."

Joe alerted Art to the footprints he had found and then let him get to work. They did not want to disturb either Art or Jerry while they were working, so they searched a parking lot behind some trees located a short distance from the crime scene. They looked for surveillance video cameras in case the offender had come into the parking lot. There were none. They canvassed the area, asking business owners if they had seen someone wearing black sweat clothes or anyone suspicious lurking about. No luck.

As they searched the parking lot, Joe spotted what looked like blood by one of the parking spaces.

When they returned to the crime scene, Art and Jerry were finishing up their work and securing samples for analysis.

"I think there's some blood in the parking lot," said Sam.

"You'll need to show me where it is," said Art.

"We cast the shoeprint behind the yew and additional shoeprints around the blood trail leading to the rocky shore," said Jerry.

"We took a lot of blood samples from the area. Maybe the offender left some DNA," said Art. "We're taking the bicycle in for further analysis in our lab."

"Be careful with it," said Joe. "It's a very expensive bike."

"How expensive?"

"You can't buy a new one for less than five grand."

"Then I shouldn't try to ride it, huh?" quipped Art.

"Probably not. It's a little more sophisticated than the three-wheeler you ride."

"You're as funny as a colostomy bag, Joe."

"Did you get anything worthwhile, Jerry?" asked Sam.

"It's tough to get evidence from an outdoor crime scene like this," replied Jerry. "We have a lot of blood samples to analyze and several castings of shoeprints that may or may not belong to the offender. Maybe Kendra can turn up something significant when she does the post."

"What about the missing head?"

"I've called in a diver to check the shore. We're staying until he completes his search. I'll let you know if it's found."

Joe escorted Art to the parking lot and showed him the suspected blood evidence. Art kneeled and tested it.

"It's blood," said Art. "Good catch."

Art took a sample and said they would test it against the blood collected at the scene.

By the time the cleanup crew had finished, the scene was released. Joe and Sam were ready to return their squad car to Area 3 and head home. Tomorrow, they would need to notify the victim's next of kin.

Chapter Two

J oe pulled his Camaro into the driveway of the house he shared with Destiny Alexander. He had called her before leaving his Area 3 office to let her know he was on his way home. When he entered from the garage, the usual greeting he received from Autumn, their Lhasa Apso, did not happen, and he assumed Destiny must be walking her around the block. Nice, he thought. He was tired and wasn't looking forward to walking the dog, even though it was just around the block.

He poured himself a glass of water from the pitcher in the refrigerator and drank the whole thing. He did not realize he was so thirsty, but working outside on a sunny day with no break or lunch had dehydrated him. After downing the water, Joe poured himself a glass of Pinot Noir and sat down on a stool at the island to relax and wait for Destiny and Autumn to return.

Before he had time to sip his wine, he heard the front door open, and Autumn came running in, panting and jumping up on his leg, begging for attention. Destiny followed close behind.

"Hi," she said, leaning over and giving him a kiss. "Busy day?"

"Yeah. Good to be home," said Joe.

"You'd better give Autumn some attention before she starts barking at you."

"Has she had a T-R-E-A-T yet?" asked Joe, spelling it out so Autumn would not respond to the word.

"No."

Joe reached down and petted Autumn, speaking to her and rubbing her ears. Then he said the magic word. "You want a 'treat?'"

Autumn gave him a woof and began turning in circles. Getting up from his stool, he dug a treat from a package in the cupboard. Looking down at her, he said, "Speak." Autumn replied with another "woof," and Joe handed her the bone-shaped treat. She snatched it from his fingers, carried it over to her bed, and started crunching on it. This had become a ritual each night when he came home.

"You said you had a busy day," said Destiny. "Care to share?"

"Yeah, but not before dinner."

"That bad?"

"Yeah. That bad," he replied as he reached for his glass.

Destiny poured herself a glass of white wine from a bottle in the refrigerator and sat beside him. "Tell you what…Why don't I cook tonight so you can relax? You look tired."

"Thanks, but I think it would be better if I shared the cooking duties. That way, I can get my mind off today's work."

Joe wasn't usually bothered by the murders he was called on to investigate. Given his many years working homicide, he had seen almost everything, and he seldom had trouble compartmentalizing. Close the door, and it is out of mind. But today's murder had stuck to him like a leech. He needed a distraction.

"You want to try that new salmon recipe tonight?" asked Destiny.

"Yeah. I would."

"You prepare the salmon, and I'll make that roasted brussels sprout dish we like. And we already have salad fixings and some of your vinaigrette left over from yesterday."

"Sounds good," said Joe. "I've been wanting to try that recipe."

Their dinner of salmon with creamy white wine sauce and roasted brussels sprouts with balsamic vinegar and honey was declared fit for a king. Afterward, they cleaned up the kitchen and adjourned to the couch in the living room.

Destiny snuggled up to Joe and said, "I've never seen you bothered by an investigation before. What happened?"

"Oh…A cyclist was killed on a bike path along Lake Michigan early this morning. After stabbing her in the chest multiple times, the offender decapitated her."

"Really!"

"And the victim's head is currently unaccounted for."

"Omigod."

"There's a good possibility it was thrown in the lake. Evidence techs requested a diver, but I haven't heard they found anything."

"That's terrible. Any witnesses?"

"One. A jogger. He saw a guy run from the scene. Said he looked like a ninja."

"A ninja," she said, unable to stifle an incredulous response.

Joe slowly shook his head. "I know it sounds crazy. But that's how he described him."

Destiny thought for a moment and then said, "Ninjas have been associated with deaths and beheadings. You think there could be someone so obsessed with Japanese warrior culture that he sees himself as a ninja assassin and has started acting out?"

Joe sighed. "Oh, man. I hope not. That's all we need…some nutcase running around beheading people."

"Did your witness specifically describe what he was wearing?"

"Yeah. Black hoodie, sweatpants, black ski mask."

"Sword?"

"No. Sam asked about that, and he said he didn't see a sword or any other weapon. I doubt the offender was acting out as a ninja. More like some guy wearing black sweats and a ski mask."

"Did he see him attack the woman?"

"No, he reported seeing the suspect crossing the bike path and running away the moment he saw him."

Destiny nodded as she considered the situation.

"You know," said Joe, "I can understand someone having a motive and using a knife to kill a person. I've seen it before. It's up close and personal. But why would the offender take the time to decapitate the victim after he killed her? It seems so extreme."

"Well, it could be a multitude of reasons. Mental illness, hate, anger, wishing to make a statement of some kind, acting out, throwing off the police. You name it. Hopefully, your investigation will determine a motive."

"In other words, it could be anything."

"More or less."

"Great."

"Sorry, but without more information, it's nearly impossible to pinpoint the reason. A stabbing like the one you described reflects a high degree of emotionally charged aggression that probably built up over time. You're right about it being up close and personal. There's a good chance it wasn't a random act."

"Targeted attack?"

"Yes. Unless it was the work of someone deranged, then logical thinking goes out the window."

"I'll share this with Sam," said Joe. "Maybe we'll learn something that'll give us a lead in the coming days."

Chapter Three

Joe met with Sam first thing in the morning, and they decided to research their victim, Jennifer Anne Logan, before contacting anyone who may be living at her residence. Joe suggested they split the research topics, with Sam focusing on her finances and Joe researching her biographical data.

They reconvened two hours later with the information they had acquired.

Joe began. "Jennifer Anne Logan was born in Chicago forty-five years ago to Patrick and Kathleen McDonald, now deceased. She has one sibling, a sister named Cassidy. Logan graduated from Northwestern University and shortly after began working in real estate."

"Her future husband's company," interjected Sam.

"Yeah," continued Joe. "Nineteen years ago, she married the multi-millionaire real estate developer William J. Logan. He was twenty-four years her senior."

"Must have been love," quipped Sam.

"So cynical," kidded Joe.

" Sometimes, love is green."

Joe acknowledged Sam's cynical comment with a chuckle and then continued. "Anyway, her husband died five years ago, and she never remarried. She inherited the majority of his wealth and retired from the real estate business. Here's an interesting tidbit: she was a dog show judge. Probably didn't need to work, given her late husband's wealth."

"You got that right," said Sam. "Her husband never had children with his first wife. She was killed in a car-pedestrian accident. Sometime after he married Logan, he was diagnosed with ALS, and he made her the co-owner of his company and transferred his assets to her name several years before he died. After he passed, she sold his real estate company for an undisclosed amount. Her net worth has been estimated to be well over one hundred million dollars. She's been living off the proceeds from her investments and some income from her judging assignments."

Once they had learned a few things about Jennifer Logan, Joe and Sam prepared to drive to the address listed on her driver's license. She lived on North Dearborn Parkway in the exclusive Gold Coast neighborhood.

When they pulled up to the tan stone mansion, Sam remarked, "So, this is how the other half lives."

"Try the top two percent," added Joe. "It would take a serious income just to pay the taxes on a place like this."

Walking to the black wrought iron fence that fronted all the homes on the block, Joe released the gate, and they walked up the stone steps to the door. After ringing the doorbell several times, the only response was the faint sound of a dog barking inside.

Sam looked at Joe and said, "Let's try around back."

When they reached the beautifully landscaped backyard, they walked up the steps to the French doors, peered through the glass, and knocked. Nothing. They were about ready to leave when they saw a woman step into view.

Joe knocked loudly, held up his badge against the glass, and yelled, "Hello! Chicago Police Department!" The woman froze.

"Chicago PD. Open up!"

She responded to his command, slowly walked to the door, and opened it a crack.

"Yes, can I help?" she said with a heavy Hispanic accent.

Joe and Sam were holding up their IDs for her to see. "Chicago Police Department," repeated Joe. "I'm Detective Erickson, and this is my partner, Detective Renaldo. Do you live here?"

"Oh, no. I clean house," she replied. Sam gave Joe a look.

"¿Podemos entrar?" asked Sam in Spanish. (Can we come in?)

"Supongo," she replied. (I suppose.) Clearly uncomfortable letting them in, she reluctantly opened the door and stepped back.

Once inside, Joe asked, "Is this where Jennifer Logan lives?"

"Yes, I clean house Wednesdays."

"What's your name?"

She looked even more nervous, so Sam spoke to her in Spanish again. "No te preocupes, no somos de Inmigración." (Don't worry. We aren't from Immigration.)

She looked relieved and then smiled, "Okay."

Joe repeated his question. "What's your name?"

She looked at Sam for guidance, and he nodded. Then she looked back at Joe and said, "Elena Sanchez."

"Thank you, Elena. Does anyone else live here besides Jennifer Logan?"

"No. Just her."

Joe looked at Sam and said, "You want to explain to her what happened?"

"Sure." Sam spoke to her in Spanish, informing her about her employer's death. After hearing the news, Sanchez collapsed into a nearby chair and began crying. Sam talked with her while Joe looked on, feeling helpless since he didn't speak Spanish.

"Surely Logan had an attorney," said Joe. "I'm going to look for her office and see if I can find anything about next of kin or an attorney."

Sam asked Sanchez if Logan had an office, and she indicated it was upstairs.

Joe slipped on gloves as he began climbing the curved Art Deco staircase to the second floor. After opening doors and finding four bedrooms, each with a bathroom and a fireplace, Joe opened the door to the one nearest the stairs and saw it was used as an office. *Should have opened this door first,* he thought. It was an impressive room with a fireplace, attached bathroom, leather couch, and a huge flatscreen television on the wall opposite an antique walnut partners' desk. The leather desktop was replete with pictures, a computer, a printer, and a Rolodex containing cards with names, addresses, and phone numbers. One wall was filled with photographs of dogs, award plaques, rosette ribbons, and shelves with silver bowls, platters, and wine bucket trophies.

Picking his way through the Rolodex was tedious, but Joe finally found information under "F" for the Fredericks Law Office. He leaned down and took a photo of the card with his phone's camera. Continuing his search, he found most of the names on the cards meant nothing to him. Just names and phone numbers, some of which were probably those recorded by her late businessman husband. Construction firms, banks, and city offices.

He kept flipping through the cards, and under R, he found the RCR Financial Group. Assuming they may have something to do with managing her assets, he took a photo of that card, too.

They needed to access her computer as well as her cell phone, which Kendra found in Logan's fanny pack. But first, they would need to get a search warrant for those two items. Then, the phone and computer would be sent out to the state's Regional Computer Forensics Laboratory, where technicians would open the devices and download her messages. Typically, the technicians would have her messages back to the detectives in about one week's time.

Joe looked up the address of the Fredericks Law Office, which was located in the Loop on South Wabash. He noted the location of both the law office and the financial group since only their phone numbers and email addresses were recorded on the Rolodex cards.

Looking through the desk, he found information about dogs, upcoming judging assignments, several breed standards, and letters from the American Kennel Club. Photos displayed on her desk showed an attractive blonde-haired woman winning awards at dog shows with small black dogs posed on a raised platform surrounded by flowers. Older men and women in each photo held rosette ribbons and silver trophies, and the placards next to the dogs read, "Best in Show." The woman holding the dog's leash in each photo resembled Logan's driver's license photo. But while looking around the room, Joe did not see any pictures of her late husband anywhere. Interesting.

He stepped to a polished, antique wooden file cabinet, but found it locked. They would need a search warrant for that as well.

After he finished surveying the room, Joe went back downstairs. Sam and Elena Sanchez were sitting next to each other, conversing in Spanish. Hearing dogs barking, he asked, "Where are the dogs?"

"Downstairs," replied Sanchez, and she pointed to a door.

Opening the door, Joe descended the steps to the basement level. He opened one door and found a well-stocked wine cellar. Then he opened another door that revealed the home's mechanical room with a furnace and water heating systems. Again, he heard the sounds of dogs barking and opened yet another door. Inside were a series of kennel cages containing two cute little black dogs. Their appearance was scruffy, and their heads sported long, erect ears with hair jutting from their cheeks and chins. When he entered the room, they began barking aggressively and nonstop. Walking to their cages, he put up his hands for them to smell, and he began talking to them in a gentle voice, the same voice he used with his own dog. At first, they barked furiously, but when their curiosity got the better of them, they eventually calmed down, and most of their barking ceased.

Looking around the room, Joe saw photos of little black dogs mounted on the wall and a framed poster with a picture resembling the dogs in the cages. In large letters, it read, "Love is an Affenpinscher." Storage cabinets lined another wall, and a grooming table and stool sat in the middle of the room. A large-screen television hung from a wall opposite the grooming table.

He looked up "Affenpinscher" on his phone and found pictures of dogs that resembled the ones inside the cages. Putting his hands up to the cages once again, Joe said, "So, you're Affenpinschers, huh?" They sniffed his hands, and one of them stuck its nose up to the door and licked his hand.

At that moment, Sanchez and Sam entered the room, and the dogs began barking like crazy.

"I just got them quieted down, " said Joe.

"What are you? The dog whisperer?" joked Sam.

"Sanchez walked up to the cages and said sternly, "Shh! No bark!" And the little dogs obeyed, giving only occasional woofs and snorts.

"She's the dog whisperer," said Joe.

Sanchez spoke to the dogs in Spanish, and they seemed to pay attention, their bright eyes focused on her as she spoke. After a few moments, she turned to the detectives. "I take care of them. When Miss Jennifer is gone. Good dogs."

"Then, you have a key to the house?" asked Sam.

"I know code to lock. On front door."

They left the basement area and climbed to the main floor, where they discussed the situation with her. Someone would need to return to the house every day to feed and exercise the dogs until arrangements could be made for them. "I do that," she said.

Once they had finished speaking with Sanchez and were walking to their car, Joe asked, "You think she can be trusted? That house has a lot of valuables in it."

"Logan gave her the combination to the front door," said Sam. "And she trusted her to care for her dogs when she was gone. I'd say so."

"You get her address information?"

"Yeah. In speaking with her, I sensed she's trustworthy."

Once they were seated in the car, Sam asked, "Where to now, Boss?"

"Let's grab some lunch. I found the name and address of an attorney's office and an investment firm in the Rolodex on her desk. I think we should pay the attorney's office a visit."

Following a quick lunch, they drove to the Wabash Avenue address for the Fredericks Law Office and took the elevator to the fifth floor. The doors opened onto a posh lobby with leather chairs sitting on large oriental rugs. Seeing the receptionist's desk, they walked up to it. Upon seeing them, a woman in her thirties stood and greeted them.

"Good morning," she said with a smile. "Do you have an appointment?"

Joe and Sam showed their IDs, and Joe said, "Chicago PD. We need to speak with someone who represents Jennifer Logan."

Her eyebrows raised as she said, "Oh. Well, okay. That would be Mr. Benowitz. Let me check if he's available."

She sat down, picked up the phone, and pushed several buttons. After a moment, she said, "There are two detectives from the police department who've asked to see Jennifer Logan's attorney." She listened for a moment and then said, "They didn't say." Nodding, she listened for a few seconds and replied, "Okay."

After replacing the receiver, she stood and said, "He can see you now. If you'll follow me, please?" Leading them down a hallway, they stopped at a door, which she partly opened, and said, "Mr. Benowitz?"

A male voice inside said, "Send them in."

She smiled and opened the door for them. They stepped through into a large office, revealing a short, balding man around sixty who was rounding his desk. He approached them and said, "I'm Simon Benowitz, Ms. Logan's attorney."

Holding up their IDs, Joe and Sam introduced themselves. "Thank you for seeing us," said Joe.

Straightening his tie, he said, "You're here because you have an interest in my client?"

"In a manner of speaking," replied Joe. "I regret to inform you Ms. Logan was found murdered yesterday."

Silence as the news sank in. After a moment, Benowitz said, "Uh…Why don't we sit down over here," indicating the leather couch and chairs.

After they were seated, Benowitz asked, "You said she was murdered?"

"She was. We're investigating the case," replied Sam.

"This is terrible. I just spoke to her last week. What happened?"

"She was killed by an assailant while riding her bicycle along a bike path near the lake," said Joe, choosing to leave the decapitation detail out of his explanation.

"Oh, my…Do you have a suspect?"

"Not yet," said Sam.

"It's a little early in our investigation," added Joe. "But we're following up on several leads."

"I see."

"It would be helpful if you could provide us with contact information regarding her next of kin," continued Joe. "She apparently has a sister?"

"That's correct. Cassidy. Cassidy O'Leary. She lives with her husband in Hinsdale. Let me get her address information for you. She'd be her next of kin." Benowitz rose from his chair, sat down at his desk, and began working his keyboard. After a few moments, the printer spat out a sheet of paper, which Benowitz handed to Joe.

"That's her phone number and address."

"Were they close?" asked Sam. "Ms. Logan and her sister?"

"No. They were somewhat estranged, sorry to say."

"Was there any hostility between the two?"

"Hostility? Not that I know of. Jennifer told me once they'd simply grown apart over the years. Cassidy didn't care for Jennifer's husband. I think that was the main reason."

"Oh?"

"You know why?" asked Joe.

"Will was rather pompous and often condescending toward others."

"I know you can't reveal details, but did she have a will?"

"She did. She had us draw it up after her husband passed away."

"Good to know."

"Will her death be in the news today?" asked Benowitz.

"The crime may be reported, but her identity hasn't been released. That's why we need to contact her sister right away," replied Sam.

"Is there anyone else we need to contact?" asked Joe.

"Family, no. Her parents are gone, and she only has the one sister. But, given her wealth, her financial advisor needs to be notified. I can do that for you."

"Would that be RCR Financial Group?"

"I see you've done your homework. Yes. I've spoken to Bill Morgan many times over there. He'll be devastated."

"We appreciate your help."

"Is there anything about Ms. Logan we need to know?"

"Well, she never remarried after Will passed. But she had a number of men she had relationships with. But they only lasted a short time."

"She shared that with you?" asked Sam.

"Let's just say she was rather candid about her love life."

"She have any enemies? Men who didn't take a breakup well?"

"I'm afraid I can't respond to that. I have no idea."

"Any names come to mind?"

Benowitz chuckled. "I know what you're looking for, but while she was forthcoming about finding new lovers, she was discreet about who they were."

"I see."

Joe looked at Sam and asked, "You have any other questions for Mr. Benowitz?"

"Not at this time."

Rising from their chairs, they thanked him for answering their questions. As they were getting off the elevator, Joe asked, "You think a relationship gone bad could be the motive behind her death?"

"I think we need to find out who her lovers were. The male ego can be a fragile thing."

"You think one of them could've been angry enough to cut her head off?"

"It's possible, I suppose," replied Sam.

Looking at the paper with her sister's address, Joe said, "I think we need to make a trip to Hinsdale."

Looking at his watch, Sam replied, "Yeah, but it's a little late in the day to drive up there."

"Right. We'd better head back to the office. We can make the notification tomorrow."

Chapter Four

The city of Hinsdale lies 20 miles from the Loop, but given traffic on the Eisenhower Expressway, travel there would normally take around forty minutes. Hinsdale is one of the wealthiest communities in Illinois, with a population of slightly over 17,000.

The GPS unit guided Joe and Sam to Cassidy O'Leary's address, a mansion located on Woodmere Drive. The light tan stone and stucco exterior was accented by perfectly manicured shrubbery and landscaping.

When their car came to a stop, Sam looked at the house and said, "Looks like Logan's sister did all right for herself."

"Yeah," replied Joe. "Quite impressive."

They walked up to the dark brown, mahogany arch-top front doors. Moments after they rang the bell, one of the double doors opened to reveal a man in his mid-forties wearing khaki shorts and an olive-green golf shirt.

"If you're selling something, we're not interested." He was about to shut the door when Joe and Sam held up their IDs. "Chicago PD, sir," said Joe. "Detectives Erickson and Renaldo. We're here to speak with Cassidy O'Leary. Is she here?"

Surprised by their request, he responded, "Uh…yeah. She is."

"We need to speak with her."

"What's this about?" he asked.

"Official police business," stated Sam. "And you are?"

"Sean O'Leary. Her husband."

"Okay, Mr. O'Leary. Would you tell your wife we're here and need to speak with her?"

He looked displeased by their presence, but he begrudgingly agreed, saying, "All right. Hold on a minute, and I'll get her."

O'Leary closed the door, and a couple of minutes later, both of the double doors opened, revealing O'Leary and a woman standing beside him, smartly dressed in a blue floral top and coordinated shorts."

"I'm Cassidy O'Leary," said the woman. She was attractive, about forty, with ash-blonde hair and large expressive eyes. "You told my husband you wished to speak with me?"

"Yes," said Joe. "Can we come in?"

Cassidy and her husband exchanged glances and then stepped away from the doors, allowing Joe and Sam to enter.

Once inside the foyer, Joe said, "We're here to deliver some bad news, I'm afraid. There's no easy way to say this, but your sister, Jennifer Logan, was killed day before yesterday."

Silence.

"Omigod," said O'Leary softly. He put his arm around his wife, who was covering her mouth with her hands, her eyes revealing the shock.

"What happened?" he asked.

"I'm sorry to report her death was a homicide," explained Sam. "Our condolences."

"She was murdered?" said O'Leary softly.

"She was," replied Joe as Sam nodded.

Cassidy's hands fell from her face. Looking at her husband, she stammered, "This…This is horrible."

"Uh…why don't you come into the living room?" said O'Leary, his attitude changing from disagreeable to accommodating. They were led into an opulent room with a high ceiling surrounded by ornate crown molding. A navy-blue sectional with end tables and lamps sat on a large gray and blue oriental rug.

"Have a seat," he said, indicating two matching overstuffed chairs. He seated himself next to his wife. He pulled a handkerchief from the back pocket of his khakis and handed it to Cassidy, who used it to dry her eyes.

In a shaky voice, she asked, "Wh-what happened?"

"Your sister was killed by an assailant while riding her bicycle along a bike path near the shore of Lake Michigan," said Joe. "We're in charge of investigating the case."

"Was anyone else hurt?" asked O'Leary.

"No," replied Joe. "The attack appeared to be perpetrated by someone specifically targeting your sister-in-law."

"What?" asked Cassidy, trying to make sense of it all. I…"

"Do either of you know if she had any enemies?"

"Probably some disgruntled dog show person she didn't put up," replied O'Leary.

"Put up?" asked Sam.

"Put up for the win," clarified Cassidy. "She's a dog show judge. She told me some dog people are crazy."

"I don't think she meant that literally," remarked O'Leary.

"So, you've talked recently?" asked Joe.

"We've never been that close," replied Cassidy. "But in the last year or so, our relationship has become more cordial. It's not that we had a big fight or anything like that. It's more about having little in common. We've sort of pursued different paths over the years."

"We were told you didn't care for her husband."

"Well…" hesitated Cassidy.

"He was a horse's ass," added O'Leary, speaking for his wife. "Not to speak ill of the dead or anything, but he rubbed people the wrong way, including us."

"I think she had to put up with a lot," added Cassidy. "But he was a means to an end. It meant she didn't have to work anymore, so she could indulge her passions."

"And they were?"

"Breeding and showing dogs. Then she got into judging, which she told me she loved. When she became an AKC judge, she gave up showing her dogs, saying it was a conflict of interest."

"Affenpinschers," stated Joe.

"Uh-huh," she said, nodding. "She loved them."

"And what about her husband?" asked Sam.

"He tolerated the dogs as long as they made her happy. But he didn't lift a finger to help her. She did everything herself or hired somebody to help out. He didn't want anything to do with them."

"During one of our interviews, her lawyer revealed your sister had a few relationships after the death of her husband, but she ended each one of them. Do you know the names of any of the men she had relationships with?"

Cassidy shook her head and said, "Sorry. She never confided in me about the men in her life. We weren't close enough for her to talk about that." She looked at her husband, who shrugged.

There was an uncomfortable pause, and O'Leary filled it by asking, "Do you have any suspects?"

Once again, Joe and Sam explained it was still early in their investigation, they had no suspects yet, and they were presently pursuing leads.

"Will you be planning her funeral services?" asked Joe.

"I suppose we will. She doesn't have anyone else," answered O'Leary.

"Then, I'll give your contact information to the appropriate authorities so they can inform you when you can schedule a funeral or memorial service." He purposely omitted references to the words "Medical Examiner, autopsy, and releasing the body" to avoid upsetting them further.

"Thank you," replied Cassidy.

When it was time to leave, Joe left his card with Cassidy and asked the O'Learys to call him if they remembered anything or had any questions. After being shown out, Joe and Sam were soon on the way back to Chicago.

As they drove back on the Eisenhower Expressway, Joe said, "You know, the O'Learys could be inheriting a fortune."

"Yeah," said Sam. "It'll be interesting to find out who Logan's beneficiaries are. You never know. Maybe she left everything to charities, and the O'Learys get nothing."

"Wouldn't that be a bite!"

"By the looks of their home, they don't need it," remarked Sam.

"Yeah, but the rich never seem to have enough."

"Ain't that the truth."

Chapter Five

The next day, one of the headlines in the Tribune read, "Noted Dog Show Judge Killed." The article reported the homicide death of Jennifer Logan along a bike path near the shore of Lake Michigan. It did not mention her decapitation, a fact not released to the public. It only said she was attacked by an assailant with a knife while riding her bike. Word was out.

A week later, Joe and Sam received a message from the Regional Forensics Computer Lab, giving them access to Logan's email messages and computer data. They split the inspection, so Sam looked into her phone information while Joe checked her computer data.

By the time the morning ended, Joe had found a series of emails from a man who had purchased an Affenpinscher puppy from Logan. The man complained that the eight-month-old pup had a temperament issue and had been biting and snapping at him and his kids.

Her responses showed Logan tried to guide him in diagnosing the cause of the dog's hostile behavior, but he reported nothing seemed to work. She asked what the family had done to socialize him and if he had noticed how his kids treated the puppy. Had they hit or kicked him? Teased him? Had he taken the puppy to obedience class? Angered that she was accusing his kids of abuse and frustrated that he paid several thousand dollars for a dog with temperament issues, he demanded that she take him back and refund his money. Logan stated she would take him back, but refused to refund his money. If she found the dog had problems, she would replace him with another puppy. Behavioral issues could be due to a number of things, including a poor home environment and mistreatment.

The customer's responses became more heated, and in one of his last emails, he threatened to get an attorney and blast her name all over the internet for selling vicious dogs if she did not refund his money. She responded, "You signed an agreement that states I will take the puppy back and replace it with another one. I don't make refunds. By signing it, you agreed to these terms, and I consider it binding." His final email to her contained a bristling, one-word message: 'BITCH!' Joe wondered if his anger could have festered and motivated him to kill her?

Once Joe printed out their email correspondence, he began investigating the man who had the beef with Logan. His name was Mark Naughton. He was forty-one years old, married, and lived in Evanston. Joe found Naughton had no criminal record and was employed by a marine engineering firm. Not your typical violent offender, but his issue with Logan could have provoked him into getting even.

After lunch, Joe and Sam got together to compare notes. Sam also saw Logan's email exchanges with Naughton. Her texts included exchanges with numerous people, mainly about meeting for dinner and seeing friends at dog shows. They agreed they should speak with Naughton about his whereabouts at the time of Logan's murder.

That afternoon, Joe and Sam drove to Watson Engineering, Mark Naughton's workplace. The marine engineering firm was located on West Jackson Boulevard in the West Loop neighborhood. The mostly glass, sixteen-floor office building had a public parking garage, and they used it to park and take the elevator up to the eighth floor, the location of Watson Engineering.

The elevator doors opened onto a soaring lobby. The first thing they saw was a large steel Matt Myers sculpture that reached to the ceiling and dominated one side of the room. Modern art paintings hung from the walls. Joe and Sam walked on the travertine floor to the information desk, where an attractive, smartly dressed young woman rose from her seat to greet them.

Showing his ID, Joe said, "Detectives Erickson and Renaldo, Chicago PD."

Unfazed by their introduction, she said, "Good morning, detectives. What brings you to Watson Engineering?"

"We need to speak with Mark Naughton. Is he here?"

Picking up the phone, she said, "Let me see if he's in." After pressing several buttons, she waited a few moments and then said, "Mr. Naughton, there are two police detectives asking to speak with you. She paused as she listened, then replied, "Very well."

Rising, she said, "He says he has some time. Follow me, and I'll take you to his office." Service with a smile.

Joe and Sam followed her down a corridor until she stopped before a door. She opened it a crack and said, "Mr. Naughton, the detectives are here to see you."

A voice from inside said, "Show them in, Brandi."

Brandi opened the door, and they stepped through into Naughton's office. Joe saw that it was decorated with framed pictures of C1 Corvettes. He wondered if Naughton owned one or just liked them. Whichever it was, it could act as a friendly gateway into a more uncomfortable discussion.

Naughton was standing beside his desk when they entered, and he stepped forward as soon as they came into the room.

Holding up their IDs, Joe said, "I'm Detective Erickson, and this is my partner, Detective Renaldo."

"Mark Naughton," he said as he shook their hands.

Before Joe could remark about the Corvettes, Naughton said, "I don't understand. Is my family all right?"

"As far as we know," replied Joe. "We're not here about your family. We'd like to speak with you about Jennifer Logan."

"Jennifer Logan? What did she do? File a complaint about me with the police?"

"No," said Sam. "She got murdered."

There was a pause as Naughton took in the news of her death. "Murdered?"

"Yes."

"Great," he sighed. "Now, I'll never get a refund on the little Nazi bastard."

"Excuse me," said Sam. "Nazi bastard?"

"The dog I got from her. An Affenpinscher."

"I'm not sure I understand."

"They're toy dogs, originally from Germany."

"Oh."

"Why don't we sit down over here?" said Naughton, indicating a table with chairs in one corner of his office. After taking seats around the table, Naughton began.

"Look, I bought an Affenpinscher puppy from Logan several months ago, and he's a nasty little shit. I tried to return him and get my money back, but she refused."

"Sounds like you're pretty angry about it," said Joe.

"You'd be angry too if you shelled out three grand for a dog that bites the hell out of you and your kids."

"When you got the puppy, did you sign some sort of an agreement?"

"Yeah."

"And what did the agreement say?"

"I don't recall the specifics. I'd have to read it over again."

"So, what did you do? Take your anger out on her by killing her?"

"Are you kidding me?" said Naughton. "I never touched that bitch."

"You had motive," said Sam.

"Yeah, I may have had motive, as you say. But I didn't do it. How would I get back my three grand if she was dead?"

"Maybe the satisfaction you got from killing her was worth three grand."

"No way."

"Where were you on the morning of June 9th?" asked Joe.

"June 9th?"

"Yeah. The morning Jennifer Logan was killed."

"Christ," muttered Naughton as he removed his cell phone from the holster on his belt. "I should be able to tell you that. Just a minute." He pulled up his calendar and then looked up at Joe. "We were out of town, taking my son to a Boy Scout camp downstate. In Makanda."

"And you can prove that?"

"If I must."

"You must," said Joe, drawing a scowl from Naughton.

"We went down the night before and stayed over. I can get you a copy of the motel bill and gas receipts if that'll suffice."

"It may."

"Look, you guys. I didn't like the woman, I'll admit that. And she really pissed me off over this dog business. But I didn't want her dead. Why would I?"

Joe gave Naughton his card and said, "Here's my contact information. You can email me and attach copies of your receipts or fax them to me. I'll expect them by tomorrow. Don't make us come back here and march you out in cuffs. Got it?"

"Yeah. I got it."

Joe and Sam rose from their chairs.

"So, what's going to become of your little 'Nazi bastard?'" asked Sam, the animal lover who had several cats.

"Probably have to put him down."

"Well, don't do that. Have you tried a dog psychologist or a dog whisperer?"

"No. You put stock in that stuff?"

"Can't hurt."

"And you might check into Affenpinscher Rescue," said Joe. "Rescue organizations take dogs and put them up for adoption."

"Who's gonna want a dog that bites?"

"You might be surprised. They have people who work with dogs and try to get to the bottom of their temperament issues."

"If you care about your dog," said Sam, "then get him some professional help."

Joe had intended to ask him about the Corvettes that decorated his office. But after experiencing his hostile attitude, he decided it was not a good time to bring it up.

Chapter Six

When Joe returned to his office, he called the International Kennel Club of Chicago to seek answers to questions that arose after his conversation with Mark Naughton. He was particularly interested in the agreement Naughton had signed.

The woman who answered identified herself as Carol.

"Hello, Carol. I'm Detective Joe Erickson with Chicago PD, and some questions came up during one of our investigations. I need some assistance."

"Is this about Jennifer Logan?"

Joe didn't want to admit he was the lead detective on the case and have her ask a series of questions he could not answer, so he said, "No, this relates to what's customary when breeders sell a puppy. Can you help me out with that?"

"Well, I'll try."

"Great. My first question is about agreements between seller and buyer. Do most breeders have written agreements with specific points listed for both the breeder and the seller?"

"Yes, they do. I would say that ninety-nine percent of professional breeders use such agreements. They aren't contracts. Those are legal documents that require attorney involvement. Rather, an agreement spells out in writing what's expected of the breeder and buyer regarding the purchase of a dog or puppy. And these agreements are signed by both parties to acknowledge their responsibilities."

"Thank you," said Joe. "Now, what if someone buys a puppy that has problems regarding health or temperament?"

"Normally, there is a period of time where the breeder will guarantee the health of the animal. They usually cover congenital issues like blindness, deafness, renal failure. Those kinds of things."

"Okay. What about temperament problems like growling, biting, or other problematic behaviors?"

"Well, those things can vary from breeder to breeder. But I can tell you what my policy is with my fox terriers. If a client contacts me and says his puppy is biting, let's say. I would ask questions that are geared toward finding out why. When did this behavior begin? Is he teething? Has the puppy been teased or mistreated by someone in the household? Is he protective of his food or toys? Has he been injured, so he's in pain and doesn't want to be touched? If I can identify a reason, then I can work with them to remediate the issue."

"What about refunding their money?"

"That's almost never done. If the problem can't be fixed, then the usual policy is to return the puppy to the breeder, and then the puppy is replaced with another one. Once the dog has been returned, there will be an attempt on the breeder's part to diagnose the problem and resolve it one way or another."

"Have you experienced such a problem in the past?"

"Once about fifteen years ago. I had sold a puppy to a family, and they complained about him growling and biting. The person I was dealing with was the wife, who was upset about his behavior. They lived here in the city, so I went to their home and observed the pup's behavior. He was fine with me, but didn't respond well to their two boys. They were eight and ten. And while I was there, he growled at the ten-year-old."

"What did you do?"

"Given how the boys acted, I suspected they may have teased him or mistreated him. I asked the wife about it, and, of course, she denied her boys would <u>ever</u> do anything to provoke him. So, I agreed to take him back and see if I could do something about it. He never growled or bit either me or my husband at any time he was living with us. So, I told the wife how he behaved with us and that I suspected her kids did something to him, and that's why he behaved the way he did. I told her I would not put another puppy into their home environment. She flew off the handle when I told her that, and in order to shut her up, I told her I'd refund their money. But that was the only time I ever resorted to a refund."

"So, there's usually a no-refund policy in these agreements?"

"That's correct."

"And replacing a puppy is the standard practice?"

"Pretty much."

"Out of curiosity, whatever happened to the puppy you spoke of?"

"He stayed with us for several months so we could show him some affection and give him a loving home environment, you know? Then, I sold him to an older couple with no kids. He was just fine with them. Never a problem."

Joe thanked her and ended the call. Based on Carol's information, he concluded that Jennifer Logan's actions indicated she was a responsible breeder and acted appropriately in dealing with Mark Naughton. Had she not been killed, Logan may have asked him to return his puppy and then provided him with a replacement. Unfortunately, that was never to be.

Joe's phone rang, and it was Kendra calling.

"I'll be performing an autopsy on the body of Jennifer Logan tomorrow at ten," she said. "Just wanted to let you know."

"Has the victim's head been found?"

"No, it hasn't. But we can't keep her on ice, forever. It may never be found, so we need to go ahead–so to speak–with what we've got."

"Thanks, I'll be there."

Joe told Sam what he had found regarding the agreements between professional dog breeders and their buyers.

"Sounds like Logan acted ethically, and Mark Naughton acted like a dick," said Sam.

"Yeah. But being a dick doesn't mean he's a killer. Only a dick."

"We'll see."

"I'll let you know when and if Naughton sends documentation of his trip."

"You know, I hope Naughton doesn't decide to put the little "Nazi bastard" down. I'd take him and try to work with him. I read that Affenpinschers aren't recommended for homes with young kids. That may be his problem."

"Think he'd like living with four cats?" asked Joe.

"Better than being dead."

"Can't argue with that."

"Maybe I'll call Naughton if his alibi checks out and tell him I might be interested in taking the dog off his hands. No kids at my place."

Chapter Seven

Destiny wasn't there when Joe arrived home that evening. She'd left a note saying she had gone to visit her mother in Winnetka and would be back around seven. He checked his phone, but she had not texted him about it. *Oh, well, doesn't matter.*

He took Autumn for her early evening walk around the block. The temperature was still around eighty degrees, and her tongue was hanging out by the time they made it back home. After he loved her up a bit, he tossed her a treat, which she took over to her bed and laid down to munch on it.

Joe did not know what to fix for dinner because he was unsure if Destiny had eaten something with her mother before she left. Pouring himself a glass of filtered water from the refrigerator, he sat down and thought about what to cook. He was hungry and did not want to wait until seven or later to eat.

Once he finished drinking his water, he looked at what was available in the refrigerator. Not much. A package of baby spinach, lemon juice, and Parmesan cheese were possible ingredients. He checked the freezer and found a package of large shrimp. With garlic, red pepper flakes, and Italian seasoning, he had everything he needed for Lemon Garlic Parmesan Shrimp. Now, if they just had pasta. He checked the pantry and... Yes! Linguine. Perfect!

The recipe took him about half an hour from start to finish, and the result was as good as he remembered it to be from the last time he made it. If Destiny had not eaten, she could reheat the remainder when she returned home.

He carried a glass with the rest of his Sauvignon Blanc into the living room and sat down on the couch. Autumn joined him, and a few minutes later, her ears perked up, and she barked. Jumping down, she ran to the door leading to the garage. She could hear that Destiny was home. Joe got up from the couch and walked into the kitchen.

A moment later, Destiny came through the door.

"Hi," said Joe.

"Hi," said Destiny.

Autumn was happy to see her, but instead of kneeling down to pet her as she usually did, Destiny set her purse down on the counter, picked up a glass, and poured herself some of the white wine Joe had with his dinner.

"How was your mom?" asked Joe.

"She could be better," she said, taking a drink of her wine.

"Oh?"

"Putting her glass down, Destiny looked at Joe and said, "She had a mammogram last month, and they saw a suspicious area. She went in for further tests, and they found a lump in her breast. A biopsy was taken, and it came back malignant."

"Oh, no. What's she planning to do?"

"Well, she's scheduled for surgery next week, so I need to be with her for a few days while she recovers.

"Of course."

"Fortunately, the tumor is small, about the size of the tip of your little finger. Her doctor said they can do a lumpectomy to remove it."

Joe was concerned and saddened by the news. His mother-in-law was a kind and supportive person who seemed much younger than her years. He tried to put a hopeful spin on it for Destiny's sake.

"Thankfully, it's small, and they caught it early. I'm sure she'll be fine after they remove it."

"I know, and maybe I'm getting too emotional about it. But it's unnerving to know your mother has cancer."

"Do you know if there's any history of breast cancer in your family?"

"I asked her about that. She didn't think so."

"Even so, it might be a good idea if you got tested to see if you carry the gene that elevates your risk. It would be good to know."

Staring down into her wine, she said, "Yeah. I guess it would be good to know that."

"But if there's no history of it in your family, you're probably all right."

"Hope so."

There was a pause. Destiny looked depressed, so Joe decided it was best to change the subject. "I made Lemon Garlic Parmesan Shrimp. You want me to warm it up for you?"

"I thought I smelled something good when I walked in. Sure. If you don't mind."

After Destiny finished her dinner, they adjourned to the living room and sat on the couch. Joe put his arm around her, and she snuggled up against him. They remained that way for a while, not talking. Finally, Joe asked, "You okay?"

"I guess."

"I understand what you're feeling. When my mother was diagnosed with Alzheimer's, I've always wondered if I'm predisposed to get it. Hope not."

"It's a scary thought."

"Do you know where she's going to have surgery?"

"Here in the city. University of Chicago Medicine. Her doctor said if it was his wife, he would want her to have it done there. So, they must be very good."

"She could stay here for a few days after she's released. Take some time to recuperate before she returns home."

"I'll ask her, but I think she'd most likely prefer being at home. If that's the case, I need to be there so I can drive her back and forth to her follow-up appointments. You don't mind, do you?"

"Of course not. Whatever works best."

After some time passed, Destiny sat up. Joe reached down and picked up the glass containing the remainder of his wine from dinner, and was about to take a drink when she asked, "How's your investigation going with the woman who was killed on the bike path?"

"We may have a suspect. But he claims to have an alibi. I guess we'll know more tomorrow. He had a grievance with the victim over a puppy he bought from her. Apparently, the dog has temperament problems—he bites. The guy demanded a refund. She stated she would replace the pup with another one, but wouldn't refund his money. I learned it's standard practice with breeders. He didn't find that to his liking and pitched a fit."

"That doesn't seem serious enough for such a vicious attack."

"I don't know. He was pretty pissed about not getting his three thousand dollars back."

"Did he sign an agreement?"

"He said he did, but 'couldn't recall' what is specified."

"That's convenient. Occasionally, someone's bottled-up anger boils over into an act of aggression. But decapitating her after she was dead? Any way you look at it, that's an extreme thing to do. Unless, of course, he's some kind of psychopath."

"That's hard to know. He seemed normal enough, but I've never met a psychopath who revealed he was a psychopath."

That brought a chuckle from Destiny. "I know. It would be nice if they did."

"Sam got his dander up when the guy said he may have to put his puppy down. You know what an animal lover he is."

"He has cats, doesn't he?"

"Yeah. He told me he might be interested in taking the pup off the guy's hands rather than seeing it put down."

"Either way, the guy would be out three grand."

"Knowing Sam, he might make him an offer he can't refuse."

Chapter Eight

Shortly before ten o'clock the next morning, Joe was inside the Office of the Cook County Medical Examiner, donning scrubs and a facemask, preparing to observe Jennifer Logan's autopsy. When he was ready, he walked into the autopsy room, where Logan's headless body was on the stainless-steel table and covered by a sheet. The various instruments used to dissect the body were laid out and ready for use.

A standard autopsy takes about three hours, but Joe usually left once the major part of the procedure was over, and the Medical Examiner began dissecting tissue samples. Not having the deceased's head would be problematic since the brain, tongue, and oral cavity could not be examined for abnormalities.

Kendra and her assistant, Kenny Miller, entered the room and began by removing the sheet and then conducting a thorough visual examination, followed by swabbing the body for evidence. Then, they clipped and collected her fingernails so they could be checked for DNA.

Once Kendra had completed the major portion of the procedure, she observed that Logan was a physically fit woman with a low-normal body mass index. She had never given birth and had had a tubal ligation procedure at some point. There was no evidence of disease or conditions that could affect her overall health. The cause of death was a knife wound that sliced into her aorta, causing massive hemorrhaging. Unconsciousness and death would have followed quickly. Four other knife wounds were examined, and while each one would not necessarily have proved fatal, taken in their totality, the victim's survival rate would have been seriously compromised.

After ninety minutes, Joe left. He sought out the nearest restroom where he could wash his hands and splash water on his face in an attempt to rinse away the death. It was his usual practice after attending an autopsy procedure. After dropping the face mask and his scrubs into a designated container, he headed for the exit. Knowing Kendra well, he was confident she would forward a copy of her autopsy report in a couple of days.

As he drove back to his office at Area 3, he thought about Logan's role as a dog show judge. He decided to call the American Kennel Club, the organization that governs dog shows throughout the country. But first, it was nearly noon, and he needed to eat something. And there were no leftovers from last evening. He stopped at an Indian restaurant he and Destiny occasionally frequented on North Fletcher Avenue. Following a satisfying meal of Chicken Ghee Roast, he returned to his office.

A few minutes before one o'clock, he got a cup of coffee and walked to his desk. As he was sitting down, Sam walked up and asked about the autopsy. Joe let him know nothing was found that could lead them to a suspect unless the swabs and her nails revealed foreign DNA.

Sam handed him copies of a fax transmission sent from Mark Naughton earlier that morning. Joe looked them over and saw they were copies of receipts from a motel stay in Makanda and a service station receipt for fuel. Just as Naughton had told them.

"He couldn't have killed her," said Sam.

"Right," replied Joe. "Guess we look elsewhere."

Sam returned to his desk, and Joe glanced at his watch. It was past one o'clock, so he could make the phone call. Then, to his annoyance, he realized that New York was an hour ahead, and he could have placed the call when he arrived. Oh, well. He found the American Kennel Club's number on their website and dialed it.

When a woman answered the phone, he identified himself and asked if she could spare a few minutes to answer some questions.

"What kind of questions?" she asked.

"I'm investigating the murder of a woman here in Chicago. She was an AKC judge," explained Joe.

"Oh, no! That's terrible. Who was it?"

"Jennifer Logan."

"That's too bad."

"It is. I was wondering…Do judges ever get reported for infractions of any kind?"

"You mean, like unprofessional behavior?"

"Among other things."

"You wouldn't believe the number of complaints we get about judges. Anymore, people think they have the right to complain about anything. It's just the times we live in."

"What are some of the complaints? Could you give me some examples?"

"Well, the most common one is posting on Facebook."

"Really?"

"Oh, yeah. People can post any nonsense they want, but there are rules about what judges can and cannot post on Facebook."

"What about things like incompetence or rudeness?"

"Not so much."

"I see."

"As it happens, when we investigate, it often turns out to be a case of poor sportsmanship on the part of the person who lodged the complaint. We have to look into all of these allegations, of course, and it wastes a lot of our time. Unfortunately."

"Who complains, primarily?"

"Professional handlers, owners, exhibitors, breeders, show staff, basically everybody."

"My dog didn't win, so…?"

"Yeah. That happens."

"What if AKC finds the complaint is justified? Would it affect their license?"

"It would depend on the nature of the complaint. All judges are approved by AKC, but we don't have licenses per se. But they could be issued a warning, be suspended from judging for a period of time, or, worst-case scenario, have their approval revoked so they can no longer judge. But that would involve extreme circumstances, like the child abuse case in Chicago, for instance. You might want to check that out since it happened right there in your own city."

"I'll do that. I read about what it takes to become a judge," said Joe. "It seems to be a long, involved process with a lot of requirements."

"That's true. You can look on our website for a full explanation of the qualifications if you want. You'll see they're quite stringent. Only the most knowledgeable and experienced individuals can become judges or judge a specific breed."

Joe was pleased with the person's willingness to answer his questions, but he did not know if she would be inclined to provide more specifics related to Jennifer Logan. Since he seemed to have established a good rapport with her, he thought maybe he could obtain more details.

"My next question may seem like a privacy violation, but someone brutally killed Ms. Logan, and we need to apprehend her killer. So...I was wondering. Were there any complaints filed against her?"

"Oh...I don't know if I can answer that," she said.

"She's dead, so privacy is not in question now. I really need to know so we can determine if someone had a motive to kill her."

"Oh, dear. Well..." She sighed and, a moment later, said, "Let me check."

Joe could hear the clicking of her keyboard, and after a short time, it stopped. There was a pause, and then she answered.

"There was one complaint filed two months ago."

"Could you tell me the nature of the complaint?"

"Uh...the person alleged favoritism."

"Favoritism. As in favoring a particular exhibitor over another?

"Without reading the complaint, I can't say for sure. But I'd say probably."

"I don't suppose you could tell me the name of the person who filed the complaint?"

Chuckling, she said, "No. I'm afraid that would definitely involve a privacy issue. Sorry."

"I assumed that would be the case. So, I would need a warrant to get that information, right?"

"I'm afraid so."

"Well, like they say, 'if you don't ask, you don't get.'"

"That's right."

"Thank you, uh…Sorry. What's your name?"

"It's Judy."

"Thank you for your time, Judy. You've been most helpful."

Joe ended the call and thought, *Great. Getting a search warrant for an out-of-state organization should be fun!* But the call did provide him with some valuable information. Could the person lodging the complaint be so angry that it motivated them to murder Logan? She did tell her sister that some dog show people are crazy.

He walked to Sam's desk and explained what he had learned from Judy at AKC.

"Have you ever applied for a search warrant for a company residing out of state? In this case, New York?"

"No. I can look into it. Sounds like we need to find out what's going on with the person who lodged the complaint, huh?"

"My dog didn't win, so I'm going to kill you and cut off your head!" said Joe.

"I've heard of nuttier motives."

"I'll check out her Facebook page," said Joe. "Maybe there's something there."

For the rest of the day, Joe went through Logan's Facebook page and looked at all her postings and messages to see if there were any clues as to why someone may have wanted her dead. He discovered a message from an angry exhibitor complaining about not awarding her dog points while she continued to put up a particular professional handler. That one looked promising.

Noting both the names of the person complaining and the professional handler cited in her message, Joe finally had a lead to follow up on. But when he began delving into the people involved, Sam tapped him on the shoulder and asked, "Are you going to stay here all night?' Time had slipped away, and his shift had ended.

Chapter Nine

When Joe returned to the office the next day, he looked up the address information for the professional handler, Rebecca Michaels, named in the complaint by Alice Haldeen, another exhibitor. He found Michaels's address information in the Registered Handlers Directory on the AKC website. She lives outside of Crystal Lake, Illinois, a city of 40,000 people, forty-five miles northwest of Chicago.

Joe called the phone number listed for Rebecca Michaels, and after several rings, a woman answered.

"Rebecca Michaels."

"This is Detective Joe Erickson with the Chicago Police Department. I'm investigating the death of Jennifer Logan. I assume you knew her."

"Yes. I showed under her a number of times."

"I'd like to speak with you. Will you be home today?"

"I will. I'm preparing to leave for a show in Wisconsin on Thursday, so I'll be getting my dogs ready."

"Fine. I'll plan on meeting you at your residence later this morning if that's a good time."

"Sure. I'll be here. Come to the kennel building next to the house. You know the address?"

Joe repeated the address he had copied from the AKC website, and she confirmed it. After ending the call, Joe told Sam about the meeting. He grabbed the keys to their assigned squad car, and they prepared to leave. But before they left, Joe picked up the GPS device from his car and entered Michaels's address.

Overriding the GPS directions, Joe took I-290, the Eisenhower Expressway, out of the city since it was less heavily traveled than the I-90 route suggested by the GPS. After two highway changes, they arrived at Crystal Lake an hour and fifteen minutes later. Michaels's home was located two miles outside of town on an acreage. Next to the house was a white concrete block kennel building with a series of dog runs on one side. Parked next to it was a huge black, brown, and white motorhome.

Joe and Sam walked to the kennel building. When they opened the door, they heard a buzzer, and then a cacophony of barking ensued from another room. A moment later, a woman wearing a brown vinyl apron appeared. She was a small, solid woman around fifty years of age. Looking back inside the dog room, she clapped her hands several times and loudly uttered, "Shush! No bark!" Then she closed the door, and the barking began to die down.

Running her fingers through her short, dark brown hair, she turned to Joe and Sam and said, "Sorry about that. I'm Becky Michaels.

"We're Detectives Erickson and Renaldo," said Joe. "I spoke to you on the phone earlier."

"I assumed that," she replied. Nodding toward the door, she said, "Hearing the buzzer sets them off. They know I have a visitor. Untying her apron, she said, "Tell you what, let's go sit in my motorhome. It'll be quieter in there."

Michaels hung up her apron and led Joe and Sam to the shiny motorhome, where she opened the door and invited them to follow her inside. They climbed several steps up and into the massive vehicle. Walking past two leather captain's chairs for the driver and a passenger, they saw several shelves containing rows of wire crates, apparently for housing her show dogs. Farther back, the interior consisted of opposing tan leather benches with a table in between, a kitchenette, and a living room with matching leather furniture. Opulence on wheels.

Indicating one of the benches next to the table, she said, "Have a seat. Can I get you anything?"

"No, thanks," said Joe.

"Nothing for me," said Sam. "Nice rig you have here."

Sliding onto the bench across from them, she replied, "I just got it last year.

My old one was on its last leg. I travel a lot, and it's a home away from home. I show a lot of dogs, mostly toys, and this is the only practical way I can travel with them. I don't have the hassle and inconvenience of moving dogs in and out of a motel room. And since I'm parked on the grounds of the exhibition building and not miles away from a motel, I can haul my equipment and the dogs back and forth on my golf cart."

"How many dogs do you show?" asked Joe.

"Anywhere from six to ten. I have six right now."

"And you do this all by yourself?"

"My niece travels with me. She acts as my assistant."

It was time to cut the small talk and get down to business. "What can you tell us about Jennifer Logan? You said you showed under her."

"Well, she was a good judge. I liked her."

"In what way?" asked Sam.

"She knew her breeds, and she was very thorough when going over the dogs. She knew what to look for and wasn't heavy-handed with them like some judges are. She also expected a lot from people showing under her."

"Could you explain what you mean by that?" asked Joe.

"Dogs are well-trained and presented suitably. Handlers and exhibitors dressed professionally. She was particular, but I got the impression she enjoyed what she was doing."

"What about away from the shows?" asked Sam. "Did you socialize?"

"Outside the ring? We didn't fraternize. I only knew her professionally."

"So, you weren't friends."

"No. Simply acquaintances."

"Did you know you were named in a complaint filed against her with AKC?" asked Joe.

Nodding, Michaels replied, "Alice Haldeen. Yeah, I'm aware of that. Someone from AKC interviewed me regarding her complaint."

"The allegations stated Logan favored you over other exhibitors, thus denying wins to better dogs."

Michaels laughed derisively. "Better dogs? That's a load of crap."

"Care to explain?" asked Sam.

"I know who filed the complaint. Let me tell you something about Alice Haldeen. She's a breeder attempting to become a handler. But she doesn't present her dogs satisfactorily. They aren't groomed especially well, and she doesn't dress appropriately. I wear a business suit when I show a dog unless it's too hot. And then I wear a skirt and blouse. She wears pants that need ironing and a blouse that looks ten years old. I know she's not a handler yet, but come on. Look professional, at least."

"What about the quality of her dogs?"

"Well…they move well, I have to say that. But I've never had the opportunity to go over them to check their structure. You can have a dog with super nice structure, but if you don't present him well, and if he doesn't behave properly, someone else is going to win. Simple as that."

"Her dogs don't behave?" asked Joe.

"A dog has to be trained to behave appropriately when being shown. Her dogs are not always good on the table, and that makes it harder for a judge to go over them and check their structure. And not to be judgmental or anything, but Alice looks sloppy. She's overweight, and she doesn't move the dog around the ring especially well."

"So, you think this complaint has no merit," said Joe.

"It's a load of crap. But I guess it doesn't matter now, does it?"

"We appreciate your being so candid with us."

"You know, I'm really sorry she's dead. Jennifer Logan was very good at what she did. We could use more judges like her."

"Anything else you can think of?" asked Sam.

Michaels looked hesitant and then smiled. "You interested in rumors?"

Joe looked at Sam, who shrugged. "Why not?"

"This is just a rumor, mind you," said Michaels, "so it may not be true. But I heard she liked to sleep around. But that could have been started by someone who was jealous of her good looks. Take it for what it's worth."

"Well…We'll keep that in mind," said Joe. "Thanks for your time. We'll let you get back to your dogs."

Joe and Sam left the motorhome and drove back to Chicago. They concluded an interview with Alice Haldeen should be next on their agenda.

When they returned to their office, Joe heated the leftovers he had brought from home and ate a late lunch. Afterward, he began a search for Alice Haldeen. He found she lived in Beaver Dam, Wisconsin, which was three hours away and too far for them to interview her face-to-face. Maybe she would agree to a Zoom meeting. Not ideal, but better than a phone conversation.

After finding her phone number, Joe called. A young girl's voice answered. He could hear dogs barking in the background.

"Haldeen residence."

"This is Detective Joe Erickson with the Chicago Police Department. I need to speak with Alice Haldeen."

"That's my mom."

"Is she home?"

"Yeah."

"Could I speak to her, please?"

"M-O-O-O-O-M!" she yelled, not bothering to cover the phone's microphone.

In the background, Joe could hear a woman yelling, "What is it?"

"PHONE!"

A few moments later, a woman's voice came online. "Hello?"

"Is this Alice Haldeen?"

"Yes."

"I'm Detective Joe Erickson of the Chicago Police Department. I'm investigating the death of Jennifer Logan."

"She's dead?"

"She is. She was found murdered about two weeks ago. I thought maybe you heard."

"No. I haven't. So, what's that got to do with me?"

"During our investigation, we found that you filed a complaint against her with the AKC. Is that right?"

"Yeah. I did."

"We'd like to interview you about it, but you live too far away for us to travel to your home and answer some questions. We were wondering if you would agree to a Zoom meeting."

"No. I don't do Zoom meetings."

"Okay...."

"All I can say is that she's been unfair to me, and she always puts up the same handler. I got tired of it and filed a complaint."

"I need to ask you some questions."

"I'm not answering any more questions. I filed a complaint against her. End of story. Now, I'm busy washing dogs and don't have time to talk to you. Goodbye." Click.

She hung up on him, and Joe was not pleased about it. *What's her problem?* he thought. He decided to investigate her further. Her response to his question about the complaint revealed anger, and he wondered if rage could have led to her killing Logan.

Alice Haldeen had a Facebook page that showed she bred Shih Tzus and Maltese, both long-haired breeds. Besides photos of her dogs, there were also pictures showing two children and what appeared to be a male companion. Further research into her background disclosed that she was thirty-nine years old and married to Larry Haldeen. She also maintained a website touting her dogs and offering Shih Tzu and Maltese puppies for sale.

Joe needed to interview her, but Wisconsin was way out of their jurisdiction. Then, an idea flashed in his mind. He checked the website of the International Kennel Club of Chicago and found there was a dog show scheduled in a week. The venue was in one of Chicago's suburbs, and he wondered if Haldeen would be exhibiting her dogs. There was no way to check entries, so he thought it might be worth his time to attend and watch the Shih Tzus show. If she was in attendance, she would now be in Illinois, and he could question her whether she liked it or not. Maybe Destiny would like to go with him and check out the Lhasa Apsos. If Haldeen is not present, they can simply make an enjoyable day out of it.

Chapter Ten

When Joe returned home, he saw Destiny's car in the garage. She had been gone two days, staying with her mother, so he was eager to find out how they were doing–both Destiny and her mother.

When he entered the kitchen, Destiny was busy preparing what Joe assumed to be dinner. Autumn came running up to him, but Joe momentarily ignored her and stepped toward Destiny. He gave her a kiss and said, "Welcome home."

"Thanks. Good to be home."

Joe looked down at Autumn and asked, "You want a treat?" Autumn responded with her usual excitement. He tossed her a treat, and she took it to her bed and began crunching away.

Turning his attention back to Destiny, he asked, "How's your mom?"

"I took her in to see her doctor yesterday. He told her the tumor was localized and they'd treat it by performing a lumpectomy. She's scheduled to have it done next week. The surgeon will go in and remove the tumor along with a certain amount of the tissue surrounding it. In her case, about the size of a ping-pong ball. Then, it'll be sent to pathology to make sure all the tissue around the tumor is clean. If it is, then they'll stitch her up, and she can probably go home the next day. There's only a slight chance she may need to have radiation treatments afterward to prevent the cancer from returning. It simply depends on what the surgeon finds. After that, she just needs to continue having periodic mammograms."

"It's a good thing they caught it early," said Joe. "How's she holding up?"

"Better than me, I think."

Joe put his arm around her and gave a little squeeze. "She'll be fine."

Looking back at him, she smiled. "I hope so."

Joe picked up a glass and poured Pinot Noir from a bottle on the counter. "You want one, too?" he asked.

"Sure."

Pouring another glass, he asked, "What are you making?"

"Zucchini, feta, and leek gratin. I haven't made it before, but I saw the recipe and thought it sounded good."

"It does."

"It's about ready to go in the oven. You hungry yet?"

"I probably will be by the time it's done."

"Okay, it should be about forty minutes," she said as she opened the oven door and slid the pan in. After setting the timer, she picked up her wine glass and sat down by Joe.

"How would you like to go to a dog show next week?" he asked. "There's one happening not too far from here."

"A dog show? Sure. Is this work-related?"

"Yeah, but I think it could be fun, too. I've never been to one. Have you?"

"No."

Joe explained the reasons why he wanted to attend the show and how he hoped he would be able to speak with judges who knew Jennifer Logan and interview Alice Haldeen.

"I'm thinking that one of the judges working the show will be able to provide me with some personal insight regarding our victim. Judging assignments would have brought her into contact with other judges over the years. I'm hoping to find someone who knew her well."

"What about the woman who filed the complaint?"

"I'm gambling that she'll be showing one of her dogs at this venue. She doesn't live that far away."

"Do you know what kind of dogs she shows?"

"Shih Tzus and Maltese."

"Oh. Shih Tzus are kissing cousins to the Lhasa Apso. Did you know that?"

"No."

"Untold years ago, the Shih Tzu breed was developed by mating a Lhasa Apso to a Pekingese. Through selective breeding over time, the Shih Tzu breed came about."

"I guess you did your research, huh?"

"Of course. Do you know much about this woman?"

"She's married and has a couple of kids. They live in Beaver Dam, Wisconsin, so they're way out of our jurisdiction. That's why I'm hoping to find her at the dog show since she lives just four hours away."

"What are the dates of this show?"

"Next Saturday and Sunday," said Joe. "I'm off one of those days. It won't interfere with your mom's surgery, will it?"

"No. Her surgery's on Tuesday."

"I'll take Tuesday off so I can be with you."

"I appreciate that." She leaned over and gave Joe a peck on the cheek. "The dog show sounds interesting. I've never seen one up close and personal before. I've only watched the ones they have on television."

"I thought it might be fun to watch the Lhasa Apsos show, too."

"Yeah. It would. Let's plan on it. It'll take my mind off Mom."

The zucchini, feta, and leek gratin was quite tasty, so they decided it was worth adding to their repertoire of menu items. After cleaning up the kitchen, they adjourned to the living room.

Just as they sat down, Destiny received a call from her friend, Madison Powell. Known as "Maddie," she had been the target of a killer a year ago during one of Joe's investigations. Due to her involvement in the killer's apprehension, Destiny grew close to Maddie, and they became friends. Maddie filled a gap in Destiny's life after her best friend, Liz, was killed in a small plane crash the previous year.

After she realized it was a call from Maddie, Destiny rose from the couch and said, "I'm going to take this in the office so you can watch TV. Knowing Maddie, it might be a long conversation."

Joe picked up the remote, pulled up Netflix, and began looking through the series he had placed on his favorites list. After scanning the list a few times, he settled on a Norwegian crime drama. There was something about those dark Scandinavian mysteries that appealed to him, and he couldn't fault them for the procedural errors that annoyed him so much while watching American crime shows.

An hour into the series, Destiny returned and sat down on the couch. She snuggled up to Joe, and he filled her in on what had happened so far. By ten o'clock, Destiny had fallen asleep, and Joe was beginning to nod off, so he ended the episode, turned off the TV, and awakened Destiny.

"Hey," he said, nudging her gently. "You want to go to bed?"

Sleepy-eyed, she said, "I guess I was tired. Now, I probably won't be able to go back to sleep."

"I can fix that," said Joe, leaning over and giving her a kiss on her forehead.

"Oh, yeah?"

Joe rose from the couch, holding Destiny's hand. "Come on."

Chapter Eleven

Saturday came, and Joe and Destiny left early and drove an hour to the site of the dog show. After paying a parking fee to the attendant at the gate, they found a parking place and began making their way toward the main exhibition building. It was surprising how many cars and vans were parked on the showgrounds, some of them with wire pens set up next to them. Joe noticed a large number of motorhomes parked a distance away from the proceedings. It was a warm day, and he could hear some of their generators running. As they got closer to the building, they saw people walking dogs into and out of the entrance, and they could hear dogs barking. This was a bigger event than Joe had imagined.

"This is huge," he said to Destiny.

"It is. There must be a lot of dogs here."

Upon entering the large exhibition building, they approached a table where club members were collecting entrance fees from spectators. They saw what appeared to be hundreds of people, some seated outside the eight show rings observing dogs being shown, while others crowded around the rings, waiting for their turns to have their dogs judged. Joe and Destiny had never seen so many different dog breeds in one place. At one end, several vendors had set up stalls selling supplies and equipment. The other end was reserved for grooming, and it was packed with various exhibitors busily brushing, combing, and blow-drying dogs, evidently preparing them for their time in the ring.

Seeing the AKC superintendent's desk, Joe said, "Let's go over there and see if we can find out what time the Lhasas and Shih Tzus show. After Joe asked about times, a woman sitting at the table suggested they buy a show catalog from the club. She pointed to a table where club officials were selling catalogs. After shelling out twenty bucks for the thick show catalog, Joe saw that it listed all the dogs, their owners, the judges, and the judging schedule. Eventually, he found the listing for Lhasa Apsos.

"Looks like the Lhasas show at 10:30 in Ring 4. That's two and a half hours from now."

"That gives us plenty of time to look around," replied Destiny. "Let's find a place where we can get some coffee first."

They looked around and spotted a food bar off to one side. They walked over to it, got overpriced cups of coffee, and then sat down at one of the tables a few feet from the counter.

Joe searched the catalog for the Shih Tzu listing, and when he found it, he began reading through the entries.

"Ahh," he said, smiling.

"What?"

"Alice Haldeen. The person who refused to speak with me. She's scheduled to show one of her dogs. Looks like Shih Tzus show at one o'clock. It says they show in Ring 5."

"Let's hope she's here," said Destiny.

"Yeah. How's the coffee?"

"Not bad."

"Joe took the top off his coffee and took a sip. "You're right. Not bad."

Handing the catalog to Destiny, Joe asked, "You want to watch the dogs being shown?"

"Sure. I think I'd like to watch the toy dogs. Let's find out what ring they're in. Shih Tzus are in the Toy Group. I wonder if all the toys are being shown in Ring 5."

"Let's walk over there."

When they arrived at Ring 5, toy breeds were listed on a large poster board at ringside. Shih Tzus were the first breed scheduled after lunch at one o'clock. That got Joe thinking about judges and who may have known Jennifer Logan.

"Find a place for us to sit down," said Joe. "I need to speak with the superintendent."

Joe left and walked to the superintendent's table. He asked a woman where the superintendent was, and she referred him to a white-bearded gentleman, who was standing behind the table talking to a middle-aged woman.

When their conversation ended, Joe stepped to the man, introduced himself, and showed his ID. "Could I talk with you a moment?"

The man looked surprised and said, "I suppose. Is there something wrong?"

"This has to do with an investigation I'm conducting."

"All right. Why don't we step over here?" he said, indicating a space several steps behind the desk.

The superintendent did not appear comfortable with Joe seeking him out, so Joe said, "I'm sorry to bother you, but I'm investigating the death of an AKC judge, Jennifer Logan?"

Recognition of her name was apparent on the superintendent's face, and he replied, "Oh, yes. That...that was terrible."

"Did you know her?"

"In passing. She was a popular judge, but I'm afraid I only knew her professionally. She judged our last show."

"I'd like to speak with all of the judges here today to see if any of them may have known her personally. It would help if any of them could shed some light on what happened to her."

"Oh...Well, we can't have any disruption in our judging schedule, I'm afraid."

"I wouldn't want that, either. I'm wondering...is there a place where the judges eat lunch? It would only take a minute of their time for me to ask if anyone knew her. And if someone did, I could meet with them after the show was over."

"Judges have staggered lunches, so not all of them eat at the same time. That way, judging goes on in some rings throughout the noon hour. It's more efficient that way."

Joe could tell he wasn't crazy about the idea, so he restated, "A short interview could provide us with information that would help us apprehend

Ms. Logan's killer."

The superintendent thought for a moment and said, "Well…the judges have a place where they can eat lunch that's away from exhibitors. I guess you could ask them, as long as it doesn't take too long."

"Thanks. I'll be brief."

The superintendent asked Joe to meet him at the superintendent's table at 11:30 and again at noon, and he would take him to the room where the judges ate lunch. When they were done, Joe walked to Ring 5. All of the chairs were occupied, so he and Destiny stood among other spectators and the exhibitors.

Seeing the strange-looking dogs in the ring, Joe asked, "What do we have here?"

"Chinese Crested. Some don't have hair on their bodies, and others do."

Joe watched as an exhibitor placed her dog on a table. The judge, an older man with white hair, looked at the dog's mouth, felt the shoulders, and moved his hands over the rear legs. Then, he asked the exhibitor to walk the dog up and down the diagonal mat, observing the dog move. When the dog returned and came to a stop before the judge, he paused a moment, looking at the dog's face, and then pointed and said something Joe could not make out. The exhibitor acknowledged his direction and led the dog around the mats that lined the inner square of the ring and came to a stop behind the next dog in line. This was repeated for each of the three dogs in the class. The process looked similar to the judging of dogs he saw on television.

"The judging goes like this," said Destiny. "Male puppies followed by the adult males, then female puppies, adult females, and then Best of Breed. Just so you know, females are called 'bitches'. No comments, please."

Joe chuckled, "Okay. How do you know this?"

"I did my homework. I'll explain as we go. They don't show the class judging on TV. Only the Groups and Best in Show. That way, all the breeds can be seen by viewers."

Joe was impressed with Destiny's knowledge of the judging process. But he wasn't surprised, given her innate curiosity about everything.

As they watched, Destiny explained, "They bring in the winning male puppy to compete against the best male adult for Winners Dog. Whichever one wins will get the championship points. Then it's the same for bitches."

Joe commented on the number of Chinese Cresteds being shown, "There aren't a lot of these dogs here.

"Chinese Cresteds aren't as common as other breeds, like Toy Poodles and Chihuahuas."

"Interesting. I've never heard of them."

The show began at eight o'clock, so they missed the judging of Toy Manchester Terriers, Miniature Pinschers, and Italian Greyhounds. But they watched the judging of Maltese, Pugs, Toy Fox Terriers, Brussels Griffons, and Havanese.

While the Maltese were being judged, Joe asked Destiny to see the catalog. Looking up Maltese, he perused the entries and saw Alice Haldeen's name. She was showing an adult male and was listed as number eleven. Looking closely at the numbers on the exhibitor's armbands, he spotted the number eleven attached to a woman's upper arm. She did not appear as Rebecca Michaels described her.

Haldeen was a full-figured woman around forty, but she did not look "sloppy" or unkempt. Her hair and makeup were done, and she looked professional in her shiny, dark blue blouse and tweed skirt. As he watched her present her Maltese male, Joe observed her walking the little white dog up and down the ring mats effectively, although she was not as nimble moving from a kneeling position to a standing position as some of the younger, thinner exhibitors.

Joe wondered if there was some jealousy or bad blood between Haldeen and Rebecca Michaels. He spotted Michaels with her Maltese, which was standing on a small table outside the ring. She was brushing and combing the dog's long white hair. When the judge had considered the four male dogs, she indicated to the exhibitors to lead their dogs around the ring and then pointed to Haldeen first and to others in order of class placement. Haldeen looked thrilled. The steward called for the winner of the puppy class, and the exhibitor brought him into the ring. After looking the two dogs over, the judge pointed to Haldeen for Winner's Dog.

Michaels ignored Haldeen when she left the ring, but Joe noticed she was keenly watching Haldeen's dog perform for the judge. Was she checking out the competition?

Once the Winner's Bitch was decided, they all left the ring. Then, the ring steward called the numbers for the Best of Breed dogs, followed by those shown by Michaels and Haldeen. The judge examined each dog after it was placed on the table and observed them move up and down the diagonal mat.

Once he had completed his individual examination of the dogs, the judge stepped back and looked over the four dogs as they were lined up and presented by their handlers. When he was finished, he gestured for the exhibitors to move their dogs around the ring, and he pointed to Michaels, whose dog she awarded Best of Breed. Haldeen was given the ribbon for Best of Winners. Exhibitors with their Pugs were waiting outside the ring since they were the next breed to be judged.

Joe noticed Michaels and Haldeen avoided each other outside the ring, but didn't know if it was intentional or because they had reason to leave in opposite directions.

"Excuse me," said Joe to Destiny. "I'm going to follow Haldeen to her grooming area, so I know where she's set up. When she's done showing for the day, I'll approach her."

Keeping Haldeen in his sights, he followed her to a grooming space that consisted of a grooming table, several dog crates, and a stool. A large metal box with a lift-up top sat on a smaller table with one of its drawers open. The box was filled with bottles, combs, brushes, and what appeared to be various grooming supplies.

Haldeen handed her Maltese to a teenage girl with purple streaks in her hair, who put him inside a crate. Then Haldeen reached down and removed a funny-looking little brown dog with small, pointed ears and a very short muzzle from another crate and set it on the table. Joe had never seen this breed of dog before. Realizing he was staring and not wanting to draw attention to himself, he turned and walked back to Destiny and sat down.

"Find her?" asked Destiny.

"Yeah."

Half an hour later, as the Pugs were finishing up, Joe saw Haldeen and several other exhibitors holding little brown dogs with smashed-in noses. He looked to see what breed was showing next. Brussels Griffons. The purple-haired teenage girl he saw with Haldeen put their Brussels Griffon on a table outside the ring. A short time later, Haldeen arrived, and the girl stepped aside. The dog was shown as an adult male, and he placed second to another dog. In the ribbon line, Haldeen congratulated the winner, a gesture that reflected her good sportsmanship.

Finally, 10:30 rolled around, and it was time for the Lhasa Apsos to show. Joe and Destiny moved to chairs vacated by two spectators outside Ring 5. But as they passed the sign posted outside the ring, they saw that Schipperkes and Tibetan Spaniels were showing ahead of the Lhasas. Joe was becoming bored since each breed was judged in the same manner.

"We have to sit through two more breeds?" complained Joe. "This may be interesting for people who have a dog being shown, but watching this process over and over is getting old."

"You don't like seeing the different breeds?" asked Destiny.

"Seeing them is fine, but the repetition is…"

"You should have brought a book."

"Next time, maybe I will."

"So, you're thinking there'll be a next time?"

"Probably not."

The entries were low for Schipperkes and the Tibetan Spaniels, so it only took fifteen minutes to complete judging them. People showing Lhasa Apsos were outside the ring, brushing and combing their dogs' hair. Joe and Destiny marveled at the long, luxurious coats of the adults and how cute the puppies looked.

"Autumn looks like the puppies," said Joe.

"Well, Liz kept her in a puppy-cut. She didn't want to keep up a full coat. Our groomer does the same thing."

After puppy dogs were judged, the ring steward called for the adult dogs. Rebecca Michaels walked into the ring, followed by four other exhibitors. When it was all said and done, Michaels's dog was awarded Winners Dog.

Haldeen won Winners Bitch with her female, which meant they would compete against two champions for Best of Breed. After all the dogs and exhibitors had left the ring, the ring steward announced the numbers of dogs competing for the Best of Breed award. Michaels walked into the ring with a different dog, one that had very long hair that dripped onto the floor. A man walked in behind Michaels with another champion. Then, Haldeen followed the Winners Dog into the ring with her Winners Bitch. All the dogs were impressive, especially the two champions with their luxurious coats. But the judge surprised everyone by awarding Best of Breed to Alice Haldeen's bitch. Haldeen looked surprised and was all smiles, but it was clear from the look on Michaels's face that she was not pleased with the decision.

"What is it with those two?" asked Joe, expressing his thoughts out loud.

"What two?"

"Two of the handlers—Alice Haldeen and Rebecca Michaels. The one who won Best of Breed and the one with the red blouse who showed the champion. They seem to despise one another."

"Sometimes, competition brings out the worst in people," said Destiny. "Winning and losing can be a kind of ego conflict, and if one of the parties perceives the other has insulted or injured the other in some way, hostility can result."

"So, winning could be an insult?"

"If you're the loser, it could be."

The judging was on time, and the last class was completed a few minutes before 11:30. Joe walked to the superintendent's desk. He was on the phone, and noticing Joe's arrival, he held up one finger, indicating, "Just a minute." A few moments later, the superintendent returned his cell phone to his pocket.

"Thanks for waiting," he said as he walked around the table to where Joe was standing. "The lunchroom is this way."

They walked past the vendors to a door that opened into a room with tables and chairs. Lunch items were set up on a long table, and two older men were busy loading their plates. Other men and women were seated at tables, eating.

"Could I have your attention, please?" stated the superintendent. "I'm sure you're all aware that one of our judges, Jennifer Logan, was tragically killed not long ago." Indicating Joe, he continued, "This gentleman is the detective who is heading up the investigation into her death. He'd like to have a quick word." With that, he gestured to Joe to take over.

"Thank you," began Joe. "We are investigating Ms. Logan's death, and I would like to speak with any of you who may have known her. I promise not to take up much of your time, but we're looking for anything that could provide us with information about the victim. I'll be in this room after Best in Show is announced. We're counting on those who knew Ms. Logan to assist us in solving her murder. Thank you. I'll let you get back to your lunch."

The superintendent escorted Joe out the door, stepped back into the room, and closed the door. Joe met Destiny, and they decided to get something to eat from the lunch counter. They had salads available, which Destiny was grateful for. Joe ordered a bottle of water and a brat, which he smothered with mustard. There was a room next to the counter that had tables and chairs, and they sat down to eat their food. Afterward, they browsed the vendors, looking at all of the items available for dogs. It ranged from grooming tools to jewelry to dog food and supplements.

At noon, Joe went to the judges' lunchroom and spoke to a few judges he had not seen during his first visit. After repeating the same spiel he said the first time, he left, hoping someone would show up after the show was over.

Chapter Twelve

S hortly before one o'clock, Joe and Destiny sat outside Ring 4, waiting for the Shih Tzus to show. While Joe was giving his pitch to the judges, Destiny secured two empty chairs next to the ring.

Once again, both Haldeen and Michaels were outside the ring, readying their Shih Tzus for judging. Their long hair was pulled up off their faces and secured with a bow on top of their heads. Neither one of them was showing class dogs, and when the ring steward called their numbers for Best of Breed judging, they carried their dogs into the ring and lined up according to their numbers ahead of the class winners.

After evaluating all the dogs on the table and watching them each move around the ring, the judge observed them one by one as she walked down the row. Then she gestured and said, "Take them around."

As the exhibitors walked their dogs around the ring, the judge pointed to Michaels for Best of Breed honors. Smiling, she moved her dog to the area next to the steward's table, where she was awarded a rosette ribbon for the win. Haldeen exited the ring carrying her dog and walked toward her grooming area. She may have been disappointed not winning, but her facial expression did not reveal any negativity. Her teenage assistant folded the small table outside the ring and carried it toward the grooming area.

By two o'clock, the Group judging was underway. Workers had adjusted the fencing to make larger rings to accommodate the number of Group breeds. Each Group took between thirty-five and forty-five minutes to judge, and by 6:30, the seven Group winners had been chosen. Once again, workers made the ring larger and added a short platform surrounded by flowers for the Best in Show judging. When a Welsh Terrier was awarded Best in Show, Joe rose from his seat and asked Destiny if she would like to accompany him to the judges' lunchroom.

"It might be helpful if you would be there…in case one of the judges is a woman and doesn't respond well to men."

"Sure. If you want."

They walked to the judges' lunchroom and saw two of the judges, a man and a woman, waiting inside. The woman was drinking from a can of Diet Coke, and the man was looking at his cell phone.

"Are you both here to speak with me about Jennifer Logan?" asked Joe.

"Apparently, we are," said the woman. She was in her late forties with masculine features. Her sandy hair was cut short, and she was dressed in a blouse, coordinated pants, and black loafers. The only jewelry she wore was a wristwatch.

"I'm Della Wellington," she said.

"Thank you for sticking around," replied Joe. "This is my partner, Destiny Alexander."

"And I'm David Esposito," said the man as he slipped his phone into a holster on his belt. He looked dapper, dressed in a blue blazer, gray slacks, and a striped tie.

After exchanging pleasantries, Joe suggested they all sit down at a table. Once seated, Joe began by asking, "Just how well did you know Jennifer Logan?"

Wellington spoke first. "We both decided to get certified as judges about the same time. We went through classes together. She was a breeder of Affenpinschers for many years, and I showed Airedales. She was never a professional handler like I was, but she was an experienced exhibitor and a fast learner. She added breeds to her roster rather quickly. We always talked at shows when we happened to be scheduled together. I liked her. She was smart and had a great attitude. When I heard she'd been killed…I…I couldn't believe it."

"Did you know anything about her personal life?" asked Joe.

"Not much. I knew her husband had passed away and left her a lot of money, but we weren't really what I'd call friends. More like acquaintances."

Joe looked at Esposito and asked, "How well did you know her?"

Esposito chuckled and said, "Pretty well, I guess you could say. We had a thing going for a while. Several months. About a year after her husband passed."

"An affair, you mean."

"If you must," he replied, apparently disliking Joe's use of the word.

"What can you tell us about her?"

"Besides being very attractive, she was driven. If she wanted something, she wouldn't let anything or anyone get in her way."

"Do you know if she made any enemies?"

"Probably, but I wouldn't have any idea who they would have been."

"What caused your affair to end?"

"She met someone she liked better," said Esposito matter-of-factly and then shrugged.

"Did that make you angry?" pressed Joe.

"It did, at first. Pissed me off, you know. But she was simply someone to sleep with, a kind of recreational activity if you will. Not a person I wanted a long-term relationship with. It was fun while it lasted."

"Did she show her dogs under you?"

"No. That would have been a conflict of interest. Anyway, I don't judge dogs in the Toy Group. I judge working dogs and herding dogs."

"Would you happen to know the name of the individual she hooked up with after she ended your relationship?"

"Oh, yeah. A veterinarian, she began taking her dogs to. Dr. Randall Winthrop. 'R-a-a-ndy,'" replied Esposito contemptuously. "I heard she broke up his marriage."

"David's right," concurred Wellington. "She had a number of different guys who accompanied her when she judged shows. I don't know any names, but it seemed to me that she liked playing the field."

"Did she ever talk about her romantic life?"

"No, she didn't discuss that, and I wasn't going to ask who the guys were. None of my business."

"I have a question," said Destiny. "Did either of you think Logan was unethical in any way? Did she play favorites with exhibitors showing under her?"

"No, I don't think she would have done that," said Wellington.

"I can't say," added Esposito. "Some people think we favor professional handlers over other exhibitors. Most of the time, the handlers are better at presenting their dogs. But sometimes, if it comes down to awarding points to a handler or an exhibitor, some judges might lean toward giving the win to the handler."

"But to favor a particular handler all the time?" said Wellington. "No. That would create a situation where people would no longer enter their dogs under that judge. The person's reputation and future judging assignments could be damaged as a result."

After several more questions, Joe brought the interview to a close. He thanked them both for their candor and wished them well. Joe and Destiny did not want to miss Alice Haldeen. There was another show here tomorrow, but he did not want her to pack up and go home before he could speak with her. And he didn't want to come back again tomorrow just to question her.

Destiny followed Joe as he walked toward Haldeen's grooming space. Her equipment was there, but the dogs and their crates were gone. Damn!

"Looks like she's moved her dogs somewhere else for the night," said Destiny.

"Yeah," replied Joe. "Let's check out the motor homes. With the number of dogs she showed today, I doubt she's staying in a motel."

Joe and Destiny walked out of the building and toward the area designated for motorhome parking. Motor homes of all sizes were lined up in multiple rows, most of which had their generators running. Many had wire pens set up near the doors to exercise their dogs. Joe and Destiny began at one end, looking for a Wisconsin license plate, a glimpse of Haldeen, or one of the dogs she showed in an exercise pen.

License plates revealed exhibitors had driven in from Illinois, Wisconsin, Iowa, Indiana, Minnesota, and beyond. "Wow," exclaimed Destiny. "People came to this show from all over the country."

After looking at about half of the vehicles, Destiny spotted a Wisconsin plate. However, the dog in the exercise pen was a German Shepherd. Not a breed that Haldeen showed.

"What do you want to do?" asked Destiny.

"Let's keep this one in mind and continue looking," replied Joe.

They began walking down the third row and saw another Wisconsin plate. The motor home was not as large as the other one they spotted from Wisconsin. *Maybe Haldeen doesn't need a large one, given the smaller dogs she shows,* thought Joe.

"Let's wait here a while and see if Haldeen comes out the door."

Five minutes later, the purple-haired girl carrying a Shih Tzu emerged from the motor home and placed the dog into the exercise pen. "You poop!" she said to the dog in a stern voice. It was the same teenager that Joe saw in Haldeen's grooming area. Maybe it was the same girl who answered the phone when he called Haldeen.

"I'm glad no one instructs me to poop like that," said Joe, looking at Destiny.

"I could do that if you like," replied Destiny.

"That's okay," smiled Joe. "I'm fine with the way things are."

Waiting a little longer paid off. From out of the motor home stepped Alice Haldeen. She had changed out of her ring attire and donned a pair of faded jeans and a black T-shirt. She was bent over, picking up the dog from the exercise pen, when Joe and Destiny approached.

"Hello," said Joe.

Haldeen looked up and said, "How are you?"

"I'm Detective Joe Erickson, Chicago PD," he said, showing his ID. "It's important that I speak with you."

"Like I told you on the phone," she said politely. "I don't want to speak with you."

"Well, you're not in Wisconsin anymore, you're in Illinois. You can speak with me here, or I can escort you to the local police station, and we can speak there."

"Christ," she muttered. Then she yelled toward the door, "Darla! Come out here...now, please."

The purple-haired teenager opened the door and said, "What?" Her attitude suggested she had been rudely pulled from some life-and-death situation.

"I need to talk with these people. Why don't you go and find us a couple of sodas? Diet Pepsi for me if they have it."

Darla sighed loudly and said, "All right."

Haldeen handed her a ten-dollar bill and said, "Get me a Diet Coke if they don't have Pepsi."

Darla took the bill and sauntered off.

"My daughter. Fourteen. Is it illegal to kill them?"

"Not in some states," said Destiny. Her reply made Haldeen smile.

"I'm investigating the death of Jennifer Logan," said Joe. "You filed a complaint with AKC claiming she was biased. Care to explain?"

"I noticed you were sitting outside the ring watching me show today. As you can see, I do my share of winning under various judges. I don't win all the time, but I'm competitive, wouldn't you say?"

"You seemed to do well."

"Well, I never won when I showed under Logan. Never. I always got dumped. She wouldn't even put up my Best in Show Maltese when I showed under her. I don't know what her problem was, but it was unprofessional. So, I filed a complaint and stopped showing under her. If I found out she was judging, I wouldn't enter."

"Did you ever have words with her or say anything that could have gotten back to her some way?"

"No. Nothing like that."

"What's the deal with you and Rebecca Michaels? It was apparent there's no love lost between the two of you."

"Can I be blunt?"

"Feel free."

"She's a jealous bitch. Simple as that."

"Because your dogs beat hers?"

"Primarily. When I started showing my dogs, I approached her, hoping she would mentor me since we often entered the same shows. From the get-go, she said she wasn't interested and made it known she resented me showing against her. Unwanted 'competition.' So, I found someone else who agreed to help me. I attended training classes regularly, and I practiced a lot until I got good, and my dogs were well-trained. And I began winning because my dogs happened to be better than hers. She didn't like it. Now that I'm working to become a professional handler, she won't even speak to me inside or outside the ring."

"Did Jennifer Logan favor Rebecca Michaels when you showed under her?"

"You bet she did. Put her up all the time."

"Sounds like you had good cause to file a complaint," said Destiny.

"I did."

"What was AKC's response?"

"Now that she's dead, there probably won't be one."

"I have to ask this," said Joe. "Where were you on June 9th?"

"Omigod," sighed Haldeen. "Let me check." She pulled her cell phone from her pocket and began poking keys. After a moment, she looked at Joe and said, "On my way to a show in Nebraska. Omaha."

"Can you prove that?"

"I have gas receipts if you need them. But…is this really necessary? You think I would kill her? I wanted to see her certification pulled so she could no longer be a judge."

Joe looked at Destiny, and over her shoulder, he saw Darla returning with two cans of soda. When she arrived, Joe asked, "Say, Darla? Did you travel with your mother to Nebraska not long ago?"

"Yeah."

"What can you tell me about that trip?"

"Bor-ring!"

Joe smiled as Darla handed a can of Diet Pepsi to her mother."

"Is that all?" asked Darla with a little attitude.

"Yeah. Enjoy your soda."

Joe watched as Darla entered the motor home and banged the door closed. He glanced at Haldeen in time to catch her eye roll.

"I hear they get better when they're around twenty-five," said Destiny.

"Yeah," replied Haldeen. "If she lives that long. But she's good help, and I pay her, so she's human some of the time."

"I have one last question. "What does your husband do?"

"Oh. Larry operates a meat locker."

Destiny glanced at Joe, whose eyebrows rose after hearing her answer.

"So, he's a meat cutter?"

"Yeah. He keeps pretty busy. And he's always overwhelmed during deer season."

Joe thanked her for her time, and he and Destiny walked toward their car. It had been a long day.

"I learned a lot coming here, and it did give me one lead to check out," said Joe.

"Yeah. I'll bet Haldeen's husband has had a lot of practice lopping the heads off animals. Couldn't be that much harder to lop the head off a person."

"You've got a point there."

"Do you think he would punish Jennifer Logan so brutally for discriminating against his wife? That's pretty extreme."

"No matter how you look at it, it's extreme. I'll need to check his alibi for the day Logan was killed."

"Yeah," agreed Destiny. "I learned a lot today, too. Who would have thought that showing dogs can be a cut-throat business? Jealousy, contempt for others, poor sportsmanship."

"Sounds like professional sports."

Destiny smiled and said, "My, you're cynical."

"On the positive side, I saw a lot of cute dogs," said Joe. "I kinda liked those Brussels Griffons. You think Autumn would like a friend?"

"No."

Chapter Thirteen

Joe had barely settled into his chair at work Monday morning when he and Sam were called out to investigate a report of a human head found washed up on the shore of Lake Michigan. The location was in the vicinity where the body of Jennifer Logan was found.

When they arrived, uniformed officers had secured the scene and closed off the bike path fifty yards in each direction. Showing their IDs to the uniformed officer, Joe and Sam ducked under the crime scene tape and stepped to the shore. On the rocks, they saw what looked more like an alien creature than a human head. The water, along with lake creatures, had seriously damaged the outer tissue, and what remained was little more than a skull covered with some muscle, one eyeball still in the socket, and a mess of matted hair. What ragged skin was left had turned white. The teeth were in full view as the tissue around the mouth was mostly gone. It was not a sight for the faint of heart.

Joe saw a police sergeant conferring with a young man near a bicycle that was lying off the path. They stopped talking when Joe and Sam walked over.

"Detective Joe Erickson," said Joe. "My partner, Detective Renaldo."

"Sergeant Charles Atkins," replied the sergeant. "This is Stan Hopewell," indicating the young man standing beside him. "He said he was riding his bike and got a leg cramp, so he stopped to work it out. He was walking toward the lake when he noticed something odd by the shore. Turns out, it was a human head. When he realized what it was, he called 9-1-1."

"I about shit my pants," remarked Hopewell.

"Yeah. Severed heads can have that effect," said Sam.

"Not every day you come across something like that," said Joe. "What time did you first see it?"

"About forty-five or so minutes ago," replied Hopewell.

Looking at Joe, Atkins asked, "Missing any heads lately?"

"As a matter of fact…We'll have to wait for the ME to do some tests first," replied Joe. "We had a decapitation murder two weeks ago. The victim's head wasn't recovered."

"Uh! Can I go?" asked Hopewell. "I can't really tell you anything more. I just saw it and called 9-1-1."

Joe spotted the ME's van pulling up. "Sam, why don't you get Mr. Hopewell's contact information? I'll be back in a bit."

Sam saw the ME's van over Joe's shoulder. "Okay. Should we send Hopewell on his way?"

"Yeah. Let him go after you get his information."

Joe walked to the ME's van and saw Ward Dahlstrom step out. Dahlstrom was not a conversationalist and preferred to do his job with as few words and interruptions as possible. At the rear of the van, Dahlstrom had opened the doors and was removing his equipment when he saw Joe.

"Morning," said Dahlstrom.

"Yes, it is," replied Joe. "Did they tell you what was found?"

"Yup."

"I think there's a good chance the head belongs to the decapitated body discovered a couple of weeks ago. The victim was identified as Jennifer Logan. Kendra collected the body and has since conducted an autopsy."

"Okay." He shut the doors and began walking to the crime scene. Once there, he suited up in Tyvek coveralls, booties, mask, and gloves.

"Where is it?" he asked.

Joe pointed. "Down there. Next to the water."

Dahlstrom acknowledged with a nod and slipped under the yellow tape, carrying his kit as he walked down toward the shore. He was only there about ten minutes when he walked back to the van with his kit in hand. He returned with a large plastic bag and a white, five-gallon bucket with a lid.

Sam joined Joe, and they watched as Dahlstrom put the head into the plastic bag and placed it in the bucket. After snapping on the lid, he carried it back to his van and began removing his protective gear. Joe and Sam followed him.

"You'll let Kendra know?" asked Joe.

"Uh-huh."

After he climbed into the van to leave, Joe said, "Thanks, Ward."

"Yup," he said and started backing the van off the path for his return to the Cook County Office of the Medical Examiner.

"Man of few words," said Sam.

Joe looked at Sam. "Yup."

Sam chuckled, and they returned to the crime scene. Joe stepped to Sergeant Atkins, who was conferring with a uniformed officer. "You can remove the tape and open the bike path. There's no need for a forensic team on this one." Atkins instructed the uniformed officers to clear the scene while Joe phoned Kendra to leave a message. She must have been between autopsies because she picked up.

"Good morning, Joe. To what do I owe the pleasure?"

"Dahlstrom is on his way to you with a gift."

"Let me guess. You found a head?"

"You're way 'a–head' of me, Kendra."

"Oh-h-h," she groaned. "That was bad, even for you," she said, chuckling.

"I just wanted to give you a heads up."

"Okay, okay. You can stop now. I'll let you know as soon as I've done the examination. I can probably make an identification based on dental records. You won't have to wait for DNA."

"Thanks, Kendra."

"I assume you're 'head–ing' up the investigation," she said.

"Touché. Yeah. I am."

"Well, good luck. Later."

Gallows humor. You had to have a sense of humor to do the work required of a medical examiner. Joe had a sneaking suspicion Dahlstrom had a sense of humor, too, but was reluctant to show it. Kendra, on the other hand, always exercised her sardonic wit, and that was one of the reasons he liked working with her.

"What did she say?" asked Sam.

"She thinks she can make an identification based on dental records."

"That's good. Let's hope it belongs to Logan. We don't need another decapitation on our hands."

After closing the crime scene, Joe and Sam drove back to their Area 3 office.

Joe called the police station in Beaver Falls, Wisconsin, and explained the situation to the Chief of Police. He needed to see if Larry Haldeen had an alibi for June 9th so he could determine if he was a suspect. Chief Richter was agreeable, saying he knew Haldeen and would question him personally. Joe thanked him and ended the call.

Sam walked to Joe's desk and asked, "Where are we going with this?"

Joe told Sam about the dog showing business and the fact he discovered that the aggrieved individual's husband works as a butcher.

"So…He's skilled with a knife," said Sam.

"Yeah, but if he can establish his whereabouts for June 9th, he's probably off the hook," said Joe. "I've got the Chief of Police in Beaver Falls, Wisconsin, checking out his alibi."

"Could a person who shows dogs be so pissed off that she would murder a judge who had some bias against her?" asked Sam.

"I know what you're saying, but we've encountered stranger motives. Like the guy that killed his girlfriend because she burned his steak?"

"Well, she did ruin a perfectly good piece of meat."

Ignoring Sam's comment, Joe continued, "You know, when I interviewed Alice Haldeen, she didn't strike me as an unreasonable person. Contrary to what Rebecca Michaels said, I found her likable. But it's possible she's just a good actress. It's hard to tell."

Sam suggested putting this investigation on hold until they heard from Kendra, but Joe said he wanted to interview the veterinarian with whom Logan had a fling. "If she broke up his marriage and then dumped him, he could have a strong motive to want her dead. Betrayal is a powerful emotion."

Joe located the business address of Dr. Randall Winthrop, but it was too late in the day to speak with him since his clinic would be closed by the time they arrived. Just before his shift ended, Joe received a call from Kendra.

"I had some time this afternoon, so I conducted an examination of the head that was found this morning. X-rays were a match to Jennifer Logan's dental records. The head was too degraded to extract any helpful evidence."

Joe thanked her and informed Sam, who was relieved the head did not belong to another victim. He also explained to Sam that he was taking tomorrow off so he could be with Destiny while her mother was having surgery.

"Tell Destiny I hope her mother's surgery goes well," said Sam. "Is it serious?"

"Don't know yet. We'll have to wait and see."

Chapter Fourteen

Destiny had driven to her mother's home in Winnetka and brought her back to Joe and Destiny's place so she could stay overnight in the city. This way, they could take her to the hospital the next morning. Her mom would not be able to drive herself home after her surgery, and if more extensive work needed to be done, she could recover at Joe and Destiny's home.

Vivien Alexander was a wealthy woman. Her late father was the Vice-President of the Chicago and North Western Railway. But she never put on airs about having money or being privileged. And she made sure her only child was raised without feeling entitled.

Vivien resembled her daughter and looked much younger than her sixty-six years. In fact, Vivien and Destiny could probably pass for sisters. She took good care of herself and seemed to maintain a positive and pragmatic view toward her upcoming surgery.

"It just goes to show the importance of getting a mammogram every year," stated Vivien. "You catch this thing early, and you can deal with it before it's too late."

"You'll come through this just fine," assured Joe.

"Yes, I will," she replied with confidence.

"How about a glass of wine?" asked Joe.

"I would love to have one, but…I can't. No alcohol for forty-eight hours before surgery. Doctor's instructions."

"Oh. I wasn't aware of that. Sorry," replied Joe. How about—"

"Water would be fine," she smiled. "I'll take you up on the wine in a few days."

Joe poured her a glass of filtered water from a pitcher in the refrigerator. After visiting for a few minutes, he made a dinner of tuna steaks with lemon herb couscous. Vivien was impressed with Joe's culinary creation, but had to eat light per her doctor's orders. She ate half the tuna steak and a small serving of couscous.

"Joe, this was wonderful. Thank you."

"Yes, it was," added Destiny. "You outdid yourself."

"Yes, you did," added Vivien. "I wish I could have eaten more."

"Thanks," replied Joe. "I'll make it again when you come for a visit. Then you can eat as much as you want."

Vivien chuckled and said, "I'm going to hold you to that."

"She's not kidding," said Destiny.

"I'll make you something special once you're released from the hospital and feeling better."

Reaching over and touching his hand, she replied, "I appreciate that."

Rather than watch something on television, Vivien challenged Joe and Destiny to a rousing game of Scrabble. Given their extensive vocabularies, Destiny and Vivien excelled at this game. Joe was no slouch, either, although he remembered how they had beaten him the last time they played.

After two games, it was getting late, and Vivien was growing tired. She and Destiny had won a game each, while Joe was a close third each time. He didn't care about losing. Winning was not important to him. It was simply an enjoyable way to pass the time. They had to get up early in the morning to get Vivien to the hospital by her seven o'clock check-in time. Her surgery was scheduled for 9:30 a.m.

The next morning, Joe was up at five and had coffee made. Vivien had to fast, so Joe and Destiny decided to wait and get something to eat at the hospital cafeteria rather than eat in front of her.

Once Vivien had checked in, changed into a gown, and was lying on a bed in a surgical prep room, Destiny was allowed to join her and keep her mother company. They sent Joe to the cafeteria, where he ate breakfast and returned to the surgical waiting room with a cup of coffee. Destiny had purchased a book for him to read, a police procedural novel by Peter W.J. Hayes. He opened it and began reading.

Before he knew it, Destiny joined him. Looking at his watch, he realized he had lost track of time. He asked, "They're taking her in?"

"They took her in a little early. The doctor said the procedure should last about an hour."

"That's good."

"Unless they get in there and find something they're not expecting," she said.

"Don't go there," said Joe. "You need to think positive."

"I know," she replied. Opening her iPad, she began reading.

"Did you go to the cafeteria?" asked Joe.

"No, I don't have any appetite. I'll get something after Mom's out of surgery."

For the next hour, Joe and Destiny read. Hayes's book was a page-turner, and Joe found the story riveting. An hour passed, and Joe noticed Destiny stirring. Looking up, he saw a nurse walking toward them.

"Doctor Edelman would like to speak with you," she said.

Rising, Destiny looked at Joe, who could see fear in her eyes. The nurse took them down a hall and opened a door to reveal a tall man in scrubs. He looked to be in his fifties.

"You're Vivien Alexander's daughter?" he asked.

"Yes," replied Destiny.

"Your mother came through the surgery just fine. She's presently in the recovery room. You can see her when she wakes up. The nurse will come and get you. I removed a small tumor about the size of a pencil eraser, and it was sent to Pathology. They confirmed it was malignant, but the tissue surrounding it was clean, so I'm confident I got everything."

"Thank goodness," breathed Destiny. "Did you have to remove much tissue?"

"The amount was a little smaller than a ping pong ball. If she's concerned about it cosmetically, she shouldn't be. The incision was located on the outside of the breast, and the excised tissue won't be noticeable after it heals."

"Thank you, Doctor," said Destiny as a tear rolled down her cheek. "Thank you."

"You're welcome," he smiled. "Looking at Joe, he said, "She should make a full recovery."

"Thanks," said Joe. "When do you think she can go home?"

"We'll keep her overnight for observation, but she can most likely go home sometime tomorrow. Now, if you'll excuse me, I have another surgery scheduled."

Dr. Edelman left the room, leaving Joe and Destiny looking at one another. Destiny hugged Joe and released her pent-up emotions.

"Hey, it's okay," said Joe in the most soothing way he could muster. "She's going to be fine."

After a few moments, the nurse opened the door and asked them to return to the waiting room. Joe wasn't seated for more than five minutes when his phone rang. It was Sam.

"How are things?" asked Sam.

"The surgery went well," replied Joe. "She's in recovery right now."

"Good to hear."

"What's up?"

"I took a call from the Chief of Police in Beaver Falls, Wisconsin. He reported that Larry Haldeen was in Canada fishing when Logan was killed."

Joe let out a sigh. "Great. Another suspect off the list." One more thing on his plate today.

"So, that leaves…"

"The veterinarian. Dr. Randall Winthrop. We can check him out tomorrow."

"Sounds good."

When the call ended, Joe went back to reading his book while Destiny walked to the cafeteria to get something to eat. After half an hour, she returned and handed Joe a coffee before sitting in an adjacent chair with her iPad.

"Thank you," said Joe as he began removing the top of his coffee cup. "You find anything good to eat?"

"Yogurt. I was so famished I ate two cartons."

Joe chuckled and said, "Nervous eating."

"No, just hungry."

About an hour later, a nurse led them to the recovery room, where they found Vivien awake but groggy from the anesthesia. The nurse told them she would be moved to a private room after she spent the appropriate amount of time in recovery. Destiny wanted to stay with her mother, but Joe felt the area was too crowded with him there, so he returned to the Waiting room.

By noon, Vivien had been moved from Recovery to a private room and was beginning to feel some discomfort from the surgery. Destiny told Joe he didn't need to be there with her and suggested he run any errands or go home. She would call him when she wanted to be picked up. But Joe was enjoying his book and decided to remain in the Waiting room reading until Destiny was ready to go home.

After eating lunch in the cafeteria, Joe called Dr. Randall Winthrop's office to set up a meeting tomorrow. A young woman answered.

"The Pet Doctor. Can you hold?"

"Yeah."

A minute later, the voice returned. "Sorry about that," she said. "How can I help you?"

"This is Detective Joe Erickson with the Chicago Police Department. I need to set up a meeting with Dr. Winthrop for tomorrow."

"Let me see…" There was a pause, and then she said, "He's booked solid tomorrow. It looks like he could see you sometime next week."

"This is a police matter. I'm not calling about a pet. We need to see him sometime tomorrow, so you'll need to make time."

"Oh. Well…I guess the best time would be right when we open at eight o'clock. He usually doesn't start seeing clients until 8:30."

"Eight o'clock works. Pencil us in. Thanks for your cooperation."

By 2:30, Destiny was ready to go home. Her mom was tired and needed to sleep. She walked into the Waiting room where Joe was engrossed in his book.

"I think it's time we head home," she said. "Mom needs to sleep, and there's nothing I can do but sit around. I'll come back in the morning."

"You look tired," said Joe.

"I am. I didn't sleep well last night. This has been pretty stressful."

"Have you eaten any lunch?"

"No."

"You want to stop somewhere?"

"I'd rather go home."

Chapter Fifteen

By the time Joe finished his jog the next morning, Destiny was dressed and ready to drive to the hospital.

"Did you eat?" asked Joe.

"No, I'll get something at the hospital cafeteria. If they release her, I don't know if she'll come here or go back to Winnetka. If she insists on going home, I'm going to stay with her."

"That's fine. Let me know what you decide."

She started to open the door to the garage, then turned and said, "Oh, I walked and fed Autumn already."

"Okay."

She left, and Joe looked down at Autumn, who was standing at his feet, looking up at him. He kneeled down and petted her.

"You've been fed. Don't try to con me into getting more."

As if she understood, she turned, walked to her bed, and laid down.

Joe and Sam arrived at The Pet Doctor right at eight o'clock. People were already bringing in their dogs and cats. Two young women behind the counter were accepting the caged animals and taking them somewhere in the back.

An elderly gray-haired woman handed a soft-sided cat caddy to the assistant, who assured her by saying, "You should be able to pick him up after three o'clock."

Before releasing her hold on the caddy, the woman peered through the netting to see the kitten and said, "You be a good boy for the doctor now, Teddy." Then she released her hold on the caddy, and the assistant took the kitten through a doorway behind the counter.

The woman looked at Joe sadly and said, "He's losing his manhood today."

That brought a smile to Joe's face. "I'm sure he'll be okay," he said. "I lost my manhood a couple of years ago, and I've been fine ever since."

She looked at Sam with confusion on her face. "He's never complained," said Sam.

"Oh my," she said. Then she turned and walked slowly out the door.

The vet assistant with the nose ring was looking on, and she asked, "Did you have to wear a cone, too?"

"He did," replied Sam. "A lot of people stared."

She laughed and then asked, "Have you been helped?"

"Not yet. I'm Detective Joe Erickson, and this is my partner, Detective Renaldo. We have an appointment with Dr. Winthrop."

"Oh, yes. I talked to you on the phone yesterday. I'll tell him you're here." Then she left as another assistant, who had Latino features, came through the door.

"Have you been helped?" she asked.

"We have," said Sam.

She smiled as a middle-aged man in a light blue smock came through a side door. "I'm Dr. Winthrop. We can talk in my office."

Joe and Sam followed him to the rear of the building to a small office space with a desk piled high with papers and brochures. Two plastic chairs were placed in front of the desk. A bookcase with medical books, binders, and notebooks filled the wall behind his desk.

"Why don't you have a seat? Samantha told me who you were. Detectives Erickson and Renaldo, right."

"That's right," said Sam as they sat down.

"Maybe you can tell me what this is about?" asked Winthrop.

"Jennifer Logan," replied Joe. "Her name ring any bells?"

Winthrop sighed and said, "Oh, yeah. Has she done something?"

"She's been murdered."

Winthrop's jaw dropped, and his face turned pale. "Uh...I wasn't aware of that. Murdered, you said?"

"That's right. It was in the paper."

"I must have missed it."

"We're investigating the case," said Sam.

"Oh, man…this is terrible."

"When's the last time you saw her?"

"Well…a month or so ago, I suppose. She brought one of her dogs in for a dental exam and cleaning."

"We were told you two had a relationship at one time," said Joe.

Winthrop's facial expression reflected his displeasure at breaching the subject before saying, "Yeah. We did."

"And it broke up your marriage," stated Joe.

"It was the straw that broke the camel's back, so to speak. My wife…It gave her a reason to file for divorce when she found out."

"We also heard that Logan dumped you sometime after that. Is that correct?" asked Sam.

"Really…Do we have to go into this?" asked Winthrop, clearly annoyed by the line of questioning. "It's a private matter, and I'd prefer not to discuss it."

"Prefer or not," said Joe. "Logan was murdered, and it appears you could have a motive."

"That's a crock. Why would I kill her or anyone else?"

They could see that Winthrop was growing more hostile with each question, so they pressed him to see if his hostility might reveal something incriminating.

"She dumped you. Why was that?" asked Sam.

"You'll have to ask her. Oh, but I guess you can't, can you?"

"We're asking you."

He paused and used the moment to compose himself. Looking at Joe, he said, "She had what you'd politely call…a strong libido. And after our initial passion dimmed somewhat, she found excitement with someone else."

"You still sound angry," said Joe.

"Only when I'm forced to talk about it. I didn't like the fact that she dumped me for some other guy after causing my divorce. But…I have to admit it was good while it lasted."

"You ever think about punishing her for what she did to you?"

"Think? Maybe. Act on it? No. Absolutely not. Like I said, I could never kill anyone. Look, I still see her occasionally. Her dogs are still my clients. If I'm homicidal about what she did, why would I agree to keep seeing her dogs? It's all in the past."

"That's rather noble of you."

"Her money spends like anyone else's. And her dogs deserve the best of care."

Winthrop looked at his watch and said, "I have several surgeries scheduled this morning. Are we done here?"

Joe looked at Sam and then said, "Where were you on the morning of June 9th?"

"Why? Was that when she was killed?"

"It was," said Sam.

Winthrop sighed loudly and pulled out a planner from his desk. After a minute, he looked up. "I had an emergency that morning. I was here a little before six o'clock."

"Can you prove that?"

"You can ask Samantha, my assistant. Ask her about the Boxer that was brought in after being hit by a car. She assisted me during the surgery. I'm sure she'll remember."

"She here today?"

"Yeah. She's the one with the nose ring."

Joe and Sam exchanged looks, and then they rose from their seats.

"Thanks for your time, Dr. Winthrop. I think we're done, at least for the time being," said Joe.

"Have a good one," said Sam.

Before Joe and Sam went out the door, Winthrop said, "There's one thing I'd like to say about Jen."

"And what's that?" asked Joe.

"I'm guessing one of her relationships got her into trouble."

"How so?"

"I don't want to get into any salacious details, but...she was insatiable. Her needs may have caused her to make a bad decision. I'm serious. She was something else."

"We'll keep that in mind," said Sam.

Joe and Sam walked to the counter and saw the assistant with the nose ring. "Are you Samantha?" asked Joe.

"Yes," she replied, rising from the computer.

"Dr. Winthrop told us you assisted him on a surgery a while back. A Boxer that was hit by a car?"

"Oh, yeah. Broken hip."

"When was that?"

"I got called in early that morning."

"I mean, what date?"

"Oh. Let me look." She sat down at the computer and began working the keyboard. After a minute, she looked up and said, "June 9th."

Sam looked at Joe, whose expression revealed disappointment.

"Thanks for checking," said Sam. "Did the patient live?"

"He did," she smiled. "Thanks to Dr. Winthrop."

As they turned to go, Samantha said, "My condolences about your manhood."

In no mood for humor, Joe ignored her as he pushed through the door. Sam gave her a smile and a thumbs-up. They left the vet clinic and began driving back to their office.

"Now, what?" asked Sam.

"I don't know," replied Joe. "This has been pretty frustrating so far."

Chapter Sixteen

As Sam started driving away from the vet's office, Joe checked his notebook and saw the reference he'd noted after examining Logan's bicycle. There was a sticker on it advertising a bicycle shop, and he thought it would be a good idea to look into it.

"I think we should check out the shop that serviced Logan's bike," said Joe.

"Okay," said Sam. "What's the address?"

Joe gave him the address of Owens Cycle Shop on West Chicago Avenue. When they entered the brick building, they saw a showroom with new bicycles of all kinds. Stepping to the counter, they waited as a man paid his bill for having his bike serviced.

The counterman looked at Joe and Sam and said, "I'll be with you in a moment." Then, he escorted the customer through a door off the showroom, presumably to pick up his bike.

When the counterman returned, Joe and Sam produced their IDs and introduced themselves.

"I'm Jim Owens, the owner. What can I do for you?" he asked, taking their presence in stride.

"We're investigating a recent homicide. The victim rode a Roubaix SL8 Comp bicycle, and I saw it had a white sticker with your shop's name on it."

Owens ran his fingers over his chin and said, "We don't sell many of those. But if it had our sticker on it, we must have serviced it for the owner."

"Her name was Jennifer Logan. Do you remember her?"

"Oh, yeah…homicide. She dead?" he asked, surprised and concerned.

"She is," said Joe. "She was attacked and killed along a bike path near the lake on June 9th, and we're interviewing anyone who had a connection with her."

"Jeez. That's a shame. She was a good customer."

"Did she happen to purchase her bike here?"

"She did. In fact, I sold it to her a couple of years ago. She always had it serviced here, too."

"Who did the work on it?"

"It wouldn't have been me. Let me check. We keep records on all of our customers." Owens stepped to his computer and pulled up Logan's file. "She had it serviced on the second of April. Getting it ready for the riding season."

"Did she interact with anyone besides you?" asked Sam.

He looked at the record and said, "It looks like Miguel serviced it. She may have spoken to him if she wanted something specific. He's one of my best mechanics."

"Could we speak with him?"

"I suppose. Let me get him for you."

Owens went through a door and returned a couple of minutes later with a slight Latino man in his forties. "This is Miguel Rodriguez."

"Do you remember working on a Roubaix SL8 Comp bicycle for Jennifer Logan?" asked Sam.

Rodriguez nodded. "Miss Logan," he replied in a heavy accent. "I remember. Nice lady."

"So, she spoke to you about her bike?"

"Yes. She had me work on her bike. She wanted it tuned up. Wasn't shifting right. Very particular about her bike, she was."

"Did you ever see her outside the shop?"

"Oh, no. Just here."

"How is it you remember her?" asked Joe. "You must work on a lot of bicycles."

"Not on bikes like hers. Roubaix lot of money. She was particular."

"As in 'demanding?'"

Rodriguez shrugged.

Joe looked at Owens and asked, "Was she satisfied with the work that was done?"

"She was. Miguel is the only mechanic I trust to work on pricey bikes. When he tunes up a bike, it's next to perfect."

Rodriguez smiled and nodded in agreement.

"Good to know."

"You need Miguel for anything else?" asked Owens.

"I don't believe so."

Rodriguez looked at Owens, who said, "You can go back to work now."

"Thank you," he acknowledged with a nod and walked back through the door into the shop.

"I know this may seem like a strange question," said Owens. "But what became of her bicycle?"

"It's being held for evidence," said Sam. "At some point, her next of kin can claim it."

"The reason I ask is the fact it's a valuable bike. I'd hate to see it fall into the hands of someone who doesn't know how to take good care of it."

"Not everybody should have a Ferrari, you mean?" asked Joe.

"Exactly."

Joe picked up a business card from the counter and then thanked Owens for his assistance. They returned to their office and began looking into Jim Owens and Miguel Rodriguez. They found Rodriguez was legally here on a Green Card. Owens, on the other hand, had been convicted on an assault and battery charge as a result of his role in a bar fight when he was twenty-two years old. But he has been clean ever since. He took over the shop from his father, who started the business. Neither man appeared to have a motive for killing Logan.

"A lot of nothing today," said Joe.

"Yeah," agreed Sam. "A lot of nothing."

Chapter Seventeen

Joe had just arrived at Area 3 the next morning when he received a call from his fellow detective, Gary Nelson. He was surprised that Nelson would call him. What was this about?

"Yeah, Gary…"

"You guys caught a case a while back where the victim's head was cut off, right?"

"Yeah, we did."

"Well, it looks like the killer's struck again."

Joe was silent for a few seconds.

"You still there?" asked Nelson.

"Uh…yeah," replied Joe. "Where are you?"

Nelson provided the address, and after ending the call, Joe said to Sam, "We need to go to the 606 Trail near Wood Street."

"What's happened?" asked Sam.

"A decapitation."

"Another one?" exclaimed Sam.

"Apparently."

The 606 Trail was the unused, former Bloomingdale railway that was developed into a recreational park. As he drove to the location, Joe explained the call from Dirty Gary, as he was known to his fellow detectives. Fifteen minutes later, they arrived at the crime scene. The 606 Trail was popular with bicyclists and joggers. The blue lights on three cruisers were flashing, lighting up the area like a morbid carnival.

A section of the trail had been cordoned off, with uniformed officers guarding the perimeter. A few gawkers had gathered outside the crime scene tape. Gary Nelson and his partner, Mike Tattaglia, were talking with a young woman seated in a police cruiser. The Medical Examiner's van was present, and a few yards away, Joe recognized Kendra Solitsky, dressed in white Tyvek. She was kneeling and examining the body of the victim.

Joe and Sam walked to the cruiser to speak with Nelson and Tattaglia. The woman sitting in the cruiser was dressed in jogging clothes. Her eyes were red and swollen from crying, and she was using a handkerchief to dab at them. When Nelson noticed Joe and Sam, he turned and walked to the front of the cruiser to speak with them.

"What do you have so far?" asked Joe.

"A woman by the name of Kristy Allerton was jogging and came upon the body. Coming across the decapitated victim was pretty upsetting, but she managed to call 9-1-1. That's her in the cruiser," said Nelson, indicating her with a head gesture.

"Is the victim's head missing?" asked Sam.

"No. It was found several feet from the body. Why do you ask?"

"The case we investigated about three weeks ago was a headless body. The head washed up a coupla weeks later on the shore of Lake Michigan."

"Nice."

"Sure was."

"Got an ID on the victim?" asked Joe.

"Not yet. Female, thirties, wearing jogging clothes."

At that moment, Tattaglia stepped into the conversation. "The ME told us you caught a similar case a few weeks ago."

"Yeah," said Sam. "A bicyclist on a trail next to the lake."

"Any suspects?" asked Nelson.

"None yet."

"We've interviewed various persons of interest, but they've all had alibis," added Joe.

"The woman who discovered the body—did she see the offender?" asked Sam.

"She said she saw a runner up ahead," replied Tattaglia. "She could only describe him as someone wearing a black hoodie. Could be sweats or a jogging outfit, I suppose."

"Our witness saw something similar," said Sam. "A guy wearing black sweats. He had the hood pulled up, and his face covered with what looked like a mask."

He said the person resembled a ninja," said Sam.

"A ninja?" sneered Tattaglia.

"That's what he said."

"I think we should talk to the lieutenant about you taking over," said Nelson. "Sounds like these two cases are related."

"Yeah," agreed Joe. "Good idea."

Out of the corner of his eye, Joe saw Kendra walking toward them carrying her kit. She ducked under the tape and began removing her hood, mask, and gloves. The detectives walked toward her, eager to discover what she had to say.

She looked at the four detectives and said, "Looks like I'm Miss Popularity today."

"I thought you were Miss Popularity every day," said Joe.

"Flattery will get you everywhere."

"Well?" asked Nelson, wanting to get to the facts. He wasn't one to engage in banter.

She handed Nelson a plastic bag containing a wallet. "Name's Leah Sarandon. Cause of death was multiple stab wounds to the chest."

"And the decapitation?"

"Given the stab wounds, she was most likely dead when that occurred. I'm calling in Evidence Techs on this one. There may be some of the offender's DNA on the body. And I saw some shoe prints on the path."

The woman who was sitting in the cruiser hesitantly walked up to them. "I'm sorry, but…can I go now?"

"Not yet," said Kendra. "Evidence Technicians will want to take prints off the soles of your shoes. To distinguish your shoes from the other shoe prints on the path."

"All right," she said. "Guess I'd better call in and tell them I'm taking a vacation day today. ” She pulled a phone from her pocket and slowly walked back to the cruiser and sat down.

“Looks like we have company,” said Kendra.

Joe turned to look and saw a television crew approaching. “Wonderful,” he said. “Just what we need.”

“I’ll take care of this,” said Nelson. He intercepted the news crew before they could get close to the crime scene. He forced them to remain a good distance away to prevent them from getting footage of the victim. The reporter tried asking him questions. But it was against policy to comment on an ongoing investigation, so he could not speak to them other than to instruct them not to come any closer. He directed one of the uniforms to make sure they kept their distance. The crew eventually left after filming a short report for the news.

Forty-five minutes later, the Evidence Techs arrived. Big John Gustafson and his assistant, Lenny Andrews, suited up. Andrews began by taking prints of Kristy Allerton’s jogging shoes while Big John photographed the scene. He also took prints of the victim’s shoes. Next, they photographed and cast shoe prints found on the path. Following the casting work, they took swabs from the body, her clothing, and the blood from the surrounding ground area. Two hours later, they had completed their forensic work and were preparing to return to their lab.

Once their investigation was complete, Big John released the body, and Kendra loaded the victim into the ME’s van and drove to the Office of the Medical Examiner. Before leaving, Kendra told Joe she would be conducting the autopsy tomorrow afternoon, and she would inform him of the time so he could attend.

It was mid-afternoon when the crime scene was released, and the cleanup crew had finished their work. The yellow crime scene tape was taken down by uniformed officers, and Nelson and Tattaglia left to make the notification. Assuming Lieutenant Bellamy would hand over the case to them, it was Joe and Sam’s job to find out who Leah Sarandon was and why someone would want to murder her so viciously.

Chapter Eighteen

Joe entered the garage and saw that Destiny's Mercedes was not there. Checking his phone, he noticed she had texted him, saying her mother wanted to go to her own home to recuperate. She would call him sometime that evening. He had been so caught up in the investigation that he had forgotten all about checking his messages. Not the first time.

After taking Autumn for her evening walk, he made a green salad and warmed up the leftovers from the previous night. Crime scenes always tired him out due to all the standing around, walking, interviewing witnesses, and dealing with the scene itself. You seldom had a moment to sit down, and a lot of the time, you had no opportunity to eat.

After dinner, Joe moved to the living room and began reading the book he had started while in the hospital waiting room. It was a police procedural set in Boston, and he found the police work to be a realistic depiction of how detectives handle cases, not like some of the ridiculous things he had seen on network television.

Fifteen minutes after he began reading, his phone rang. It was a call from Destiny.

"How's your mom doing?"

"Pretty well. They released her at noon, and she was eager to get home."

"Is she having much discomfort?"

"She's refusing to take the pain meds they prescribed for her. She swears she's not going to take anything with codeine in it. Instead, she decided Ibuprofen was enough to do the job. But given the surgery, there's bound to be pain. I have to take her in for a checkup tomorrow."

"Glad to hear she's doing well."

"Thanks. Everything okay at home?"

"Yeah. How long do you think you'll be at your mom's?"

"A couple of days. She's supposed to stay off her feet and not lift anything, so I want to stick around and make sure she follows her doctor's instructions. You know how she is."

Joe chuckled, "Oh, yeah."

"Anything new at work?

"As a matter of fact…there was another decapitation murder today."

"You're kidding."

"Nelson and Tattaglia caught it. But Nelson had heard about the case we're investigating and called me. We went to the scene. The victim was a woman in her thirties who was jogging in a park."

"That's terrible. Any witnesses?"

"No. Just the jogger who called it in. She wasn't much help. Said she saw what looked like a runner dressed in a black hoodie way in the distance. Couldn't provide any more details. We're going to talk with the lieutenant tomorrow and see if the investigation can be transferred to Sam and me since they're most likely related."

"I'm sorry you have to investigate such gruesome homicides. What's with people, anyway? Killing someone isn't enough? Their heads have to be cut off?"

"I know. It's bizarre."

"To do something like that, the offender's probably acting out of rage and has some kind of vendetta against his victims."

"Hopefully, we can find a connection between the two. We don't know much about the second victim yet."

"If I can help, let me know."

In the background, Joe heard Vivien calling her daughter's name. "Sounds like you're being paged."

"I am. Look, I'll call you again tomorrow. Gotta go. Love you! Hug Autumn for me."

"Love you, too!"

After the call ended, Joe returned to his book. By nine o'clock, his head was nodding, and he found he was reading the same paragraph for the third time. He looked at Autumn, who was curled up beside him.

"Time to turn in, Autumn."

Joe entered the bedroom and shed his clothes. After brushing his teeth, he set the alarm and settled into bed. He was tired, but sleep wouldn't come. After lying there for over half an hour, he retrieved his book from the living room and returned to bed. After reading for another half hour, he began to feel groggy. He placed the bookmark, laid the book on the bedside table, and turned off the light. Sleep came soon after.

Chapter Nineteen

Detective Nelson sought out Joe the next morning, and they went to Lieutenant Robert Bellamy's office to discuss transferring the Leah Sarandon murder from Nelson and Tattaglia's caseload to Joe and Sam's.

They explained the circumstances to Bellamy, who listened intently.

Looking at Joe, Bellamy asked, "What's this do to your caseload?"

"It'll give us a full load," replied Joe. "But I think we need to have one team investigate both. We're reasonably sure they're connected."

"And what's this do to your caseload?" he asked Nelson.

"It will release us to focus on the drive-by shooting at the high school," replied Nelson.

Bellamy considered it for a moment and then said, "Okay. It's logical one team investigates both." Looking at Joe, he said, "It's yours. Good luck with it."

They thanked him and left his office.

"You made the notification yesterday?" asked Joe.

"Yeah. She lived with a partner in Uptown. He's a doctor with a private practice."

"How did he take it?"

"Pretty upset."

"Did he know anything?"

"He wasn't up to answering any questions. He was a mess. I'll forward the file to you."

Joe walked to Sam's desk and let him know that the Sarandon case was now officially theirs to investigate.

"Bellamy was okay with that?"

"Yeah. He said it made sense for us to investigate both."

Joe and Sam began looking into Leah Sarandon's background to see if there were any obvious links to Jennifer Logan.

Leah Marie Sarandon was born in Oak Park, Illinois, thirty-six years ago, the youngest of four children. She graduated from Western Illinois University with a degree in accounting. For the past six years, she has been employed as a certified public accountant with Crockett & Associates. Court documents revealed she had been divorced from Kevin John Halliwell for two years. No children. Her address confirmed she lived in the Uptown neighborhood. There were no apparent links to Logan.

Joe's phone rang. It was Kendra.

"Sarandon's autopsy is scheduled for this afternoon at 3:30. I'm assuming you wish to attend?" she said.

"I'll be there," said Joe. "Anything I need to know?"

"Nothing yet. I took DNA samples from fingernail scrapings. She was a nail-biter, so there wasn't much I could collect."

"Okay. See you this afternoon."

Joe and Sam arrived at Sarandon's apartment on West Lawrence Avenue shortly before eleven o'clock. They rang, and a male voice answered.

"Yes?"

"Detectives Erickson and Renaldo, Chicago Police Department. We need to speak with Travis Scott."

"Hold on. I'll get him."

A minute later, another male voice answered, "This is Travis Scott."

"I'm Detective Joe Erickson, Chicago PD. We need to speak with you. We're investigating the death of Leah Sarandon."

There was a pause, and then he said, "All right." Seconds later, the door buzzed, and it unlocked for them to enter.

Taking the elevator to the third floor, Joe and Sam found Apartment 3C and rang the bell. Moments later, the door opened as far as the chain allowed. Joe and Sam held up their IDs for the thin-faced man to see. Seemingly satisfied with their identification, the man released the chain and opened the door for them to enter.

"Come in," he said. Scott was forty-something, with thinning dark hair and rimless glasses. As they entered, a little black dog began barking.

"No-no, Fritz," he commanded.

"Is he an Affenpinscher?" asked Joe, since he looked like the dogs at Jennifer Logan's residence.

"He is. I'm surprised you know that." Reaching down and picking up the dog, he said, "Excuse me a second." Then he placed the dog in another room and shut the door. "Little turd–he can be obnoxious, sometimes." Following him into the living room, they saw another man who resembled Scott.

"This is my brother, Leland."

"Gentlemen," he said, acknowledging them. Then he looked at Scott and said, "I'll leave you alone so you can talk in private. I'll be back around five."

"Thanks, Lee," replied Scott.

Scott's brother left. The apartment Scott shared with Sarandon was neat and decorated in an eclectic style that mixed contemporary, antique, and post-modern pieces. Abstract paintings and prints hung from the walls.

"Have a seat," said Scott, indicating the couch.

Scott sat adjacent to them in an overstuffed chair.

"I'm sorry for your loss," said Joe.

"Thank you," replied Scott, folding his thin fingers together.

"I know this is a difficult time for you, but the sooner we can acquire information, the sooner we can move forward with our investigation. We need to apprehend this offender."

Nodding, Scott replied, "I understand."

"Let me start by asking if Leah had any enemies."

"No, she always avoided confrontation. She was more comfortable with facts and figures than being around people. I can't imagine why someone would want to hurt her."

"Was she in contact with her ex-husband?"

"No. He moved to Virginia. She hasn't heard from him in a long time."

"Was there any trouble at work?"

"I doubt it. She worked mostly on tax stuff. She would have told me if there was."

"She was jogging on the 606 Trail near Garfield Park when she was attacked," stated Sam. "Did she jog there often?"

"Almost every day. She liked to stay in shape because her job called for her to sit at a desk all the time. She claimed jogging helped keep her weight down. She liked the trail because it was a…safe place to run." After noting that, he shook his head slowly. "Ironic, huh?"

"Do you know if Leah knew a woman by the name of Jennifer Logan?" asked Joe.

"Jennifer Logan," said Scott, repeating the name. "I don't know. I don't remember her ever mentioning that name."

"Out of curiosity, where did you get your dog?"

Scott looked at Joe with a confused look. "What's that got to do with anything?"

"Humor me."

Scott looked at Sam and then back at Joe. "I'm not sure. He's Leah's dog. She already had him when we started seeing each other. Why do you ask?"

"A dog show judge, who was an Affenpinscher breeder, was killed in the same manner as Leah. About a month ago. We're trying to establish any connections with other people."

"Oh, man…I suppose I could look through Leah's files and see where she bought Fritz. But he's three years old now. I don't know how that could be relevant."

"We have to look at everything," said Sam. "No stone unturned, so to speak."

"Okay."

"Where do you work?" asked Joe.

"I'm a neurologist," replied Scott. "I have my own practice on Lakeshore Drive."

"You don't have any angry or unstable patients, do you?" asked Sam.

"No. Nothing like that. I mostly treat people with Parkinson's Disease and a few other neurological conditions."

"You said she didn't have any enemies. What about a person with a grudge or someone she may have had a disagreement with?"

Scott shook his head as he replied, "Not that she ever told me."

"Who were Leah's friends?" asked Sam. "It would be helpful if you could give us names?"

"She only had one that I know of. She didn't have what you'd call a circle of friends."

"And that would be?"

"Heather. Heather Ford. She's a friend from college."

"Would you happen to have Ford's contact information?"

"I don't. She probably has it on her phone."

"Her phone was taken as evidence. We don't have access to it right now."

"Well, I know she works as an accountant for the city. Something to do with the fire department. Sorry, but that's all I know."

"We can work with that," said Sam, who entered it in his notebook.

"Do you know what veterinarian Leah took her dog to?" asked Joe.

"Oh, jeez," he said. "Let me think. Uh…it was…I can see it…oh! The Pet Doctor."

Joe looked at Sam, acknowledging a connection. They continued to probe for more answers, but after a few more minutes, they concluded there was nothing more they could glean from Scott. Joe handed him his card and said, "If you could check and find who Leah bought her dog from, we'd appreciate a call, one way or the other."

"Certainly."

"Did Leah have a computer?" asked Joe.

"A laptop."

"An Evidence Technician from the police department lab will need to take it for evidence purposes. They'll give it back when they're done with it. The same with her phone."

"I don't know what they could find on it," said Scott.

"We have to be thorough in these investigations," explained Sam. "We have to check everything we can."

"What about next of kin?" asked Joe.

"I've already called her mother."

"Thanks for your time, doctor. Again, our condolences for your loss."

They left his apartment and traveled back to their office. Joe began making notes of their conversation until twelve o'clock. He had no leftovers to bring to work, so he walked to a nearby diner and ordered lunch. As he was paying the cashier, he received a call from Travis Scott.

"I found where Leah bought Fritz," he told Joe.

"That was quick," replied Joe.

"Well, being an accountant, she kept good records, so I found it right away. She bought him from Jen-Lo Kennel."

"Jen-Lo Kennel," repeated Joe. "Were there any names on the document?"

"There were two. Leah's and the breeder. Her name is Jennifer Logan."

Bingo! "Thank you," replied Joe. "That's helpful."

"I hope it leads you to the person responsible."

"So do I."

On his way back to his office, Joe began thinking about the connection between the two victims. *Is this only a coincidence? Or is there more to it? After all, it's been three years since the sale of the dog. Did they stay in touch during this time? Did they have any people in common? Is it possible Leah Sarandon processed Jennifer Logan's taxes? Or became aware of something illegal? That is something they could check out.*

Back at his desk, Joe called Crockett & Associates to see if Jennifer Logan was a client. He was transferred to another extension, and after listening to a minute of classical music, his call was answered.

"Colleen Francis," replied a woman with a smoky voice.

"This is Detective Joe Erickson with the Chicago Police Department. I'm investigating a homicide, and I was wondering if you could answer a couple of questions.

"Homicide. Well, possibly," replied Francis slowly, hesitant about agreeing before hearing the nature of his questions.

"Could you tell me if Jennifer Logan was a client?"

"That's privileged information."

"Well, she's dead. She was murdered about a month ago. I don't think she'll object to a yes or no answer."

"She was murdered?" said Francis, her voice registering shock.

"I take it she was a client, then?" asked Joe.

After a moment, Francis replied, "She was. I just got back from vacation. I wasn't told about her…This is awful."

"It is," said Joe. "And one of your accountants was murdered in the same manner a couple of days ago."

"Who was that?"

"Leah Sarandon?"

Silence. "Dear god…"

"I take it you knew her, too?"

"I'm her supervisor…or was."

"We're trying to establish if there's a link between these two women. Could you tell me if Ms. Sarandon ever worked on Ms. Logan's account?"

"Well…"

"Look," said Joe. "I know your company probably has a policy of keeping clients and employees protected. Now, I could get a search warrant to obtain this information, but it would save us both a lot of hassle if you could just give me a yes or no answer."

With a heavy sigh, she said, "All right. Hold on. Let me check."

He heard the clicking of a keyboard, and after a minute, Francis said, "No. She never worked on any of Jennifer Logan's accounts."

Shit! thought Joe. He was hoping there would be another connection between the two women. "Thank you for your time, Ms. Francis. Chicago PD appreciates your assistance."

Looking at the clock, he saw it was nearly time for him to drive to the Office of the Medical Examiner to attend Leah Sarandon's autopsy.

Racking his brain during the drive, he became increasingly frustrated. They had nothing to go on. All their possible leads had dried up. He hoped that the autopsy would reveal something new. Anything, no matter how small, could help.

The autopsy determined that a knife with a seven-inch blade was the weapon used to kill Leah Sarandon. It supported the same offender theory.

The cause of death was a stab wound that penetrated the right ventricle of the heart. Death would have been instantaneous. Six other stab wounds to the chest and neck were, on their own, survivable with immediate medical attention. But taken in their entirety, she would have bled out in a matter of minutes.

The victim's head had been removed between the second and third cervical vertebrae. Blade marks on the second cervical vertebrae suggested the offender did not know anatomy and tried several times to slip the knife through the disc that separated the two vertebrae.

Kendra had not reviewed her autopsy report on Jennifer Logan beforehand. She had no reason to do so. Given the nature of the stab wounds on Sarandon, Kendra was reasonably certain that the offender was left-handed. This was new information and not noted in Logan's autopsy report. When Joe asked about it, Kendra said she would check her notes again to see if Logan's wounds corresponded to a left-handed offender.

A left-handed offender. Finally, something useful, thought Joe. Only ten percent of the population is left-handed. The rest of the autopsy failed to provide any additional evidence other than a knife with a seven-inch blade was the murder weapon, just as it was in the Logan attack. When he returned to his Area 3 office, he told Sam about what the autopsy revealed.

"Well, that's something," said Sam. "A left-handed offender with a seven-inch blade. Should be a snap to find."

"Yeah," replied Joe. "Easy as pie."

Chapter Twenty

The next morning, Joe and Sam met to discuss the double murder and where they needed to focus their attention in the coming days.

"I think we need to interview Sarandon's friend, Heather Ford," said Sam. "She may be able to shed some light on one or both women."

"Agreed," replied Joe. "We don't know much about Sarandon yet. Maybe there's something in her background that can give us a lead."

"What do you think about our veterinarian? Dr. Winthrop?" asked Sam.

"He seemed a little too laid back about his breakup with Logan. Still a client after she broke up his marriage and then dumped him? Really?"

"Yeah. I would have told her what she could do with her dogs, and it wouldn't be pretty."

"It doesn't make sense...unless they were still seeing each other occasionally."

"A 'friend with benefits' sort of thing?"

"Maybe," considered Joe. "If what Winthrop said was true–that she had an insatiable sex drive–then maybe he was someone she slept with on an occasional basis. To 'fulfill' her needs."

"That could explain why her dogs were still his clients."

"Something could have set him off. Like she dumped him permanently. Under that suave exterior, there could be an angry, vengeful man."

"And...He performs surgery," added Sam. "Sounded like he was good at it."

"I see where you're going. If Winthrop can handle a scalpel, he could probably wield a knife."

"Right."

"Did you notice if he was left-handed?"

"I didn't."

"Neither did I."

"But how would he kill Logan if he was in surgery?" asked Sam. "He couldn't be in two places at the same time."

Joe slowly shook his head and then stopped. "Unless…Miss Nosering was covering for him. This is getting too complicated. If there's a link, we need to find it. It has to be more than using the same veterinarian."

Sam thought for a minute and then asked, "Do you suppose Sarandon could have known something incriminating about Winthrop? Or figured out who killed Logan? And that's what got her killed."

"The killer knew she knew, you mean?"

"Yeah."

"Could be. I think we need to interview Heather Ford before we go further."

"I think so, too."

"I'll track her down and set up an interview," said Joe.

"And I'll find out if Winthrop is left-handed."

When they ended their meeting, Joe went to his desk and called the First Deputy Fire Commissioner's Office. He figured that office could put him in touch with Heather Ford. But a representative referred him to the Chicago Department of Human Resources, since that office was responsible for hiring applicants and would have her up-to-date contact information.

Joe called the number he was given, and a woman answered.

"Department of Human Resources."

Joe introduced himself and told the woman he was investigating a crime and needed to contact Heather Ford.

"I'll need to transfer you," she responded. "Hold on, please."

After a few moments, another female voice answered.

"Elizabeth Spencer. How may I help you?"

"This is Detective Joe Erickson from the Area 3 homicide unit. We're investigating a death, and we need to speak with the victim's friend. Her name is Heather Ford, and we were told she's an accountant working with the Fire Department. Can you check on that for me?"

"What's your badge number?"

Joe gave her his badge number and a phone number to call to verify his identity.

"Hold, please."

He waited on hold for several minutes, presumably while Spencer confirmed his identity. Finally, her voice came back online.

"All right, Detective Erickson. Tell me again. What's the name of the individual you're seeking?"

"Heather Ford. F-O-R-D."

"Thank you."

He was put on hold again. A minute later, she returned.

"Heather Ford is employed as an accountant with the Chicago Fire Department."

Joe began to get aggravated. "I know that," he said, stifling his temper. "I need her contact information. A phone number would be sufficient."

"Hold, please." And once again, he was placed on hold. A few seconds later, she returned and said, "You can reach her at work. The number is 312-555-8890."

Joe thanked her and called the number. A recording played and asked, "If you know your party's extension, you can enter it now." He didn't know it and pressed zero, hoping for an operator. Instead, the call was ended.

He muttered a few curse words and decided to check the Illinois Driver's License database. He found several Heather Fords there, but he narrowed them down to a woman the same age as Leah Sarandon. Noting her address in the West Loop neighborhood, he checked the White Pages for a phone number. No landline listed. In lieu of a phone number, he planned to contact her at home. Hopefully, she will be there after work.

Ford undoubtedly has a cell phone. Finding her cell phone number would have been preferable. However, police are precluded from obtaining cell phone numbers without a search warrant or a subpoena unless there is a need to provide immediate assistance or to prevent imminent harm. That would be carefully monitored with strict protocols to prevent misuse.

When 4:30 rolled around, Joe and Sam drove to Heather Ford's address on

West Jackson Boulevard, hoping she had returned home after work. Traffic was unusually heavy, and they arrived shortly after five o'clock. Ford's apartment was in a vintage brown brick building that was once a 19th-century hotel. The neighborhood where she lived was known as one of the most vibrant cultural areas in the city.

Upon entering the vestibule, Joe found the intercom system and checked the directory for Heather Ford's name. Seeing the name H. Ford, he pushed the button and waited. A short time later, a scratchy audio voice responded.

"Yes?"

"Heather Ford?" asked Joe.

"Yes."

"Chicago Police Department. We need to speak with you."

The door leading to the apartments buzzed and unlocked without another word. They took the elevator to the third floor and sought out Apartment 3A. Joe pressed the video doorbell and held up his ID. After a few moments, the door unlocked and opened a crack. "Yes?" said a female voice.

"Detectives Erickson and Renaldo," said Joe, still holding his ID for her to see.

Ford removed the chain and opened the door for them to enter. She was a petite woman with strawberry blonde hair that was worn short. Her dressy blouse and black slacks suggested she had not had the time or inclination to change out of her office attire.

"I assume you're here about my friend, Leah. Right?"

"We are," said Sam, returning his ID to his pocket. "Our condolences for the death of your friend."

"Thank you. Come on in." She led them to the living area and indicated the muted green couch, saying, "Have a seat."

Joe and Sam sat down as Ford sat on a matching loveseat. The two pieces of furniture dominated her small apartment, which was decorated in a leisurely Coastal style.

"We're investigating Leah Sarandon's murder, and we'd like to learn more about her, hoping it will lead us to the offender," said Joe.

"Of course. Anything I can do to help. Of all the people for this to happen to…"

"What do you mean?"

"She was such a kind, mild-mannered person. I doubt she's ever offended anybody."

"I understand you've known each other since college?"

"We attended Western Illinois University together. Both of us majored in accounting, so we had several classes together. That's how I got to know her."

"What more can you tell us about Leah?" asked Sam.

"Oh, god." She took a big breath as tears welled up in her eyes. "This isn't going to be easy for me. She was my best…friend."

"We understand."

"Well…she was quiet, not the most sociable person. I mean, when we were in college, she didn't go out to the bars or party like a lot of students did. And she wasn't the kind of person to hook up with guys. She studied a lot at the library. Straight-A student. Really smart."

"What did she do for fun?" asked Joe.

Ford chuckled. "You're going to think this is crazy."

"Try me."

"She loved to watch horror movies."

"Really."

"I know it contradicts her quiet, shy personality, but let me tell you, she loved them. Got off on being frightened and shocked. And she liked to get involved in political discussions. Women's rights were important to her."

"Was she involved politically here in the city?"

"Not so much. She wasn't fond of large crowds, so she didn't feel comfortable attending events."

"We heard she liked to work out," said Sam.

Nodding, Ford said, "She started jogging in the rec center when we were students. She said she was putting on weight from eating all that starchy residence hall food, so she took up running to burn off calories. She continued jogging when she moved up here."

"What about boyfriends while living in the city? She have many?"

"No. Not until she met Travis–Dr. Scott. She really fell for him. And he for her, evidently. They eventually moved in together. She spoke very highly of him."

"What did you think of him?" asked Joe.

"Nice enough. Kind of nerdy but nice. I can see why they were compatible."

"Did Leah have any enemies? Anyone she may have had a disagreement with? Over her political views, maybe?"

Shaking her head, Ford replied, "No. Not that I know of. Certainly not something that would motivate someone to kill her." She paused and said, "Sorry," as she dabbed a tissue at her eyes.

"Take your time," urged Sam.

After a moment, she continued. "If she had a discussion with someone with an opposing viewpoint, she would approach it on an intellectual level. To her, it was a debate, not an argument. Her emotions never entered into it. In fact, I don't think I've ever seen her angry."

"Do you know if she may have done something or was privy to some information that could have been dangerous?"

"Not really."

"She ever talk about work? Something she was concerned about?"

"She worked in accounting. How dangerous can debits and credits be?"

"Money is a powerful motivator for murder. Theft, embezzlement, cooking the books..."

"I suppose you're right about that. But she didn't talk much about work."

"Did she ever mention the name Jennifer Logan?" asked Joe.

Again, she shook her head. "Not that I remember."

"What about her dog?"

Ford looked at him incredulously. "You think Fritz is a suspect?"

"Just answer the question, please."

"Fritz. She called him her hairy child."

"Dr. Scott referred to him as a 'little turd!'"

She chuckled. "Leah spoiled Fritz rotten. He's a one-person dog. He didn't like anyone else, especially Travis. I think Fritz was jealous."

"I see."

"What's with the dog questions? I don't understand."

"The breeder who sold Fritz to Leah…She was murdered in the exact same way as Leah was. A month ago. We're trying to determine if there's something that would lead a person to brutally kill these women."

Silence. Fighting tears, Ford looked from Joe to Sam, saying, "This is so sick. Really freakin' sick!"

"It is," said Sam. "That's why we needed to speak with you."

"And if you think of anything, no matter how small or insignificant it might seem, you need to call us. We have to stop this offender before anyone else is killed," explained Joe. He placed his card on the coffee table and continued. "You can call me anytime, day or night."

Ford nodded. Joe looked at Sam and said, "Do you have anything else you'd like to ask Ms. Ford?"

"I don't think so." Looking at Ford, Sam stood and said, "Your cooperation is most appreciated. Thank you."

She rose from the loveseat and began leading them to the door. As they were about to leave, she said, "I hope you catch the sick bastard who did this."

"We'll do our best," assured Sam. "We'll get him."

Outside, as they were walking to their car, Joe said, "You were pretty confident about our solving this case. If we're going to nail this offender, we need to find something substantial to go on. Right now, we don't have zip other than the fact he's a lefty."

"Something will turn up."

"Let's hope. Because right now, hope is all we've got."

Chapter Twenty-One

For dinner that evening, Joe grilled a thick ribeye steak and paired it with a Caesar salad. Once everything was cleaned up and put away, he and Autumn retired to the living room. It wasn't long until Destiny called.

"How are things?" asked Joe.

"Mom's doing fine. The doctor seemed pleased with how her incision looked."

"That's good."

"She wants to do things because she's feeling better, but I won't let her. I think she's getting annoyed with me saying 'no.'"

"She's been independent for a long time," replied Joe. "You're not going to change her."

"I know. The Affannatos are coming to visit tomorrow. I'm sure Loretta will be bringing food."

"I wish I could be there. She's a great cook."

"She is. When I come home, I'll describe how wonderful it was."

"Thanks a lot," replied Joe with mock sarcasm.

"Just kidding."

"I know. When do you think you'll be coming home?"

Destiny chuckled, saying, "If she doesn't kick me out first, I'll be home the day after tomorrow."

"You timed that right. That's one of my days off."

"How's Autumn getting along?"

Joe looked down at Autumn. "She's confused by your absence. She walks around like she's looking for you. Similar to what she does the first few days when you go out of town on a job."

"Sounds like she'll be happy to see me."

"Better be prepared for some sloppy kisses."

"From you?"

Joe laughed. "Yeah. Me, too."

They ended their call, and Joe settled in with his book. By ten o'clock, he had grown drowsy and re-read the same paragraph over and over. Giving up, he stuck the bookmark in place and went to bed.

* * *

As Joe jogged the next morning, he could not help but think about the case. It was frustrating that he and Sam could not latch onto a solid lead. So far, they had failed to connect the two victims other than through their dogs and their veterinarian. How could that be relevant? There had to be something they had not discovered yet. Perhaps concentrating their efforts on the first case would lead them to the link and a motive.

Shortly before ten o'clock, Joe received an email from Roger Morgan, a technician at the Regional Computer Forensics Laboratory. They had successfully opened Jennifer Logan's phone and laptop so detectives could access her messages. Joe alerted Sam, and an hour later, they began searching through her messages, with Sam taking her phone and Joe her laptop. They both found multiple messages exchanged between Logan and a woman named Aurora Adams. Evidently, Logan and Adams were close friends, given the topics they discussed and the number of personal messages sent over a significant period of time. They needed to interview her.

While exploring Adams's social media accounts, Joe found she lived in Chicago and was employed by the Grayson Trading Company, an investment firm. He found their offices are located on South Riverside Plaza in the Loop's commercial district. According to the Illinois Driver's License database, Adams is forty years old and lives on South Sangamon Avenue in the West Loop neighborhood. Nice place to live. He took a screenshot of her license and then another one of her photo, which he enlarged. She appeared to be an attractive woman with dark brown hair. After printing out the screenshots, he placed them in Logan's file. Further research revealed Adams was divorced and the owner of a two-year-old Lexus.

Sam walked over to Joe and tapped him on the shoulder to get his attention. "I found something interesting."

"Oh, yeah?"

"It seems Logan had some kind of relationship that went south over a year ago. Some nasty email messages were exchanged between the two of them."

"I located one of Logan's close friends," added Joe. "I think we need to speak with her. She may know something about that bad relationship. You get a name for this guy?"

"Yeah. Noah Sinclair."

"You know anything about him?"

"Not yet."

"Okay. While you're checking him out, I'll try contacting Aurora Adams."

Joe called Grayson Trading Company's general number. After identifying himself, he asked to speak with Aurora Adams. His call was transferred, and a woman's voice answered.

"Aurora Adams. May I help you?"

"This is Detective Joe Erickson with Chicago PD. I understand you were a friend of Jennifer Logan, is that correct?"

There was a pause before she spoke. "I was, yes."

"My partner and I are investigating her case, and we need to speak with you."

"Okay."

"What's a good time and place?" asked Joe.

"Let me check my schedule." Joe heard her using her keyboard, and a minute later, she said, "I have today open at 3:30, and tomorrow open at 11:15, if either of those work for you."

"Let's do 3:30 today. Will this be at your place of business?"

"That's correct." She gave him the address, and after thanking her, he ended the call.

Joe looked for Sam, who was not at his desk. He assumed he was getting coffee or using the john, so he picked up his empty coffee cup and walked to the break room. Sam came out as Joe was about to go in.

"I was able to arrange an interview with Logan's friend, Aurora Adams, at 3:30 today," said Joe. "She works in the commercial district in the Loop, so it'll take some time to get there."

"Gotcha," replied Sam. "Let me know when you're ready to leave."

After filling his coffee cup, Joe returned to his desk and sat down. He began to delve deeper into Logan's email messages with Aurora Adams. It appeared that Adams acted as a confidante for Logan, someone with whom she could discuss things that were bothering her. High on her list was Noah Sinclair. It seemed Logan was impressed with his performance in bed, but over time, she grew tired of him since he was becoming more and more controlling and possessive. She mentioned to Adams that Sinclair "blew up" and threatened her when she delivered the news about ending their relationship. Following an angry phone conversation, she told Adams that she refused to take his phone calls and blocked his emails and texts.

From Joe's past experience, both of the decapitation crimes were committed by an angry offender, and this jilted beau appeared to be a good candidate for further investigation. He hoped Aurora Adams could cast some additional light on this guy.

After lunch, Joe began reading some of the last emails exchanged between Logan and Sinclair. Their responses were filled with angry words.

Joe and Sam drove to the Loop and parked across from the Riverview Plaza. The address of the Grayson Trading Company was on the fourth floor of the tower. When the elevator opened, they saw a bustling office complex with many offices and cubicles. Flat screens listed the names of companies and their current stock prices. Employees were busy on their phones and working on their keyboards. It looked and sounded like an intense working environment.

Walking to the main reception desk, they were greeted by a woman who looked like she could have stepped straight out of a Hollywood casting call for a new Bond girl. She stood up from her chair as they approached.

"Good morning, gentlemen," she said with a smile that revealed perfect teeth. "What can I do for you today?"

Showing their IDs, Joe said, "Detectives Erickson and Renaldo. We have a scheduled appointment with Aurora Adams."

The fact that they were detectives did not seem to faze her as it occasionally did with some people.

"Of course," she said. "Let me tell her you're here."

Picking up her phone, she pressed several buttons and waited for a moment. Joe could see her expression change when someone answered. "Your 3:30 appointment is here…Detectives Erickson and Renaldo." She listened for a few seconds and then hung up. Making eye contact with Joe, she said, "She'll be with you in a moment." She held eye contact with him a little longer than necessary. Joe glanced at Sam, who had an amused expression.

"Thank you, Claudia," said Sam, having read the nameplate she was wearing.

Glancing back at him, she replied, "You're welcome." Brushing her long, dark hair back, she was about to sit when her face registered seeing someone.

"Ah. Here she is now."

Joe and Sam turned to see a woman walking toward them, her shoes clicking against the hardwood floor. She looked much more attractive than her driver's license photo. Dressed in a tailored silk suit, she projected a business-like demeanor.

"Hello," she said, shaking their hands firmly. "We can talk in my office. If you'll follow me…"

She turned, and Joe got a subtle whiff of her perfume. Nice. They accompanied her to a small office. Closing the door behind them, she said, "Please sit down," indicating the two chairs facing her desk.

After they were all seated, Adams leaned forward with her arms on her desk. Looking at Joe, she said, "You told me on the phone you're investigating Jennifer's death?"

"That's correct," replied Joe. "From what we understand, you were a close friend of hers, is that right?"

Nodding, Adams said, "Right. She was one of my closest friends."

"How did you get to know her?"

"A number of years ago, she came to us as a client. But after we had some dealings regarding her stock portfolio, we soon grew to be friends. It seemed to have been one of those–uh– inexplicable connections, I guess you could say."

"In other words, you hit it off," said Sam.

"We did."

"Did you know her before her husband passed?"

"No. We met shortly after."

Adams looked back at Joe, saying, "Do you have any suspects?"

"There's a person of interest we'd like to ask you about."

"Noah Sinclair?" she presumed, her eyebrows rising.

"What makes you think he's a person of interest?" asked Joe.

"He hated her."

"Why's that?"

"Well, as she explained it to me, he turned out to be a real asshat. She enjoyed being with him at first. Successful businessman. Multi-millionaire. Seemed to be a real catch."

"And then?"

"As their relationship developed, he became more and more controlling. He wanted to know where she was, what she was doing, who she was with. It was like he didn't trust her when she was out of his sight. She tolerated it for a while because she found him…desirable. But she wasn't about to put up with that crap for long. When he accused her of being with some other guy, she got angry, and he got physically abusive. After that episode, she broke it off. Told him to take a 'flying fuck.' Her words, not mine."

"How did he take it?" asked Joe, seeking to confirm what he read in Logan's email correspondence.

"He was livid. He exploded at her when she told him."

"What do you mean by 'exploded'?"

"Screamed and yelled profanities, grabbed her by the arm so hard he left bruises. She called the police and reported the incident. Then she filed for an Order of Protection against him."

"When did this take place?" asked Sam.

"Oh…maybe six months before…" Adams hesitated to finish the sentence. It seemed her business-like demeanor was beginning to crack.

"Before she was killed?"

Adams nodded. She reached for a water bottle and took a drink. "Sorry."

"Take your time," said Joe. When she was finished, he asked, "Did you ever meet Noah Sinclair?"

"Once."

"What was your impression?"

"A handsome, charming prick."

"Care to explain?"

"I can see why she was attracted to him. Most women would be physically attracted to a guy with his looks. And he seemed to satisfy her needs, so to speak. But there's something seriously wrong with him, psychologically."

"In your opinion, could he become angry enough to kill her for dumping him?"

Adams let out a sigh. "I don't know. It's hard to know what people are capable of. But if I were you, I wouldn't rule him out."

"Do you know if she had problems with anyone else?"

"Abusive men, you mean?"

"Anyone."

She thought for a moment. "Not that I know of. But she told me someone had filed a grievance or something with the AKC. About her work as a judge. She seemed to toss it off and said it was just sour grapes. Nothing came of it as far as I know."

"Yeah, we've already looked into that."

"Any of her other romances end badly?" asked Sam.

"One. There was this veterinarian. They had a fling, and it caused his wife to file for divorce. They didn't stay together, but they're still friendly. I mean, he continues to take care of her dogs, so…"

"So, you don't see him as a suspect?"

"I don't think so. They were still seeing each other from time to time, from what she said."

"Seeing…as in continuing an on-again off-again relationship?" asked Joe.

"If you're asking if they still got it on occasionally…yeah. They did. I loved her like a sister, but her sex life was something else. She would say, 'I have needs.' It wasn't my place to judge who she slept with. She was a dear friend, and…"

She picked up the bottle of water and took another drink. Afterward, she paused before she spoke.

"We're not judging her," said Sam. "We simply want to find out who killed her."

"It's been hard to come to grips with…what happened. The way it happened."

"We understand."

"Is there anything else you care to tell us about her?" asked Joe.

"Well…She was witty but only showed her sense of humor to people she knew. And despite being wealthy, you would never suspect it. She acted like a normal person. Except for her rather robust sex life."

"Did you know her husband?"

"No. He'd already passed when I met her. She spoke very highly of him, though. And it sounded like they had a good marriage. I'm no psychiatrist, but I think his death affected a change in her. She never mentioned having any extramarital affairs. Her promiscuity came afterward."

Joe looked at Sam and could tell he had exhausted all his questions. Looking back at Adams, he said, "I think we're done here, Ms. Adams. We appreciate your time."

Joe left his card and asked her to call if she remembered anything. Once out on the street, Sam said, "It sounds like we have a potential suspect."

"Yeah," replied Joe. "Let's look into his background when we get back to the office."

"Tomorrow," said Sam.

Looking at his watch, Joe smiled. "Yeah. Tomorrow." Sam didn't like to start something new when it was getting close to Miller time, and Joe respected that.

Chapter Twenty-Two

Joe was eager to get to the office the next day so he could begin researching Noah Sinclair. Sam investigated Sinclair's financials while Joe looked into his social and political connections.

Sinclair was all over the internet. Newspapers and periodicals showed him pictured with the governor and other political and high-profile individuals. He had a Hollywood leading man's face and a charming smile to match. Joe found he was on the board of numerous companies, universities, and charities.

The fifty-two-year-old Sinclair was a graduate of Northwestern University. He is currently the President and CEO of the Sinclair Group, a software company that developed computer programs for weapons systems. His company has received many multi-million-dollar contracts from the Department of Defense.

Twice divorced and the father of two children, Sinclair maintained a presence on Facebook, Twitter, Instagram, LinkedIn, BlueSky, and TikTok. However, the postings were not personal. There was nothing about his kids, family members, hobbies, or opinions. It became obvious that Sinclair had a public relations staff assigned to keep his name and image before the people and avoid anything personal. *Why?* Joe wondered. In any case, little was learned about his personal life.

Police reports were more revealing. There was a string of domestic abuse calls involving Sinclair, but no arrests were made. Two different women filed Orders of Protection against him. One was his first wife, and the other was Jennifer Logan. Apparently, he has a problem playing nice with his romantic partners. Joe made a note to interview his ex-wives. He looked them up and found his first wife had remarried and was living in New York. That would have to be a phone interview. Fortunately, his second wife still lived in the Chicago area.

Joe and Sam met over lunch at an Italian restaurant to discuss what they had learned about Noah Sinclair.

After the waitress took their drink order, Joe looked at the menu momentarily and then put it down. He had eaten here many times and knew what he wanted.

"What do you think?" asked Sam, glancing up from the menu. "About Noah Sinclair."

"He's a potential suspect," replied Joe. "Abusive partner with what appears to be anger issues."

"I suspected that from his ugly email messages," replied Sam. "I guess Logan wasn't an isolated case."

"Two Orders of Protection filed against him. Multiple domestic abuse calls over the years. But he doesn't seem the sort to kill in such a violent and bloody fashion. Unless…he's smart enough to disguise his actions as those of a maniac."

"Understandable for Logan. He had motive. But what about Sarandon? What's his motive for offing her?"

"Remains to be seen," replied Joe, shaking his head. "Something is missing. Something we aren't seeing."

Joe reported what he had learned about Sinclair's ex-wives, and Sam agreed that their next step should be to interview each of them.

"You suppose they were forced to sign a non-disclosure agreement that prevents them from talking about their marriages?" asked Sam. "Sinclair's attorneys could have included such a clause in the divorce agreements."

"We'll see. What did you find out regarding his financials?"

Putting down his menu, Sam replied, "The guy's loaded. It's estimated he's worth close to four hundred million dollars. He's donated a lot to charities of various kinds and likes to schmooze with important people."

"I'm not surprised. There are a lot of photos of him with city officials, business leaders, and a few celebrities at charity functions. Not just here in Illinois, but in New York and Los Angeles."

"Yeah. He gets around."

The waitress returned with their drinks and asked if they were ready to order. Sam ordered the veal scallopini while Joe ordered mostaccioli with red clam sauce.

When the waitress left, Joe quipped, "I thought you'd order a hamburger and fries."

"A few months ago, maybe I would have. Since moving in with me, Carolyn's been working on my bad eating habits. She likes to cook Italian. Says a Mediterranean diet is very healthy."

"It is if you stay away from the cream sauces."

"Yeah. I've lost seven pounds due to her cooking."

"Good for her. And you."

For a guy who used to live on hamburgers, hot dogs, and French fries, Sam was turning over a new culinary leaf thanks to Carolyn's intervention. He was getting to the age where he needed to alter his diet if he was going to remain healthy and fit. He didn't want to see Sam end up like Detective Nate Smith, who didn't take care of himself and succumbed to a heart attack at a Cubs game.

Changing the subject, Sam asked, "Did you locate Sinclair's ex-wives?"

"His first wife has remarried and lives in upstate New York. She's the mother of his two kids. His second wife is still in the area. I found her address. Lives in Forest Park. I'll set up an interview with her."

"Sounds like a plan. Oh! Something else. Did you get the email from forensics about the Berman case?"

Katie Berman was a student at Columbia College who was found beaten to death in an alley. Her homicide had been on Joe and Sam's caseload for three months, and they had been anticipating the results of DNA found under her fingernails.

"No, I didn't. When was this?"

"Just before we left."

"Oh. Was it helpful?"

"Sure was. We've got enough to make an arrest. It came back to a sex offender named Neil Lee Geisler. He was recently released from a prison in Indiana."

"It's about time we got some good news," said Joe.

"Tell you what," said Sam, "I'll look into finding this loser, and you can contact Sinclair's second wife. What's her name?"

"Jill. Jill Sinclair."

Back at work after a savory lunch, Joe researched Jill Sinclair before contacting her. He discovered she was actually "Dr. Jill Sinclair," an anesthesiologist at the University of Chicago Medical Center. Interesting. *I wonder if she was present during Vivien's surgery.*

He called the U of C Med Center and asked to be transferred to Dr. Sinclair's office. When she failed to pick up, he left a message for her to call him.

Since Sam was focused on finding Neil Lee Geisler's location, Joe decided to reach out to Sinclair's first wife, Amanda Radcliff. She resides in Alexandria Bay, New York, a small tourist community in the northern part of the state. He discovered that she and her husband owned Red Cliff Winery in a neighboring town. Their website provided contact information, including a business phone number. He placed the call.

A woman answered, "Red Cliff Winery."

"This is Detective Joe Erickson with the Chicago, Illinois Police Department. I need to speak with Amanda Radcliff."

"Speaking," replied Radcliff. "What can I do for you?"

"Your ex-husband is a person of interest in a crime we're investigating, and I'd like to ask you some questions."

"What did he do, kill somebody?"

Joe was taken aback by her response and didn't answer immediately. "Why do you ask that?"

"I doubt you'd be calling me if he got a speeding ticket."

"We don't know if he's guilty of anything. Right now, he's simply a person of interest."

"Okay. Can you tell me what kind of crime?"

Joe would have preferred not to reveal the nature of the crimes, but since she asked, he felt obligated to tell her. He was curious what her reaction would be.

"We're investigating a homicide."

There was a pause, and then Radcliff mumbled, "Wow. Is he a suspect?"

"At the present, he's simply a person of interest.

"What's the difference?"

"A person of interest has a connection to the crime. When we have evidence pointing to a person's guilt, he becomes a suspect. We don't have any such evidence on your ex."

"Hm. Learn something every day."

"I've called, hoping you can help point us in one direction or the other."

"Okay. Fire away."

"Good. So, let me begin by asking if your ex-husband was prone to violence. Did he ever get physical with you?"

"Oh…well, there are two sides to him that you need to know about. He could be sweet, romantic, and kind. He could also be a paranoid bully who questioned everything I did. I never fooled around on him, but he seemed to think I did. And for no good reason. 'Where the hell were you?' he'd ask. 'Getting my haircut.' 'And that took two hours?' 'Port to port, yeah, it did. You want to check the car's GPS?' Conversations like that. He was terrible sometimes. And it got pretty damned old. And the kids cowered and hid in their rooms when he was in one of his moods. I was afraid he'd screw them up."

"So that was the cause of your divorce?"

"The ongoing mental cruelty…along with the rest of it."

"The rest of it?" asked Joe.

She let out a sigh he could hear over the phone.

"Did he ever get physically violent with you?"

"Look, he pays for the kids' college. I don't want to piss him off."

"I won't use your name as a source. But it's important that I get to the truth."

She paused, seeming to weigh whether to reveal everything. "All right. He put me in the hospital once. He grabbed me really hard by the throat and shoved me down a flight of stairs. I broke my arm and wound up with a concussion when I hit my head on the newel post. He was all apologetic at the hospital. It wasn't the first time he grabbed me or pushed me up against a wall. But that time was the last straw."

"Do you believe he could become so angry that he would attack and kill a former lover with a knife?"

"Jesus! That's what you're investigating?"

"Sadly, it is."

"Well…we've been divorced for fifteen years. I don't see him going that far. At least he wasn't homicidal with me. But who knows? He could have gotten worse or gone off the deep end, I suppose. I've only talked with him once in the last couple of years, and that time, it was about paying his son's college tuition. Other than that, we've had no contact. And, to tell you the truth, that's just fine with me."

"The victim had multiple stab wounds, and she was decapitated."

"For god's sake!"

"Does that sound like something your ex could be capable of?"

"That's what happened?" she gasped.

"It is."

"Unless he changed, the sight of blood was something he couldn't deal with. I cut my finger once with a knife I was using in the kitchen. It was a nasty cut, and it required a couple of stitches. When he saw the bleeding finger, he began to swoon and stumbled out of the room. I thought he was going to pass out."

"Really."

"Oh, yeah. I don't know if he could cut someone's head off. He would have to have gone a little nutso to do something like that, you know?"

"Okay."

"Honestly, Noah could be a real son-of-a-bitch sometimes. But I don't know if he could be the perpetrator in your case. Not with all that blood."

They spoke for a little longer, and Joe ended the call. What she told him painted a troublesome portrait of Sinclair. Could he have evolved from an abusive and paranoid husband into a homicidal offender? People can change in fifteen years. Changed so much that the sight of blood no longer affected him? Hm. They would need to hear from his second ex-wife to get another, more recent opinion.

Chapter Twenty-Three

When Joe arrived home that evening, he saw Destiny's car in the garage. He was eager to see her, and as he entered the kitchen, she met his eyes with a smile.

"Welcome home," she said, throwing her arms around him.

"Welcome home to you, too." They kissed. It was long, lingering, and wet. And it was repeated as soon as their lips parted. "I missed you."

Destiny smiled. "I can tell. I missed you, too."

They kissed again, and Destiny said, "We should probably stop this, or it could lead to something.

"So?"

Destiny laughed and released her embrace, saying, "To be continued?"

"Oh yeah."

Joe looked down and saw Autumn waiting at his feet. He leaned down to pet her. Destiny said she had already walked her around the block and given her a treat. She looked up at him, her eyes begging for another treat.

"Sorry, Autumn," said Joe. "You've already had your T-R-E-A-T." He made his way to the counter and got a wine glass from the cupboard. "How's your mom doing?"

"She's still a little sore, of course. But she's doing fine. The doctor told her she could drive, but to take it easy. She can go back to being her usual independent self."

As Joe poured wine from a bottle of Pinot Noir, he asked, "Shall I pour a glass for you?"

"Please."

"I was thinking maybe we could go out tonight. To celebrate you being home."

"Sure. But we probably need a reservation," she said, taking the glass of wine from him.

"I already made one. I figured I could call and cancel if you didn't want to go. If you were too tired or something."

"I'm not tired," she said. "I'm happy to be back home."

Walking back around the island, Joe sat on one of the stools and sipped his wine.

Sitting beside him, Destiny said, "So…where are we going?"

"Our favorite Serbian restaurant."

"The Whiskey Cafe? Oh, yum!" she said. "We haven't been there for a while."

"I know. The reservation is for 7:30, so we won't be pressed for time."

"Perfect."

"What have you been doing while I've been gone?

"Oh…reading. I'm almost done with the book you gave me. Another thirty pages to go."

"Is that all?"

"Yeah. That and thinking about the decapitation cases. We haven't made much progress, but there's another person of interest. I interviewed his first ex-wife this afternoon. I'm going to set up a meeting with his second ex-wife tomorrow."

"How many exes does he have?"

"Two. And several ex-girlfriends. He probably holds the record for being dumped the most times."

"Unlucky at love or—"

"Sounds like a dick. A very rich dick."

"Hmm," muttered Destiny. She was not convinced a rich man would commit such a heinous act. It didn't make sense to her unless the guy was a psychopath. "Have you interviewed him?"

"Not yet. Why?"

"Statistics show that white people are less likely to commit violent street crimes. They do commit a lot of crimes, don't get me wrong. But they're much more likely to be of the white-collar variety. There's a disproportionate involvement of minorities in street crime, and that's largely due to poverty and living in an urban setting. You know that. It's possible some white guy could be the offender, but it's less likely your rich person committed these crimes."

"Given what we've found so far, neither of the victims had any ties to the populations who commit street crimes. They were both white women. And these two crimes don't appear to be random. They were targeted. But I'm not ruling anyone out."

"I wouldn't either. There are always aberrations that don't fit the norms."

Not long after their conversation, Joe and Destiny left for the Whiskey Cafe on North Lincoln Avenue, the Serbian restaurant they enjoyed patronizing. The food there was always well-cooked and impeccably presented.

After she had brought their drinks and given them time to look over the menu, the waitress came back to their table to take their order. Joe ordered the Shawarma-Spiced Skirt Steak Frites while Destiny asked for the Halibut Ceviche, a dish she had ordered months ago and deemed outstanding.

Halfway through their meal, Destiny heard a familiar voice say, "Well, hello there," and looked up to see her mother accompanied by a distinguished-looking gentleman about her age.

"Mom! I thought you were supposed to be taking it easy."

"I am, but I got bored." Turning to her escort, she said, "Dennis, this is my daughter, Destiny, and her partner, Joe Erickson. Destiny, Joe, this is Dennis Simon-Cooper, my escort for the evening. He works at the British Consulate here in the city."

"Pleased to meet you," said Simon-Cooper with a pronounced English accent. "I live in quarters two doors down from your mother. Several months ago, we met and became acquaintances. I told her I would treat her to dinner when she was feeling aces."

"You have good taste in restaurants," said Joe.

"And it appears you do as well," replied Simon-Cooper with a charming smile.

"I'll talk with you later," said Vivien. "We'd better get to our table."

"Lovely making your acquaintance," said Simon-Cooper.

Joe looked at Destiny, who didn't seem amused that her mother was out and about so soon after her surgery. "Looks like you can't keep a good woman down."

"Seems so," replied Destiny, taking a sip of her wine. "I just hope she knows what she's doing."

"Well, I don't think you'll have to worry about him fondling her incision tonight."

"Joe! That's my mother you're talking about!"

He laughed. "Just kidding."

"Sheesh!" And she returned to eating her ceviche.

As they were leaving, Joe and Destiny could not avoid her mother's table, which they had to pass on their way out. Stopping, they wished them well and said good night.

On the drive home, Destiny voiced her concerns about her mother. "I hope she's not overdoing it," she said.

"She wasn't drinking—did you notice she only had a glass of water in front of her? I'd say she's aware of her limitations and following her doctor's orders," replied Joe.

"I noticed that."

"I wouldn't worry. She's a big girl."

"I know. It isn't easy being an only child."

"I know all about that," replied Joe. "I often wished I had a brother, but it was never to be."

"At least you had two parents. My father died when I was two years old, so all I know is having my mom as a parent."

"You're lucky to still have her. She's young and vital. She has a good chance of being in your life for a long time to come. I wasn't so lucky."

"Thanks," she said and leaned over and kissed him on the cheek.

"Mm. That was nice," he said.

Joe wanted to put his arm around her, but it wasn't possible with bucket seats and a console, unlike his high school days when he was driving a car with a bench seat. Putting your arm around your sweetie who had slid next to you was a common practice. Not particularly safe, though. But he had fond memories of what happened on those seats. Thinking of it made him smile.

"What are you smiling about?" asked Destiny.

"Something that happened back in high school. I don't know why it just popped into my head."

"What was it?"

"You had to be there. It was a Marathon thing," he said, harking back to incidents while growing up in Marathon, Iowa.

"Oh."

Whew, he thought. *Got out of that one. And without lying!*

"You'll have to tell me what a 'Marathon thing' is sometime."

Joe laughed. "You know, there are some things that are best left unsaid."

Chapter Twenty-Four

J oe slept late the next morning, preferring to snuggle with Destiny. He figured his exertion the previous evening was a suitable substitute for jogging three miles. While Destiny slept in, he walked Autumn and quietly made himself breakfast so as not to wake her.

When Joe got to his Area 3 office, his first task was to find contact information for Jill Sinclair. While Joe was doing that, Sam began tracking down the location of Neil Lee Geisler, the suspect in the murder of Katie Berman.

Knowing Sinclair worked at the University of Chicago Medical Center, he called the hospital's general number and was transferred to her office. Expecting a recording, he was surprised to hear a woman answer.

"Dr. Sinclair," she said.

"Good morning," said Joe. "I'm Detective Joe Erickson with Chicago PD, and I need to speak with you regarding your ex-husband, Noah Sinclair."

"Has something happened to him?"

"No. As far as I know, he's fine."

"That's too bad."

Her cynical response made Joe smile. "Is there a time when we can sit down and interview you?"

"What's this about?"

"He's a person of interest in a case we're investigating."

"Really."

"Really," replied Joe. "We need to speak with you about him. We've already interviewed his first wife, and we need to get your perspective, too."

"Well…Okay. Let me check my schedule. Hold on." She put him on hold, and a few moments later, she came back. "I have this afternoon at 2:30 available. Now, that's tentative. There's always a chance of an emergency surgery, so it may not work out."

"I'll take my chances," replied Joe. "Hope to see you at 2:30."

She gave him directions for finding her office, and then they ended the call. It seemed her opinion of Noah Sinclair was troublesome as well. He walked to Sam's desk and told him about their interview with Dr. Sinclair.

"Got it," said Sam. "I just received an email about our suspect in the Katie Berman case."

"Yeah?"

"We're in luck. Neil Lee Geisler was picked up last night on an assault charge. He's being held at the Nineteenth."

"That's good news," said Joe.

"I called over there and told the sergeant to hold him so we can make another arrest."

That was a relief. Locating Geisler could have taken a lot of time and effort, so finding him already incarcerated made their arrest easy.

They drove to Police District 19 headquarters on West Addison and asked to interview Neil Lee Geisler. Joe and Sam had been there many times and were known to the Duty Sergeant. They explained they were there to arrest Geisler on a murder charge. Ten minutes later, Geisler was sitting in an interrogation room. Looking through the two-way mirror, Joe and Sam observed Geisler cuffed to the table. The thirty-six-year-old was a good-looking man with a neatly trimmed beard and curly brown hair. He had a split lip, possibly resulting from the assault last night. The average person seeing Geisler for the first time would not get the impression he was a habitual criminal. Offenders like Geisler don't always fit the image most people have of predators and violence-prone perpetrators, making them especially dangerous.

Joe and Sam met with another sergeant who accompanied them into the interrogation room. The sergeant unlocked the cuff that held Geisler to the table.

"Stand up," the sergeant commanded, and then cuffed him with his hands behind his back.

"What the hell is this?" protested Geisler. Looking at Sam and Joe, he said, "What do you want?"

"Neil Lee Geisler, you're under arrest for the murder of Katie Berman," said Sam.

"What the fuck?" protested Geisler.

"You have the right to remain silent," Sam began reading from a card. They always read a person's rights from a card rather than reciting them from memory, so a defense attorney could not accuse an arresting officer of miscommunicating the Miranda warning.

Geisler demanded to speak with an attorney. Forty-five minutes later, a young public defender showed up. He was apprised of Geisler's arrest pending a charge of first-degree murder. When he advised his client not to say anything, Joe and Sam's work was done. The DA's office would take it from here. The DNA evidence should be enough to convict Geisler, especially since witnesses could place him in the vicinity around the time of the crime.

That afternoon, Joe and Sam drove to the University of Chicago Medical Center on South Maryland Avenue. When they reached Dr. Sinclair's office, they found an envelope taped to her door with "Detective Erickson" written on it. Joe opened it and read her note, which said she had been called in for emergency surgery and would not be available for their meeting. She suggested reaching her at her home after five o'clock. She noted her address and phone number.

Joe looked at Sam and said, "Wonderful. She got called into surgery."

"You think she's avoiding us?" asked Sam.

"No. It sounds legit. She noted her home address and said she'd be there after five. I know you're off then, but I can go to her home and interview her if you've got stuff to do."

"Thanks, I appreciate that," said Sam. "I have an appointment with my physical trainer at the gym."

"You're going to the gym now?" asked Joe, surprised by this new revelation.

Looking a little embarrassed, Sam said, "Yeah. Something else Carolyn's been urging me to do. She hooked me up with a personal trainer who's helping me feel pain and discomfort—I mean, get into shape."

"I'm impressed," said Joe. "With Carolyn, not you."

"Very funny," replied Sam. "You might have noticed I was moving kind of slow a month ago."

"Yeah, but I didn't want to give you a hard time about it."

"Thanks."

"I thought maybe you'd hurt yourself in the throes of passion."

"You're a regular comedian today, aren't you?"

"All kidding aside. I'm glad you're taking your health seriously. Carolyn will be glad you did."

Chapter Twenty-Five

Joe traveled to Dr. Jill Sinclair's residence on Elgin Avenue in Forest Park, a wealthy community ten miles west of the Loop. His GPS took him to her address, a condo in a renovated 1920s brick townhouse.

He pressed her name on the intercom and identified himself. She buzzed him into the lobby. Her condo was one of two located on the first floor. When he rang her doorbell, the door opened, revealing a woman wearing jeans and a T-shirt emblazoned with "University of Chicago Med Center." Jill Sinclair was a tall, slim woman with fiery red hair and freckles.

"Detective Erickson, I presume?" she asked.

"That's correct," said Joe, displaying his ID for her to see.

"Please come in."

She led him to a nicely appointed living room decorated with sizeable French country furnishings. Original paintings adorned the walls. "Sit wherever," she said.

Joe chose a chair while Sinclair sat on the couch facing him.

"Lovely place you have here, Doctor," remarked Joe.

"Call me Jill. You should be thanking my sister. She's an interior designer. I gave her carte blanche when I got this place."

"It's impressive."

"You said you wanted to speak with me about my ex-husband?"

"I do," said Joe. "I found your response, shall we say, 'interesting.'"

"Noah and I don't speak. Simple as that. He can best be described as a chameleon. He could change his colors and go from sweet to nasty, depending on his mood. And you never knew which one you'd get when he walked in the door."

"As I mentioned on the phone, he's a person of interest in a crime we're investigating. Let me ask, was he ever physically violent with you?"

"No. He has a quick temper, and he was verbally abusive. But he never got physical. I told him if he ever touched me, he'd regret it because I know how to defend myself. I took self-defense classes in college. It may have been years ago, but I haven't forgotten the techniques I learned."

Joe was jotting down her answers in his notebook, and when he finished, he looked up and asked, "Was there anything in particular that would set him off?"

"He has trust issues. I don't think he trusts anybody, to be honest. The thing is, he's also a control freak. Maybe that's how he made his businesses successful, I don't know. But it didn't make for a happy marriage. The only good thing that came out of our relationship was the settlement I got in our divorce. I never signed a prenup, and I got this place and a nice retirement portfolio as a result. Let me tell you, I deserved every penny."

"Was there an event or occasion that prompted you to file for divorce?"

"Which one?" she chuckled. "I guess when he accused me of having an affair with one of my colleagues. Nothing could have been further from the truth."

"Can you describe his behavior when he got angry?"

"Yelling, swearing, throwing things. He broke an eighteenth-century vase that belonged to my great-grandmother. I could have killed him for that." She paused and smiled. "Maybe I shouldn't have said that."

"When's the last time you spoke?"

"We ran into each other at a political function a couple of years ago. He flashed that smile of his and said, 'How have you been?' Like nothing had ever happened. I just said, 'Considerably better,' and walked away."

"This may seem like a strange question, but did you ever find he had an adverse reaction to the sight of blood?"

"No, I don't recall anything like that. Out of curiosity, what's he suspected of?"

"We're investigating a homicide, and he's a person of interest because he had a previous relationship with the victim."

"Wow."

"Do you think his temper could lead him to kill a person and decapitate them afterward?"

"Mother of God! That's what you think he may have done?"

"Someone did. And we're not ruling anyone out at the present time."

Sinclair sat back on her couch and thought for a moment. "Wow," she said again. "I'm floored. I know he probably seduces women. He's good at it. But to kill somebody for pissing him off? I don't know about that."

"You were together for how long?" asked Joe.

"Two and a half years. Married for almost two."

"I just have one more question. When you were together, did he jog or run to keep in shape?"

"As a matter of fact, he did. Every morning. He was a fanatic about it. He'd go for a run right after he woke up and was usually back in about half an hour."

"Good to know. Thanks for your time, Jill," said Joe, rising from the chair. "You've been quite helpful."

"Are you married?" she asked.

"In a relationship for several years," replied Joe. "No rings, yet."

"Nice to know somebody met the right person."

"You will. Sooner or later."

"I don't know. I think it may be safer to remain married to my work."

"If it keeps you out of trouble…" said Joe.

"Thank you, detective," she smiled back. "So far, so good."

Joe left her condo and returned to Chicago amid heavy traffic, arriving home much later than usual. He had called Destiny before he drove to Forest Park to let her know he was going to be quite late. She told him she had received a call from her friend, Maddie, and they were going out to dinner. "You may get home before I do," she said.

And he did. When he entered the kitchen, he found a note from Destiny saying she had walked Autumn, and there was a salad in the refrigerator. Joe poured his usual glass of wine and sat down with Autumn on the couch to watch TV. He planned to put off his dinner until he became hungry. By the time Destiny arrived home, he had fallen asleep without eating.

Destiny leaned over and gave him a kiss on the cheek. "Hey, there, sleepy head," she said. "I'm home."

Looking up at her, half asleep, he said, "Oh, man…I must have been tired." Looking at his watch, he said, "Quarter to ten. Crap! I'm probably not going to fall asleep tonight."

"Maybe if you start reading your book, you'll grow drowsy."

"How was your dinner with Maddie?"

"It was nice. She took me to a new place with a lot of vegetarian choices. Good food. Good conversation."

"Glad you had a nice dinner. I think I'll try to go to bed and finish that book."

"I'll join you in a little while."

Joe looked down at Autumn, who was nestled beside him. "Right, Autumn?" Autumn looked up at him without moving and then closed her eyes again. "Glad you agree."

Joe rose from the couch and walked to the bedroom. After getting into bed, he read three pages and fell back asleep. So much for finishing the book.

When Destiny came to bed, she carefully removed the book from Joe's hands, placed the bookmark on the open page, and laid it on her bedside table. After she slipped into bed, she leaned over, kissed his shoulder, and then turned out the light. Joe rolled over to face her.

"Did I wake you?" she asked.

Putting his arm around her, he kissed her and said, "Mm. I'm glad you did."

Chapter Twenty-Six

Joe and Sam met the next morning to determine where their investigation into the decapitation deaths needed to go. While they were pleased with the arrest and indictment of Neil Lee Geisler, they were frustrated that their newest case was not leading them to a viable suspect. Only a person of interest, and Joe was dubious about his guilt, given he couldn't stand the sight of blood.

"The only possible suspect is Noah Sinclair. What do you think?" asked Sam.

"All accounts paint him as a dick, but why would a multi-millionaire kill two people in such a heinous manner when he could have hired it done? I can maybe understand him killing Jennifer Logan if he was obsessed with her. But Leah Sarandon? There's no connection. Logan was a very attractive, outgoing woman. Sarandon was rather plain and reserved. She wasn't his type."

"Maybe he was using a strategy to deflect suspicion. He had no connection to her, and he chose her randomly, killed her in the same manner to throw investigators off the scent."

"That would be cold," said Joe, but he was still not convinced. Sam's suggestion seemed like a long shot.

"We only need to nail him on the Logan murder. Maybe we should forget about Sarandon for the time being and focus on Logan. If we look deep enough, it might lead us to a link to Sarandon."

Sam looked at Joe and saw him staring into space. "What is it?"

"I just thought of something. What if Sarandon worked on Sinclair's accounts?"

"That's a thought," replied Sam. "You think she found something illegal?"

"Maybe."

"But that would be a completely different motive."

"It would. I'll check with her office to see if they can confirm it."

"What about Noah Sinclair?"

"Well…he's all we've got," said Joe, looking at Sam. "If nothing else, we have to eliminate him."

"We need to bring him in."

"Agreed."

When Joe got back to his desk, he called Sarandon's accounting firm, Crockett & Associates, and asked to be transferred to Colleen Francis, whom he had spoken with previously. He sweet-talked her into revealing whether Noah Sinclair was a client. She told him he was not. Another dead end.

Next, he began to track down Noah Sinclair. His residence is in Highland Park, one of Chicago's most affluent suburbs. Noting the address, he checked for his business headquarters. The Sinclair Group also had a Highland Park address.

Joe called the phone number listed on the Sinclair Group website.

A woman answered. "Sinclair Group."

"This is Detective Joe Erickson with the Chicago Police Department. I need to speak with Noah Sinclair."

"I'm sorry, but Mr. Sinclair is not in."

Of course, he isn't, thought Joe. "Do you have a number where he can be reached?"

"I'm sorry, but I can't give out information on Mr. Sinclair."

"This is police business, and it's very important that I contact him."

"I understand. I can pass along a message if you like."

"I don't like. Is he at home by chance?"

"Like I said, I cannot give out any information on Mr. Sinclair."

Obviously, this was getting him nowhere. "All right. Can you give me the phone number for Mr. Sinclair's attorney?"

"That I can do. Hold on, please."

Joe hoped it was a firm in the city, so he would not have to travel up to Highland Park. After a moment, she came back on the line.

His attorney is Mr. Wendell DeForrest of DeForrest, Brown, and Whittier. Would you like their phone number?"

"No, thank you," said Joe. "I already have it. Good day."

Joe had dealt with Wendell DeForrest several years ago. He was a crafty old fox with a homespun charm that masked a brilliant legal mind. DeForrest, Brown, and Whittier was one of the most powerful law firms in the city, so it was not surprising they would represent a multi-millionaire asshat like Noah Sinclair.

Joe made a call to the law firm and asked the receptionist to speak with Wendell DeForrest.

"Are you one of Mr. DeForrest's clients?" she asked.

"No. I'm Detective Joe Erickson of the Chicago Police Department. Would you tell him I'm calling about a police matter?"

"Let me transfer you to his assistant."

A moment later, another woman answered. "Mr. DeForrest's office," she said.

Joe introduced himself and said he needed to speak with "Mr. DeForrest."

"I remember you," she said. "It's been a few years."

"Yes, it has. Is this Fiona?"

"It is. Mr. DeForrest's in court this morning."

"Is there a time when he can see me? Perhaps this afternoon around three?" Joe remembered DeForrest telling him he always took a short nap at three o'clock each day.

"He's not available at three. In fact, he's never available at three, but he could see you at 2:30," she replied.

"That works. See you at 2:30."

Joe thanked her and ended the call. He and Sam would need to travel down to the Loop. DeForrest, Brown, and Whittier's offices were on the thirty-fourth floor of a fifty-story tower on North Wabash. Joe assumed Wendell DeForrest had not changed much since they encountered him while investigating another case involving a wealthy client.

Joe told Sam of their 2:30 meeting with Sinclair's attorney, "It's with Wendell DeForrest."

"Oh. He lawyer-up already?" asked Sam.

"I can't locate him. I can't get a phone number or find out where he is at the moment. I got the runaround at his office, but when I asked, the receptionist gave me his attorney. I'm thinking DeForrest can arrange a meeting with him."

"Rich people," mumbled Sam. He always resented dealing with the wealthy and their attorneys. "A bane to my existence."

Joe chuckled at his griping. "Why would you expect less? It's the way they all operate."

"Yeah-yeah. I'll let you do most of the talking."

That afternoon, Joe and Sam drove to the Wabash Avenue address and took the elevator to the thirty-fourth floor. They walked to the receptionist, where Joe stated they were there for a 2:30 appointment with Mr. DeForrest. She made a call, and a short time later, Fiona, DeForrest's assistant, met them.

Reaching out to shake their hands, she said, "It's been a while, hasn't it?"

"It has," said Joe.

"He's expecting you. If you'll follow me, please." Fiona turned, and they accompanied her to DeForrest's office. She opened the door and said, Detectives Erickson and Renaldo to see you, sir."

"Send them in," came the familiar deep voice of Wendell DeForrest.

As they entered his office, they saw him rounding his desk. His suitcoat was off, his collar was unbuttoned, and his necktie had been loosened. He didn't bother to adjust anything.

After he shook their hands, he said, "Have a seat, gentlemen," indicating the leather wingback chairs in front of his desk.

After they were seated, DeForrest asked, "What can I do for the city's finest?"

Joe took the lead, remembering what Sam had said: "We're investigating a murder, and one of your clients is a person of interest. Given his connection to the case, we'd like to interview him."

"Who are we talking about?" asked DeForrest.

"Noah Sinclair."

"Really," said DeForrest. "Noah's a person of interest?"

"He is. He's not a suspect, but we'd like to interview him to see if he can provide us with information about the crime."

"So, you want to determine if he is a suspect," clarified DeForrest. Nothing got past this man.

"In so many words, yes. He was romantically involved with the victim a short time ago, and given his temperament, he showed up on our radar."

"I see. Well…I'm aware of Noah's skirt-chasing. I represented him in both of his divorces, but I don't think he's capable of anything other than an occasional temper tantrum."

"If so, he may fall off our radar. But given his relationship with the victim, we need to speak with him. We wouldn't be doing due diligence if we didn't. I'm sure you understand."

"Who's the victim, if you don't mind me asking?"

"A woman by the name of Jennifer Logan. She was killed and decapitated along a bike path."

"I read about that. Quite a wealthy woman. And she's the one Noah was screwing?"

Joe smiled at DeForrest's plainspoken question. "For a time, yes. She broke it off. And from all accounts, he was none too pleased."

DeForrest sighed. After a moment, he said, "Tell you what I can do. I'll corral this mustang, and you can speak to him as long as he has his attorney present. How's that?"

Joe looked at Sam, who replied, "Fine."

"That works for us," agreed Joe.

Rising, Joe laid his card on DeForrest's desk and said, "If you could have someone call me when you have him corralled?"

"I'll see to that," DeForrest replied, rising from his chair and walking around his desk. "You should hear something in a day or two."

They thanked him and left his office. In the elevator, Sam said, "Interesting, he used the words 'corral this mustang,' isn't it?"

"We've dealt with DeForrest in the past. When he uses a metaphor like that, you can assume he's accurately describing his client."

"Think he'll come through?"

"Yeah. I don't think he'd jerk us around. Not about this."

Chapter Twenty-Seven

Two days after they met with Wendell DeForrest, Joe received a call from Fiona Garrick, DeForrest's assistant.

"Mr. DeForrest was able to contact Noah Sinclair, and he has agreed to meet with you here in our offices at eleven o'clock tomorrow morning. Does that time suit your schedule?" she asked.

"It does," replied Joe. "We'll be there."

Joe was pleased with the prompt response to their interview request. Scheduling a meeting with someone like Sinclair could have dragged out over a period of weeks. Maybe DeForrest convinced Sinclair that it was in his best interest to cooperate. Joe let Sam know about the meeting, and they continued to look into Sinclair's life.

Still bothered by the lack of a connection between Sinclair and Leah Sarandon, Joe began looking into her past job experience. After receiving her bachelor's degree in accounting, Sarandon was hired by Sonorra Solutions and worked in their accounting department. Once she passed her Certified Public Accountant exam and obtained her state license, she resigned and took a job with Crockett & Associates. Joe found that Sonorra Solutions is a subsidiary of the Sinclair Group, the company owned by Noah Sinclair. Could he have known Sarandon while she worked at Sonorra Solutions? Could she have stumbled upon some damning information about Sinclair? And did that have anything to do with her departure? Surely, she could not be using it to blackmail Sinclair, could she? Joe decided to follow up with her former supervisor at Sonorra Solutions.

One thing struck Joe as he considered this possible connection. Noah

Sinclair was always drawn to beautiful women. He was seen with them and had relationships with them. Leah Sarandon did not fit that mold. What, if anything, would Sinclair have seen in her? Or…was he afraid of what she knew? Or angry about what she was threatening to do?

Sonorra Solutions was an accounting firm. Joe found their website and called the posted contact number.

A woman answered. "Sonorra Solutions. How may I direct your call?"

Joe introduced himself and asked to be transferred to the Human Resources department. After a moment, another woman picked up.

"Human Resources. Jeri speaking."

"This is Detective Joe Erickson, Chicago PD," replied Joe. "I'm investigating the death of one of your former employees, and I would like to speak with her supervisor."

"A former employee, you said?"

"Yes. Her name was Leah Sarandon. She worked with Sonorra Solutions about ten years ago."

"Hold on. Let me see if I can pull up her information." She placed Joe on hold and then came back on the line a minute later. "Yes, she was employed with us for a period of two years."

"I'd like to speak with her immediate supervisor, please."

"Uh…let's see…uh, that would have been…Theresa Nicholson. She no longer works for us. She retired last year."

"Do you have a phone number where she can be reached?"

"I do, but it's a year old. It may not be current."

"I'll take my chances," said Joe.

"Did you say you're investigating a death?"

"Yes. Leah Sarandon. She was murdered a few days ago. I'm the lead detective on the case."

"That's terrible."

"It is. Did you happen to know her?"

"No. She left before I began working here."

"I see. Could I have that phone number, please?"

Jeri gave him Theresa Nicholson's phone number. Joe thanked her and ended their conversation, saying, "Thank you, Jeri. Your help was most appreciated." He was grateful she was willing to cooperate.

Before calling Nicholson's number, Joe began a background search on Theresa Nicholson. She was sixty-four years old and the wife of Morris Nicholson. Their address was on West Argyle Avenue in the Forest Glen neighborhood, one of the northernmost neighborhoods on the Northwest side. Joe debated between calling or showing up on their doorstep, but decided to call first. He preferred to meet with her face-to-face, hoping she could provide a link between Sarandon and Noah Sinclair. It was probably a long shot, but he needed to know one way or the other.

Joe called the number and was rolled over to voicemail. He left a message saying it was urgent that he speak with her about a case he was investigating. An hour later, Nicholson returned his call.

"This is Theresa Nicholson. You left a message saying I should call you." Her voice reflected concern.

"Thanks for returning my call so promptly," said Joe. "I was told you were a supervisor with Sonorra Solutions prior to your retirement a year ago. Is that correct?"

"Yes, it is."

"Do you recall an employee by the name of Leah Sarandon?"

She sighed. "Oh, I most certainly do. I read about what happened to her in the newspaper. It just makes me sick to think about it. She was such a nice person."

"Is there a time when I can meet with you? I'm investigating her death, and I'd like to ask you some questions. But I'd rather not do it over the phone."

"Of course. Well…I don't have anything scheduled this afternoon if that's an acceptable time."

"It is. Will two o'clock be okay?"

"Fine."

"And do you still live on Argyle Avenue?"

"We do."

"Okay. Then I will see you at two."

Joe informed Sam of the interview he had set up with Leah Sarandon's former supervisor at Sonorra Solutions. After lunch, they traveled to Theresa Nicholson's Forest Glen home. They arrived a few minutes before two o'clock.

The Nicholson home was a well-kept gray bungalow with white trim, the kind of house built in the early 1900s. Joe and Sam walked up the front steps onto a large porch and pressed the doorbell. Shortly after, a woman opened the door.

With IDs in hand, Joe asked, "Theresa Nicholson?"

"Yes."

"Detectives Erickson and Renaldo."

Nodding, she said, "You're right on time. Come in."

She guided them through the foyer into a roomy living room. The house had been renovated at some point because it featured an open kitchen, but the transoms above all the doors were retained. A fireplace with full bookcases on either side took up one wall.

"Please sit down," said Nicholson. As Joe and Sam seated themselves on the dark gray couch, Nicholson sat opposite them in a leather recliner. At that moment, a man in his sixties walked in and asked, "What's going on?" He was tall, slim, and had a head of thick silver hair.

"Morris, these are the detectives I told you about."

"Oh," said Morris. "Well, I'll let you get on with business then." He turned and left the room.

"Your husband?" asked Sam.

"For forty-one years," she replied, smiling.

"Congratulations."

"Thank you."

"On the phone," began Joe, "you said you knew Leah Sarandon. That was almost ten years ago. How is it you remember her?"

"She was a quiet person. Reminded me of our youngest daughter. She was quite smart and very capable, but she was rather shy. I took her under my wing and convinced her to get her CPA certification. And she did. But once she got it, she decided to move on."

"Was there a reason why she decided to leave?"

"Her decision surprised me. She didn't confide in me the reason why she wanted to leave. I thought she was happy in her job."

"Was she a good employee?"

"Oh, yes. I wish I had half a dozen more like her. Focused, diligent…never missed a day of work. She caught a lot of accounting errors."

"Did she ever uncover any fraud or theft?" asked Sam.

"Once," replied Nicholson.

"Was it associated with the Sinclair Group?"

"No, it was another one of our clients. We assisted with the investigation, and the person in question was fired and prosecuted."

"I see," said Joe. "Do you know if Noah Sinclair ever spoke with her?"

"The big honcho. Not that I'm aware of. I don't know why he would have any need to speak with her. If he wanted to know something, he would go through appropriate channels and ask to speak with her supervisor. That would've been me."

"Did you ever speak with Noah Sinclair?"

"No. If people from the Sinclair Group contacted us regarding a question, it would be one of their managerial staff. Not the head guy."

"Did you notice anything unusual about her behavior before she left your company?" asked Sam.

"You're asking me to remember things that happened ten years ago. Honestly, I don't recall. I just know that when she gave her notice, it came as a complete surprise to me."

"So, you don't think she was being pressured or harassed for some reason?"

"I never got that impression at the time." Nicholson stopped for a moment and then asked, "Do you think Noah Sinclair had something to do with Leah's murder?"

"Right now, we don't know," said Sam.

"He's a person of interest in another case, and we're trying to determine if there's a link to this one," explained Joe.

"I wish I could be of more help. But I'm afraid I don't know of anything that can help you. Like I said, it's been ten years."

"You've been helpful. It's possible there is no link between these two cases, and we're searching an alley with nothing in it."

"We're simply being thorough," added Sam.

"I understand."

Joe looked at Sam, and they simultaneously rose from their seats. Nicholson followed.

"Thanks for your time," said Joe. Glancing about, he said, "You have a lovely home."

"My husband's done all the work. He's pretty handy."

"He certainly is."

Nicholson saw Joe and Sam to the door. "I hope you catch the guy that did it," she said. "Leah was a wonderful person."

"We'll do our best," replied Sam.

As they walked to the car, Sam looked over at Joe. "Well, that wasn't much help."

"No, it wasn't," agreed Joe. "I'm beginning to think it will take a stroke of luck for us to make any progress in this case."

Chapter Twenty-Eight

The next day, Joe and Sam traveled to the law offices of DeForrest, Brown, and Whittier. They rode the elevator along with four others, each getting off on lower floors. When the elevator doors opened onto the thirty-fourth floor, Fiona Garrick greeted them almost immediately. She must have been standing at the elevator, waiting for them to arrive.

"Good morning," she said in a cheery voice.

"Good morning," replied Joe and Sam at the same time.

"Let me escort you to the conference room." They followed her down a hallway.

"Mr. Sinclair is already here, and he'll be represented by Mr. Leon Buress."

"Not Mr. DeForrest?" asked Joe.

"Mr. DeForrest is in court and asked his associate to sit in on your interview."

"What's he like?" asked Sam.

"Mr. Buress? He's super cute."

"If I was attracted to super cute men, I might be interested."

"Yeah, that's a shame," added Joe.

Sam gave him a dirty look while Fiona giggled. "That's funny," she said just before she stopped in front of the conference room door. She opened it and said, "Detectives Erickson and Renaldo are here." Then she opened it wide for them to enter.

When they stepped into the conference room, Buress rose from his chair while Sinclair remained seated. Buress reached across the table and shook hands with Joe and Sam, but Sinclair made no effort to be civil.

Sinclair was indeed a handsome man. With a full head of dark brown hair that Joe suspected was colored to cover the gray, he reminded Joe of the actor Timothy Dalton, who once starred as 007 in the Bond series. In other words, the fifty-two-year-old guy was a hunk.

After they sat down across from Sinclair and his attorney, Joe began, "I assume you know why we're here, Mr. Sinclair?"

Buress answered for him. "He does."

"Good. Did you know a woman named Jennifer Logan?"

"He will admit that."

Looking at Buress, Joe asked, "Has Mr. Sinclair suffered a stroke that's left him unable to speak?"

Buress bristled at Joe's remark. After a moment, he replied, "He can speak."

"Thank you." Looking at Sinclair, Joe said, "You're aware that Jennifer Logan was found brutally murdered not long ago, right? We know that you had a relationship with her that lasted several months."

Sinclair looked at Buress, who nodded for him to answer. "I read about it in the paper."

"We were told by a reliable source that you were furious when she dumped you. And that was verified through Logan's email messages. You sent her some nasty, angry stuff."

"I may have done that. But that doesn't mean I killed her."

Joe looked at his notes and then said, "A portion of your last message to her read, 'I promise I'll have your head for this, you fucking bitch.'" Looking up at Sinclair, Joe continued, "That's very telling, Mr. Sinclair, given the fact that Jennifer Logan was decapitated by her killer."

"Don't respond to that," said Buress to Sinclair. Then he turned an eye to Joe and stated, "That was hyperbole said in a moment of emotional distress. This message and the facts surrounding Ms. Logan's death are purely coincidental."

"We don't believe in coincidences, Mr. Buress. You're probably aware of that," stated Sam. Addressing Sinclair, he asked, "Where were you on the morning of June 9th?"

Sinclair looked at his attorney and said, "This is such bullshit."

"Bullshit?" said Sam, his temper flaring. "A woman you knew died horribly. We don't consider that bullshit."

"That's not wha–"

"Stop! Keep quiet, Noah," Buress interrupted. Looking at Sam, he said, "Let's take this down a notch or two, okay? My client is not denigrating Ms. Logan's death. It was a heinous act committed by some mentally deranged individual, not Mr. Sinclair."

"Where were you in the early morning hours of June 9th, Mr. Sinclair? You can clear this up by providing an alibi," pressed Joe.

Looking offended by Joe's request, Sinclair took out his phone and appeared to check his calendar. After a moment, he looked from Sam to Joe and said, "I happened to be at home that day."

"Can anyone corroborate that?"

Sinclair looked at Buress with an annoyed expression.

"Tell them," said Buress.

Sinclair sighed loudly. "All right. I was with someone."

"We'll need her name."

Sinclair looked at Buress, who nodded his response.

"This is a private matter."

"Doesn't matter."

Anger had been building in Sinclair, and this was the final straw. He exploded, "If you must know, her name is Vivien Alexander!"

The revelation that Destiny's mother might have spent the night with Sinclair left Joe speechless. Vivien was sixty-six years old, but she looked fifty and was still quite attractive. He never thought about her being sexually active. He glanced at Sam, whose expression was concerning. Nothing was said for a moment until Sam responded to Sinclair's answer, "Wasn't so hard, was it?" Sinclair glared at him.

As Joe thought about what Sinclair said, he thought perhaps it was another person with the same name.

"We'll have to verify this," said Sam. "You'll need to provide her contact information."

Buress, who seemed bewildered by Joe's reaction, said, "We'll provide that."

Sam spoke up, continuing to give Joe time to gather his thoughts. "Do you know a woman by the name of Leah Sarandon?"

"Leah Sarandon, you said?" asked Sinclair.

"Yes, Leah Sarandon."

"No, I don't know anyone with that name."

"She worked for one of your companies. Sonorra Solutions. Ring any bells?"

"That's our accounting firm." He paused as if he was running people from that firm through his head. "No, she's not someone I've met."

"Why are you asking about this person?" asked Buress.

"She was killed in the same manner as Jennifer Logan. So, I'm asking: Where were you on the morning of June 20th?"

Rolling his eyes, Sinclair consulted his phone's calendar. "I was at home on June 20th. Packing for a visit to one of our factories in Taiwan."

"Can anyone verify this? Like Vivien Alexander?" asked Sam.

"Probably not."

Shit! thought Joe. *This all hangs on Vivien's alibi.*

Looking at Joe, Sam asked, "You have any other questions for Mr. Sinclair?"

"Yeah. One. Are you right-handed or left-handed, Mr. Sinclair?"

"What the hell does that have to do with anything?" protested Sinclair.

"Just tell him," prompted Buress.

"Right," he replied, holding up his right hand and wiggling it back and forth.

Buress looked from Joe to Sam and asked, "Are we finished here?"

We are," said Sam. "He'll provide a written account of his whereabouts on the dates mentioned and provide Vivien Alexander's contact information, correct?"

"He will."

"Okay, then," said Sam. He and Joe rose from their seats. Joe was silent, but Sam thanked them for their time before they left the room.

Joe and Sam walked to the elevator without speaking. When they were alone and heading down to the first floor, Sam asked, "You think the Vivien Alexander he mentioned could be the same Vivien Alexander as your mother-in-law?"

"I don't know. Anything's possible, I suppose. We'll have to wait until we get her contact information. If it turns out to be a Winnetka address, it's her."

"How old is your mother-in-law, anyway?" asked Sam. "I've never seen her."

"She's sixty-six, but she could pass for fifty."

"My guess is she isn't a nun. What do you know about her private life?"

"Next to nothing. She does a lot of charity work, but that's about it."

"She rich?"

"Yeah. Very."

The elevator came to a stop on the fourteenth floor, and two men in suits got on. One pressed the close door button as they continued their conversation about spreadsheets and percentages. In short order, the elevator stopped, and the doors opened onto the lobby.

On the drive back to their office, Sam volunteered his thoughts about Vivien Alexander.

"One thing about Sinclair: he likes younger women. I have doubts about your mother-in-law being someone he'd want to spend the night with. Not that she isn't a desirable partner or anything, but he always goes for the younger, juicier types, you know what I mean?"

Joe looked over and smiled. "Juicier?"

"Yeah. Speaking of juicy, it's time for lunch. You want to stop somewhere?"

Joe chuckled and said, "Sounds good as long as it isn't junk food."

"No junk. I've turned over a new leaf."

Following lunch at a bistro Joe liked, they returned to their office, where Joe began searching the driver's license database for a woman named "Vivien Alexander." His search revealed five women in Illinois with that name, three of whom lived in the Chicago area. Besides his mother-in-law, two women were young enough to suit Sinclair's tastes. One was twenty-eight years old, while the other was thirty-three. The photo of the thirty-three-year-old displayed an attractive face, a young woman Sinclair could find appealing. Additionally, her height and weight suggested she had a trim physique. He printed her license record to compare it with the information Sinclair's attorney was sending. The photo of the twenty-eight-year-old wasn't especially flattering, like many people's DMV license photos. While her height and weight suggested she might have a nice figure, it was difficult to determine if she would be Sinclair's type.

Further investigation revealed that twenty-eight-year-old Vivien Louise Alexander worked as a paralegal for an attorney's office while thirty-three-year-old Vivien Renee Alexander was employed as a lab technician at Mercy Hospital. And then there was his mother-in-law, Vivien Suzanne Alexander.

Joe decided he would not mention anything to Destiny about this until the identity of the person in question was established. There was no reason she needed to know anything about this new disclosure. Destiny had suffered enough anxiety about her mother in recent days. He didn't need to add to it. Questioning his mother-in-law? Sheesh! That was something he would not look forward to doing.

Chapter Twenty-Nine

Joe didn't like keeping things from Destiny, but he chose not to mention anything about her mother's name being brought up during his investigation. If it turned out to be another person with the same name, then he would tell her. Maybe she could get a chuckle out of it. However, if it was her mother, then he would have to decide what steps to take.

Joe was mentally drained from work that day, and Destiny sensed that something was bothering him. He tried to ignore the possible connection to her mother. However, given Destiny's intuition, she may have picked up on subtle hints in his facial expressions and body language. When she expressed her concerns, he simply chalked it up to a stressful day at work.

* * *

At ten o'clock the following day, Joe received a fax from the law office of DeForrest, Brown, and Whittier containing the information they requested from Noah Sinclair. He was eager to see the address and phone number given for Vivien Alexander. And there it was. *Shit!* he thought. It was his mother-in-law's contact information. He told Sam about it.

"This could be a sticky situation, Joe. You want me to handle it?" asked Sam.

"No, we should both interview her. We know each other, and she likes me, so she may respond better if I'm there."

"Suit yourself."

"I'll call her and set something up."

Back at his desk, Joe used his cell phone to call Vivien so she would recognize his number and pick up.

"Well, Joe. This is a surprise," said Vivien. "You usually don't call. There isn't anything wrong, is there?"

"Not with Destiny or me. I'm afraid I'm calling about police business. We need to interview you regarding a case we're working on."

"Really. Well…all right, I guess."

"Is there a good time when my partner and I can travel to Winnetka and conduct the interview?"

"I'm here all afternoon. How does two o'clock sound to you?"

"Given the time, three would work better if that's okay with you."

"Perfect. Can you tell me what this is about?"

"Not on the phone, but you're not in any kind of trouble. It's about confirming an alibi. That's all I can say at the moment."

He ended the call. He could tell from her voice she was concerned, and he was hoping she would not call Destiny and alert her about the interview.

Winnetka is a small city half an hour north of Chicago along the North Shore of Lake Michigan. A lovely city where a number of feature films have been shot, it is also one of the wealthiest and priciest cities in the state.

Vivien lived in a 9000-square-foot brick and stone mansion on Indian Hills Road. It looked more like an English Manor Estate than a house.

When Joe pulled into the circular drive, Sam said, "Holy crap! This is where she lives?"

"Yup. I told you she was rich. And she lives here all by herself."

"What's a place like this worth?"

"Millions. Her father was the vice-president of a railroad, and her late husband owned a ton of real estate."

They were ten minutes late due to an accident that held up traffic on I-94. Joe rang the bell, and a moment later, Vivien opened the door and invited them in.

"We can talk at the dining room table," she said, and they followed her into an expansive dining room that resembled photos found in Architectural Digest. A long walnut table that could seat twelve was the centerpiece of the room.

"Can I get you anything?" she asked.

Joe wanted to say "three fingers of scotch" so he could settle his nerves, but of course, he couldn't. He and Sam both declined.

After indicating places for them to be seated, Vivien said, "I'm a little confused about why you need to interview me. You said it's something about an alibi?"

Joe began by explaining, "There's a person of interest in a case we're investigating, and he mentioned your name as a possible alibi for the morning of June 9th. That's what we're here to confirm."

"Well…who is it?"

"Noah Sinclair."

"Oh," she said, obviously remembering what she was doing at the time.

"I take it you know the person in question," stated Sam.

"I do. What's the crime?"

"We can't talk about it," said Joe, "but since we work homicide, you can assume…"

"Good lord!"

Joe saw she was bothered by this line of questioning, so he said, "The information you provide is strictly confidential. It won't go further than this room, so you don't have to worry about anyone finding out about it."

After a moment, she said, "All right. I'm not going to make up some colorful story. I… spent the previous night with him."

"Noah Sinclair."

"Yes."

"Okay," said Joe.

"I have an occasional need, and I found him attractive, so…" she said. "Hey, I'm not dead yet, you know."

Smiling, Joe replied, "I'm well aware of that." Refocusing, he asked, "Do you happen to remember what time you left that morning?"

"Oh…it was around ten or so."

"And Sinclair was there?"

"He was."

"And he was there with you earlier that morning?"

"That's right."

Sam looked at Joe with a disappointed look on his face.

"I'm sorry we had to dig into your private life, Vivien. But it's our job to investigate all possible leads and confirm every alibi."

"I understand," she replied. "You're just doing your job."

"And don't worry. Destiny will never know we were here unless you tell her."

"I appreciate that."

"I have one question," said Sam. "How long have you known Noah Sinclair?"

"Hm. I've seen him and spoken with him at social events for years. But this 'tryst', for lack of a better word, was a first-time thing. It happened in a moment of…"

"Need," said Joe, finishing her sentence.

Chuckling, Vivien replied, "More like weakness or questionable judgment on my part."

"We're not judging you," said Sam. "We're all human."

"Confirming his alibi takes Noah Sinclair off our list of persons of interest. He could not have been involved in the crime," said Joe.

"It means we have to continue our search for a suspect," added Sam.

"Is that good?" she asked.

"It is for Noah Sinclair."

They chit-chatted for a few more minutes before Joe and Sam returned to the city. In the car, Sam asked, "Now what?"

"Your guess is as good as mine."

That evening, before entering the house, Joe spent time in the garage looking over the Camaro project he had been working on. He was hesitant about facing Destiny after interviewing her mother. What if Vivien called her and revealed everything? After a few minutes, he entered the kitchen.

"Staring at the car again?"

Smiling, Joe said, "That's required when you build a car. You have to stare at it, studying it, so you know what to do next and how that impacts everything else. Staring helps."

She smiled and kissed him. He was relieved that she seemingly knew nothing of their interview. He felt uncomfortable not informing her about it, but like she was fond of saying, "There are always exceptions to the rule."

Chapter Thirty

As soon as Joe reached his desk the next morning, he received a call from the duty sergeant.

"I know you have a full caseload, Joe," he said. "But I just got a call from a uniformed officer from the 18th requesting detectives. He's reported a knife attack. Sounds like it could be related to your decapitation case."

"We'll take it," replied Joe. "If it seems unrelated, we can pass it on to another team."

Joe got the location and grabbed Sam, who was getting coffee. "Get ready to roll. We may have a third attack on our hands. Come on."

"On the same path?"

"No. In Lincoln Park near the Conservatory. A jogger's been attacked with a knife."

"Dead?"

"Didn't say."

They drove to the Lincoln Park Conservatory and saw the flashing lights of law enforcement vehicles about a block north. At the police barrier, Joe and Sam approached the uniformed officer, whose job was to block access to the crime scene. After showing their IDs and introducing themselves, Joe asked him for details.

"What have we got?" he asked.

"A jogger was attacked by an offender wielding a knife. He was cut up pretty bad," replied the officer.

"He?"

"Yeah. A guy."

"Is he alive?"

"He was when the EMTs left with him. Another jogger scared off the offender, but the victim had his throat cut. It was pretty bad, but the other jogger's an emergency room nurse, and she provided first aid. Probably saved his life."

"When was the victim transported?"

"About twenty minutes ago."

"Where's the nurse?"

"She's talking to the sergeant over there," he said, indicating where the two stood next to a police cruiser.

Joe and Sam walked toward a cruiser where a woman was speaking with an older uniformed officer. Her hands and arms were smeared with blood, and her jogging shorts and tank top had red stains.

With his ID out, Joe said, "Detectives Erickson and Renaldo."

When the sergeant turned toward them, Joe recognized Sergeant Taylor from other crime scenes he had been called to in the 18th District.

"Detectives," said Taylor, his voice deep and commanding. "This is Tanya Sullivan. She saw the victim being attacked and provided medical attention."

"I can see that," replied Joe, looking at the blood all over Sullivan. "Can you tell me what you saw?"

"I just told the sergeant everything," said Sullivan.

"Now you can tell us."

"All right. I was jogging and came around the foliage back there. That was when I saw someone attacking another jogger with a knife. I yelled, 'Hey!' and when the guy saw me, he took off running. I ran up to the man who was lying on the ground, bleeding, and began treating his wounds. He had stab wounds to his back, and his throat was cut. He was bleeding extensively from the neck wound."

"Can you describe the offender?" asked Sam.

"He was wearing a black hoodie and matching sweatpants. And he was wearing a black mask—like a ski mask—under the hoodie."

"Which way did he run?"

"That way," she said, pointing. "Up toward Fullerton Avenue."

"You said you saw the offender attacking the victim with a knife. Do you remember what hand the knife was in?" asked Joe.

"Oh, jeez. I…I don't recall. Sorry. It all happened so fast."

"That's okay. How far away were you when you first saw the attack?"

"Oh…forty yards, maybe."

"Could you tell if he was young, old? What race he was?"

"The way he ran away, I'd say he was young. And he was white. I saw his wrist showing between the glove and the hoodie sleeve."

"Anything else?"

"He was wearing a lot of clothes, given the temperature. All the other joggers were in shorts and T-shirts or tank tops."

"You were pretty brave yelling at him. How did you know he wouldn't come after you?"

Sullivan reached into her shorts pocket and pulled out a small canister of pepper spray. "He'd get this in the face if he came toward me," she said.

"Thank you for rendering aid," said Sam. "You may have saved his life."

"Just putting my knowledge and skills to work."

They took Sullivan's contact information and then told her she had to wait for the Evidence Technicians to arrive. She wasn't pleased when they told her she would have to give up her clothes.

"What am I supposed to wear?" she asked.

"They'll give you something to put on. Your clothes are evidence."

Sergeant Taylor had been looking on, overhearing their questioning. Joe looked at him and asked, "You have a name for the victim?" asked Joe.

"He didn't have any ID on him. I checked before they loaded him up."

"Great. Got a description?"

"Middle-aged, I'd say, around fifty. Lean body, dark hair, short beard, and mustache. And he had a tattoo of a cross on his upper left arm."

"Okay," said Joe as he wrote down Taylor's description. "Any other witnesses?"

"No," replied Taylor. "You said you're gonna call in Evidence Techs?"

"Yeah. We need to preserve the crime scene. There's a lot of the victim's blood over there, but the offender may have left some of his own."

"Okay, I'll let my guys know they're gonna be here for a while."

Sam was already on his phone requesting Evidence Technicians to process the scene. Forty minutes later, they arrived. Big John Gustafson and his assistant, Lenny Andrews, carried their equipment to the edge of the crime scene, where Joe and Sam were waiting.

Looking over at the blood evidence, Big John said, "What happened here?"

"Knife attack," replied Sam.

"Okay. Since there's no body, do I assume the vic survived?"

"Let me put it this way: He was alive when he was transported."

Big John took Tanya Sullivan back to the forensic van to sample the blood on her hands and have her change out of her clothes. She emerged with clean hands and arms, wearing white Tyvek coveralls that were two sizes too big for her. She walked back to where Joe was standing and said, "They even took my underwear."

"Yeah," said Joe. "It's possible evidence. You want someone to take you home?"

"No. I don't live that far from here. I think the walk may do me good. I just hope no one I know sees me in this outfit."

"Unfortunately, they can't afford the ones designed by Versace."

Sullivan laughed. "You can say that again."

Once dressed in their Tyvek suits, Big John ducked under the yellow tape and began shooting pictures from every conceivable angle. Andrews took prints of Sullivan's shoes to compare them with the shoe prints that were tracked in blood.

After they both had finished, they began collecting blood samples and evidence from the site of the attack.

"While you're handling the scene," said Sam, "I'm going to check to see if there are any security cameras along here and on Fullerton. Maybe we can get footage of the guy."

"Go ahead. I'll monitor things here," assured Joe. "Good luck."

After a multitude of samples were taken, the collection of evidence was complete. Big John began removing his Tyvek protection while Andrews was busy packing up the evidence bags.

Joe turned to Taylor. "You know where the EMTs transported the victim?"

"Northwestern, they said."

Joe walked to Big John, who was stuffing his protective clothing into a plastic bag. He eyed Joe and said, "Got a lot of blood samples and a few hairs. We'll see where it takes us."

"You releasing the crime scene?"

"Yeah. It's all yours."

As Big John carried his equipment to the forensics van, Joe called Northwestern Memorial Hospital in an attempt to discover the victim's condition. After several transfers, he finally spoke to Dr. Khatib, who had treated the victim in the Emergency Room.

"He arrived unconscious and in critical condition," said Dr. Khatib. "He's been rushed into surgery."

"You think he'll survive?" asked Joe.

"I can't predict that. He suffered from considerable blood loss. The blade missed the main arteries in his neck, so that is fortunate. But the slash to his throat was severe. The two stab wounds to his back were deep but missed vital organs. We should know more once he is out of surgery."

Joe informed Sergeant Taylor that the crime scene had been released, but they had to wait around for the crime scene cleaners to arrive. The cleaners' job involved using a powerful disinfectant to remove every bit of blood from the concrete walkway. Nearly an hour later, a team showed up, and within thirty minutes, they had scrubbed away all traces of the crime.

As the cleaners were finishing, Sam returned. "There are a number of security cameras along Fullerton Avenue," he stated. "We'll need to contact the 18th and have officers pick up that footage. I've made notes of all the camera locations."

"Good," said Joe. "This has to be the same offender. The description matches, and the slash to the victim's neck was probably the first step in decapitating him. But he wasn't able to get the job done because the other jogger came along, and he had to flee."

"You know what? There's one major difference here," said Sam. "This time, the victim was a man. So, the attacker doesn't appear motivated to kill only women."

"Yeah. So, what the hell ties these three victims together?"

"If this latest victim survives, maybe he can provide a clue as to the motive."

"I think we need to go to the hospital and find out more about the condition of our victim," said Joe. "The sooner we can interview him, the better."

They drove to Northwestern Memorial Hospital and spoke to a person in Admitting. They were directed to the surgical floor, where they went to the nursing station and asked the nurse on duty about a patient with knife wounds to the throat. She asked them to wait while she paged Dr. Li.

A short time later, an Asian man in his fifties walked up. The nurse, whose ID tag read "Seward," said, "These men are police detectives. They want to know about one of your patients."

"I am Dr. Li," said the man, who spoke with an Asian accent. "How can I help you?"

Showing their IDs, Joe and Sam introduced themselves and asked about a man admitted with a severe knife wound to his throat.

"Yes," replied Dr. Li. "He was in surgery for over two hours. I was able to repair the wound to the throat and treat the two puncture wounds to his back. When he arrived, he was in critical condition, and he is still in critical condition. He is currently in the ICU, so it will be some time before he can be moved to a private room and receive visitors."

"Do you have a name?" asked Joe.

"We do not. Right now, he has been admitted under the name John Doe. We hope to have his name once he regains consciousness."

"Do you have any idea when we could speak with him?" asked Joe.

"Perhaps in two or three days if his recovery goes well. Given the severity of his wound, he may not be able to speak. If not, perhaps he could communicate by writing down his answers. His arms and hands were not injured."

"Okay. We need you to call us when he is well enough to be interviewed. It's very important we speak with him," said Joe.

"I will tell my nurse to call you when he is can have visitors," replied Dr. Li. "Now, if you will excuse me, I have patients to see."

Joe left his card with Nurse Seward at the nursing station with instructions to give it to Dr. Li's nurse. "We need to know the name of this John Doe as soon as possible. When he wakes up and provides his name, we need to be called."

"Yes, sir," she replied. "We can do that."

That evening, while Destiny was visiting her mother in Winnetka, Joe didn't feel like cooking. He walked Autumn and gave her a treat before driving to a restaurant he liked. He ordered the salmon on pasta with gorgonzola cream sauce. Since he had the recipe, he could have made it at home, but it was nice sitting back and relaxing while a chef prepared it. It was a treat.

Chapter Thirty-One

The next day, Joe and Sam collected security video from businesses along Fullerton Avenue. The day after, they began reviewing the footage. It was a time-consuming task. A person matching the offender's description was spotted west on Fullerton. Additional footage showed him walking two blocks away. After that, he simply up and disappeared. One would think he would have been covered with blood, a disturbing sight that would have drawn someone's attention. Maybe the blood would not have been that noticeable after soaking into black clothing.

Joe approached Sam's desk and asked, "Have you located the offender anywhere past the third block of Fullerton?"

Shaking his head, Sam replied, "No. We seem to have lost him somewhere around that area."

"You suppose he was smart enough to plan his escape route beforehand?"

"Maybe. I think we need to walk that area and see if we can figure out how he disappeared. You game?"

"Yeah."

Joe and Sam drove to Fullerton Avenue and began walking, beginning where the offender was seen turning onto Fullerton. Joe took one side of the street and Sam the other. Joe was looking for any place the offender could duck into. He suspected the man could have changed out of his black sweats and returned to the street wearing something else, something that would allow him to blend in with others.

When he crossed the street and began surveying the buildings on the third block, he saw an empty structure that no longer housed a business. Looking around, he failed to see any security cameras on buildings directly to the left and right. Stepping to the door, he looked through the glass. It was dark, and he could only make out several cardboard boxes stacked on the floor.

The entrance door was old, and so was the lock. He examined it to determine if it could be forced open easily. With a handkerchief around his hand, he pushed on the door handle, and to his surprise, it opened. Was it not locked? Then he saw why. A strip of duct tape had been placed over the strike plate so the door latch could not engage. He entered and looked around the room, shining his flashlight to illuminate the space. While carefully examining the boxes, some of which had been stacked on top of each other, he noticed a reddish smudge. Kneeling to examine it further, he thought it might be blood. Joe stood and called Sam.

"I got something," he said.

"Where are you?"

"Third block, empty building in the middle of the block."

When Sam arrived, Joe showed him the duct tape and the suspected blood smear. They agreed they needed to call in a forensic team to dust for prints and to confirm the smudge was actually blood. And if it was, could it be a match to the victim?

Joe made the call, and they stood outside the door to prevent any curious citizens from contaminating the scene. An hour later, Evidence Technicians Art Casey and Jerry Bristow pulled up in their van. Joe and Sam had worked with them so many times that they were on a first-name basis.

Joe explained what they were investigating and the possible evidence they had found. As Art and Jerry were suiting up, Joe called the 18th and requested an officer to provide security for the scene. The area in front of the building was taped off, and Art and Jerry began by photographing the door, the handle, and the duct tape. Once done, Jerry entered and began photographing the area and the boxes. Art focused on removing the duct tape so it could be tested for DNA and fingerprints.

The uniformed officer from the 18th kept onlookers at bay, telling them to move on. While Art and Jerry were processing the scene, Joe and Sam continued their search of the area, looking for any other cameras that had not been checked out. They found one across the street outside a building housing a blood donation center. Ironic.

Joe went inside, hoping they had footage of the empty building across the street. He asked the young lady at the desk for their security footage.

"Oh, that," she said with an embarrassed smile. "That camera doesn't work. We haven't gotten around to having it fixed."

Wonderful, thought Joe. It could have not only placed the offender going inside but also coming out. How could he have known the camera didn't work?

"This facility take walk-ins?" asked Joe.

"Sure. Do you wish to donate?"

Showing his ID and introducing himself, he said, "What I wish to know is if you are the person on duty each day."

After seeing his ID, she became visibly nervous. "Uh…Yeah, I am."

"Did anyone come in here and ask about your security camera?"

"Not that I remember. Let me ask Dora." She left and returned a minute later, followed by a middle-aged woman wearing medical scrubs.

"This is Dora. She's the technician that collects the blood from donors."

Dora, a middle-aged matron who looked like she could beat the shit out of a street thug, eyed Joe suspiciously.

Showing his ID, Joe introduced himself and asked, "Was there a person who came in recently expressing an interest in your security camera?"

"Well…as a matter of fact…there was this guy a few weeks ago who commented on the security camera out front. He laughed and asked if we anticipated any armed robberies. I joked with him about protecting our facility from vampires."

"Did you mention the camera was out of order?"

"Maybe. I don't remember."

"Do you recall what he looked like?"

"Oh, boy…sorry. A lot of donors come through here, so it's hard to remember specific people. The only reason I remember him at all is because he teased me about it."

"Young, old…?"

"Younger, I think?"

"Did he make a donation?"

"He must have if I was speaking with him. I normally don't show up out front like this. And I only see people who donate."

"I assume you keep records of all the people who donate?"

"We do, but that information is confidential."

"Do you require identification from donors?"

"We do. A Red Cross donor card or a driver's license."

"I see."

"What's going on across the street?" asked the receptionist.

"Suspected break-in," replied Joe, choosing not to explain in detail.

Joe figured this line of questioning was a dead end. He thanked them for their time and left, frustrated. Would they ever get a freakin' break in this case?

He walked across the street and told Sam what he had discovered from the blood center. Sam smiled and said, "Typical."

"This guy is smart," said Joe. "He carefully plans everything out in advance, and so far, he's made no mistakes."

"Everyone makes a mistake sooner or later."

"Yeah. But how many more attacks will it take before he makes one?"

"You know...I was thinking," said Sam. "Why didn't he remove the tape from the door? It could have remained locked, and you wouldn't have found the blood smear."

"Good question. Maybe he had to make a quick exit. Or maybe he wanted others to get in here. Homeless people, addicts, kids, whoever. They could leave prints and DNA all over the place to confuse investigators. It would throw suspicion onto them and send us on a wild goose chase."

"Could be that others have already been in here, contaminating the scene."

"Yeah."

Two hours later, Art and Jerry had completed their work. Joe and Sam met them at their van as they were packing up.

Looking at Jerry, Joe asked, "That smudge on the box. Was it blood?"

"It was. And it was human."

"I'd like to know if the DNA matches blood from our recent crime scene."

"It'll take a while, but if it's a match, the system will flag it."

"In twelve weeks," added Art. "If you're lucky."

"Even with the new state-of-the-art DNA processing center downstate, DNA results are still taking a long time to come back," said Jerry. "Too bad it doesn't work like it does on television, where the cops have results in hours."

"Minutes," Art chuckled as he tied up the bag containing his protective clothing. "Ah, fiction! If this was a television show, I'd look like Brad Pitt."

"Unfortunately, you resemble a garden gnome," said Jerry.

Art was short and bald with a gnomish face that projected an amusing demeanor. But he was an excellent evidence technician.

Joe looked at Sam and caught him trying to suppress his laughter at Jerry's comment.

Looking at Jerry, Art wagged his finger and said, "Wait 'til I get you home."

When Art and Jerry had finished and released the scene, Sam turned to Joe and said, "Let's hope our victim can give us more to go on. Have you heard from his doctor?"

"Not today."

With a twinkle, Sam said, "To-mor-row—"

"Don't you dare break into that song from *Annie!*" warned Joe.

"Spoilsport."

Chapter Thirty-Two

When Joe got home that evening, he was looking forward to having two days off beginning the next day. This decapitation case was wearing on him, and he was growing increasingly frustrated with the lack of evidence and the scarcity of leads.

After voicing his frustration to Destiny, he said, "This case is going to drive me to drink."

"You already drink," she said.

"I do, but only for medicinal purposes."

"If you say so. You want a glass of wine?"

He looked at her and broke into a laugh. "No thanks. I'm tired, and I'd probably fall asleep here at the island."

"Would you like some coffee?"

"No, thanks."

"Tea?"

"No."

"Ovaltine?" she said with a German accent.

Joe cracked up laughing. "You…you are incorrigible."

"I am. Want to tell me about it?" she said as she moved to the refrigerator.

"Sure. We had another person attacked with a knife yesterday morning while you were visiting your mom."

She removed a pitcher of water and began filling a glass. "You think it was the same offender?"

"Pretty sure. Fortunately, the attack wasn't fatal this time, but the victim had his throat cut and received two stab wounds to the back. Another jogger interrupted the attack before the offender could finish decapitating him.

"Is he going to live?"

"He made it through surgery, but he's in the ICU. We have to wait until his doctor thinks he's improved enough to talk to us. If he can talk."

Destiny put the glass down in front of Joe. "So, it was a male victim this time, huh?"

"Yeah. I guess we can eliminate women haters. He didn't have any identification on him, so we couldn't look into his background."

"Three similar attacks suggest a serial killer. But the male victim doesn't fit. If I were putting together a profile, I'd be looking for someone out for revenge."

Joe took a drink from the water glass and considered what she said. "The problem we have is linking the first two victims. Revenge for what? Now that we have a third, maybe we can establish something once we know who he is."

"The offender seems to favor attacking individuals who exercise. The first was a bicyclist, right? And the next two were joggers?"

"Yeah. All three were vulnerable to an attack. It appears he carefully plans both his attacks and escapes. We traced him for several blocks today via security video, and he seemed to simply vanish. We found an empty building we think he may have used. Maybe to change out of his black clothing. Evidence Techs went over it, so hopefully, they collected some evidence that will help."

Destiny came around the island and sat down. "Not to change the subject or anything, but you didn't tell me that you questioned my mom the other day."

Great, thought Joe. *Why did Vivien say something? And how much did she tell her?* Joe decided to reveal as little as necessary.

"Her name was provided as an alibi for a person of interest in our case. We asked her about it, and she corroborated his alibi. It cleared him as a person of interest. Simple as that."

"You could have told me."

"She asked me not to, so I didn't."

"Oh?"

"I don't understand why she decided to mention it after she asked me not to say anything. What, exactly, did she tell you?"

"That you and Sam interviewed her regarding a case."

"Anything else?"

"That you were both very professional."

"Yeah. Nice that she didn't say anything about putting her in a dark room under a bright light and sweating the information out of her."

Destiny ignored his attempt at humor. Her facial expression implied puzzlement. "Weird," she said. "I'll have to ask her more about it."

"I'd just let it go," said Joe. "It's not worth pursuing."

"Maybe."

"But you're going to, aren't you?"

"It's the FBI in me. I need to know things."

"Up to you. But maybe your mother values her privacy and doesn't want you poking around in her private life."

"You know something, don't you?"

"There are some things I can't share with you. Suffice it to say that your mother provided an alibi for a person of interest. And now, we're no longer looking at him as a potential suspect."

"It wasn't that neighbor of hers, was it? You know, the Brit we met at the restaurant?

"No. It was someone else."

She looked at Joe for a few seconds, evidently trying to read his expression. Finally, she said, "All right. I guess Mom deserves her privacy. I don't tell her everything, either."

Joe chuckled, "Thank god for that."

* * *

The next day was the first of Joe's two days off. He and Destiny remained in bed longer than usual that morning. No need to jog today. While talking over breakfast, Destiny suggested going to the Art Institute that afternoon.

A new exhibition there piqued her interest, and she was eager to see it. No one had to ask Joe twice about going to the Art Institute. It was one of his favorite places to visit.

After several hours of viewing paintings, they walked to their favorite Russian restaurant on Adams and ate an early dinner. Great art and great food—a wonderful way to spend an afternoon.

* * *

Day two started out well. Joe received a phone call from Dr. Li's nurse. He had been hoping the hospital would call.

"You asked us to contact you when we identified our John Doe patient."

"I did. Who is he?"

"His name is Quentin Rosberg. He's forty-nine years old and says he's an actuary for an insurance company."

"Quentin Rosberg," said Joe, repeating the name.

"That's correct. Quentin Rosberg," she confirmed and then spelled his last name.

"And he's talking?"

"Only in a whisper. It will take some time for him to get his voice back."

"When can we see him?"

"Dr. Li said you can see him tomorrow. But you have to keep your visit short. He lost a lot of blood, and he's still quite weak."

Joe thanked her and texted Sam, giving him the victim's name and the doctor's authorization for them to visit Rosberg tomorrow. Then, he opened his laptop and searched for information on Quentin Rosberg. Even though it was his day off, his curiosity was aroused and he had to know about him.

There was only one Quentin Rosberg in the Driver's License database. He lived at an address in the Lincoln Park neighborhood. Further investigation revealed that he worked as an actuary for Chicago Mutual Insurance. No arrests. No traffic violations. Joe was looking forward to interviewing him. What could a dog show judge, an accountant, and an insurance actuary have in common? *What the hell links them together?*

Destiny walked in from the room they used as an office. "What are you going to do, today?" she asked.

"I thought I would work on the Camaro. I need to install the gauges and get them wired. Why? Did you want to do something?"

"No, just curious. I got a call from Maddie. She wanted to know if I'd like to go to lunch with her."

"Go ahead. I'll be working in the garage once I'm done with this."

"Great. I'll call her back."

Working on his Pro-touring Camaro project took Joe's mind off work and allowed him to lose himself for a few hours. He began working shortly after ten o'clock and was so engaged that he didn't hear Destiny leave. When he finished soldering the last two wires together, he checked his watch and was surprised to see it was after 1:30. He'd completely missed lunch.

As he was putting his tools away, Destiny stepped into the garage. "I'm back," she announced.

"You have a nice lunch?" asked Joe.

"I did."

"How was Maddie?"

"Fine. She told me to tell you hello."

"I was so focused on getting the gauges installed and wired that I lost track of the time. Forgot to eat."

"You haven't eaten?"

"No. I'm done here now, so I'm going to raid the refrigerator once I've cleaned up."

"Plenty of leftovers in there."

"I got a call from the hospital. Our victim is awake, and we have an ID on him. Turns out he's an actuary for an insurance company."

"Did they say when you can interview him?"

"Tomorrow."

"I assume you've checked to see if the victims belonged to any of the same organizations. Churches, YMCAs, clubs, hobbies?"

"Sam and I looked into those things and interviewed their friends. We didn't find any connections they had in common. Maybe Quentin Rosberg can shed some light on it."

"That's his name? Quentin Rosberg?"

"Yeah."

"You'll find the connection. When you least expect it. That's usually how it works."

Joe gave her a kiss and said, "Thanks for the encouragement."

"Come into the kitchen, and I'll make you something for lunch."

"That's nice of you. Thanks."

"But you'd better take a shower first. You smell like an overheated mechanic."

"And how would you know how an overheated mechanic smells?" asked Joe.

"I was with the FBI. I know things."

Chapter Thirty-Three

Joe and Sam drove to Northwestern Memorial Hospital the next morning to interview Quentin Rosberg. After checking in at Admitting, the attendant told them where to find him. They took the elevator to the surgical floor and walked to the nurses' station. Joe spoke to Nurse Seward, whom he had spoken with previously, and told her they had come to visit Quentin Rosberg.

"Let me have you speak with his doctor first." She picked up the phone and paged Dr. Li. Several minutes later, Dr. Li was walking toward them carrying a clipboard.

"Detective Erickson," he said. He looked curiously at Sam.

"This is my partner, Detective Sam Renaldo," explained Joe.

"Detective," said Dr. Li, acknowledging Sam.

"I received a call from your nurse saying we could speak with Quentin Rosberg today."

"Yes. He's been moved out of ICU to a private room. But he is quite weak, and it pains him to talk much above a whisper. He's dealing with a lot of discomfort right now due to his injuries and the surgical procedure. You'll need to keep your visit to a minimum. No more than a few minutes."

"Understood," replied Joe.

"If you follow me, I will take you to his room."

They followed Dr. Li down a hall to the elevator, which took them to the floor where Rosberg's room was located.

Stopping in front of a closed door, Dr. Li said, "This is his room. My nurse will check on you in a few minutes. Now, if you'll excuse me, I need to continue my rounds."

Dr. Li turned and began walking down the hall. Joe and Sam entered the room and saw a middle-aged man lying in bed. He was connected to several lines and wires, and a screen monitored his vitals. An IV bag hung from a stand next to the bed, and a line from it went to his arm.

When Joe and Sam stepped toward his bed, Rosberg opened his eyes. His face was puffy, and his throat was heavily bandaged. Joe and Sam made themselves known.

"Mr. Rosberg, I'm Detective Joe Erickson."

"And I'm Detective Sam Renaldo."

"We're investigating the attack on you," said Joe. "We'd like to ask you some questions if you feel up to it."

Rosberg lifted his free arm and gave them a thumbs-up. They moved closer to the side of his bed, where Joe began by asking, "Did you get a good look at your attacker?"

'No," mouthed Rosberg in a faint whisper. His bandages precluded him from turning his head, and he followed Joe and Sam with his eyes.

They could see that it pained Rosberg to speak at all, so Sam suggested he use his free hand to give thumb-up and thumb-down gestures for yes and no questions. Rosberg gave him a thumb-up.

"Do you remember if the offender held the knife in his left or right hand?" asked Joe.

Thumb-down.

"Did he say anything when he attacked you?"

Thumb-down.

"Do you have any enemies? Someone who may have an axe to grind?"

Thumb-down.

"Do you recall doing anything that could have motivated someone to attack you?"

Thumb-down.

"Do you know either Leah Sarandon or Jennifer Logan?"

Rosberg thought for a moment, and then he gave them a thumb-down.

"What about a business called Sonorra Solutions?"

Thumb-down.

"What about Noah Sinclair or the Sinclair Group?"

Thumb-down.

"Do you have any siblings that may have provoked someone to come after you?" asked Sam.

Thumb-down.

"Does an ex-wife or girlfriend hold a grudge?"

He rolled his eyes and followed it with a thumb-down.

Sam looked at Joe and then asked, "Is there anything you would like to tell us?"

Thumb-up.

Rosberg clenched his fist and whispered, "Get this guy." Afterward, he grimaced in pain and then looked first at Sam and then at Joe.

Suddenly, the door opened, and a large, rather stern-looking nurse entered the room. "Time's up, I'm afraid," she said.

"We were just about to leave," said Joe. "I'm going to leave my card on the stand here so if Mr. Rosberg thinks of something, one of his caregivers can call me."

Rosberg gave them a thumb-up. As Joe laid his card on the table, he told Rosberg, "If you think of anything, even if it doesn't seem important, we want to know so we can follow up. Have someone call me. Okay?"

Rosberg responded with a raspy whisper, "Yeah."

Joe and Sam followed the nurse out of the room.

As they left the hospital, Sam said, "Well…that was sure helpful. A big bag of nothing."

"Yeah," replied Joe. "I'm just afraid there's going to be another attack in the near future, and there's nothing we can do to stop it. The offender's not going to quit."

When they returned to their Area 3 office, Joe began researching the Chicago Mutual Insurance Company's website for their contact information. Since an actuary's job is to collect and analyze statistics, Joe didn't see how Rosberg's work could have interfaced with the lives of the two dead victims. But he had to delve into his work as well as his life to determine if there could be some kind of connection.

Joe called the contact number posted on the company's website and got an automated menu, something he had no use for. He pushed zero, hoping to get an operator to direct him, and it worked.

"Good morning. Chicago Mutual Insurance," a live female voice answered. "How can I direct your call?"

"I need to speak with a supervisor in your actuarial department."

"Certainly. Hold on, please, and I'll transfer you."

A moment later, his call was picked up. "Logistics, may I help you?"

"This is Detective Joe Erickson with the Chicago Police Department. I need to speak with one of your employee's supervisors."

"Oh," she answered, obviously taken aback by the fact that this was a call from the police. "Well…who is the employee in question?"

"An actuary by the name of Quentin Rosberg."

"Ah. That would be Mr. Schott. I'll transfer you."

Once again, Joe was transferred. After three rings, his call was answered. "Arnold Schott."

Joe introduced himself and asked to verify that he was Quentin Rosberg's supervisor.

"Yes, I am," he replied. "Has something happened? He hasn't been at work for a few days, and he never called in. We've been trying to contact him, but we haven't been able to reach him. I don't know what's going on."

"Did you call the police to do a wellness check?"

"My colleague did, and they found no one at home."

"There was an article in the newspaper, and it was reported on the local news," said Joe.

"I've been really busy lately, so I haven't kept up. Sorry."

"Mr. Rosberg's been hospitalized after being attacked while jogging. He was nearly killed by someone wielding a knife."

"Omigod," reacted Schott. "Is he going to be all right?"

"Eventually, he probably will. My partner and I are investigating the attack, and I was wondering if I could meet with you to ask some questions."

"Of course. I'm available most of today, but I'll be in and out tomorrow."

They agreed to meet at two o'clock. The Chicago Mutual Insurance Company is located in a 57-story structure on East Randolph Street. The logistics department was situated on the 29th floor. Joe told Sam about the meeting. He agreed it was a good idea to meet with Rosberg's employer, but questioned whether they could make any connections to the other victims. "Worth a try," said Joe. "We've struck out everywhere else."

Entering the expansive steel and glass lobby, Joe and Sam stepped into an elevator that whisked them directly to the building's 29th floor. Upon exiting the elevator, they encountered a large glass wall with a desk in front of it. A young man in his late twenties was seated there, typing on his keyboard.

He looked up as they approached and said, "Good afternoon. My name's Jordan. How can I direct you?"

"Detectives Erickson and Renaldo. We have a two o'clock appointment with Mr. Schott," replied Joe. "Arnold Schott."

"O–kay," said Jordan, clicking his mouse and peering at his computer screen. "Let me notify him you're here." He picked up the phone and pushed four numbers. After a moment, he said, "This is Jordan at the front desk. Two gentlemen are here to see you. They're police detectives…yes…fine." Then he stood up and said, "I'll take you to his office."

Jordan led them through a maze of cubicles and office doors. They arrived at a double door displaying a brass nameplate reading "Arnold B. Schott." He opened the door and closed it behind them once they had entered.

Arnold Schott was a thin, balding man around fifty, with glasses so thick that they magnified his eyes. Dark blue suspenders held up his gray slacks, and his bowtie matched his suspenders. He rose from behind his desk when Joe and Sam entered and greeted them.

"Good afternoon."

Holding his ID, Joe said, "I'm Detective Joe Erickson. This is my partner, Detective Renaldo. Thank you for agreeing to see us."

Indicating the two chairs in front of his desk, Schott said, "Why don't you sit down?"

After they were all seated, Schott asked, "What exactly happened to Quentin? You said he was attacked? With a knife?"

"He was attacked while jogging in Lincoln Park," replied Joe. "He sustained stab wounds to his back, and the offender cut his throat."

A horrified look came across Schott's face. "Omigod! That's terrible. Aw, poor Quentin."

"How did Mr. Rosberg get along with other members of your staff?" asked Joe.

"Just fine. He was our employee of the year a couple of years ago. That's why it was so unlike him to skip out on work. I tried calling his cell and left several messages, but…"

"How long has he worked here?" asked Sam.

"About seven years."

"How well did he get along with the administration?"

"No problems. He was a good team member. A model employee, in fact."

"Actuaries work in teams?" asked Joe.

"Sometimes. But most of the time, actuarial employees work on their own. They're assigned certain projects that analyze data and calculate likelihoods. Essentially, it's all about risk assessment."

"And that determines how much I pay for my insurance," said Sam, seeking confirmation.

"That's correct."

"Did he have a particular team partner?"

"It varies, but lately, he's been teamed with Cole Morgan."

"And they got along?"

"Swimmingly."

"Swimmingly," repeated Joe. "Could we talk with Cole Morgan?"

"Certainly. But he's not in today. In fact, he hasn't been in for a couple of days. Tested positive for COVID two days ago."

"I see."

"I hope I don't get it. You know, I had it a year ago and lost my sense of smell. I couldn't taste food for two weeks. Then my wife got it, and she had the worst cough…"

Joe nodded and glanced at Sam, who picked up Joe's cue.

"Excuse me, but we're trying to establish a link between the attack on Mr.

Rosberg and attacks on two other victims," explained Sam. "We believe the same offender is responsible."

"Good heavens. Are they alright?"

"No, unfortunately. Mr. Rosberg was the only one to survive."

Schott didn't say anything. He just blew out air and looked down at his desk.

"Is there anything you can tell us about Mr. Rosberg that could help our investigation?" asked Joe.

"Well…he's quiet and doesn't socialize much with his colleagues. But he's excellent at what he does. Always prompt and dependable. One of our very best actuaries. I can't fathom why somebody would do such a thing to poor Quentin."

They asked Schott a few additional questions, but his answers didn't prove helpful. According to Schott, Rosberg may be the next candidate for sainthood. Joe handed him his card and requested Cole Morgan's contact information.

Once they were back on the street, Joe received a phone call from a nurse at Northwestern Hospital.

"Detective Erickson. This is Dr. Li's nurse. Mr. Rosberg wrote a note saying I should call you because he remembered something."

"Did he say what it was?"

"No. All he wrote was to call you because he remembered something."

"Okay. We'll be there as soon as we can."

Joe ended the call and looked at Sam. "We need to go see Quentin Rosberg. He's remembered something."

"Great," grumbled Sam. "I hope it's relevant and not some trivial bullshit."

They drove to Northwestern Memorial Hospital and made their way to the nurses' station on Rosberg's floor. Nurse Woodward, who was on duty, recognized them. She handed Joe a note scribbled by Rosberg.

"This is what he handed Dr. Li's nurse," she said.

Joe read it and handed it to Sam.

"Thanks," said Joe. "Can we go to his room, or does a nurse need to accompany us?"

"You can go yourselves. Just…don't stay too long, okay?"

Joe and Sam walked down to Rosberg's room. Joe knocked on the door, opened it partway, and peered inside. Rosberg waved his hand weakly, indicating they should come in. Approaching his bed, they saw he had a pen and pad next to his hand. Picking it up, he wrote, "Hello," and showed it to them.

"Hello," said Joe. "We got your message. What did you want to tell us?"

Rosberg began writing on the pad and then held it up. It said, "Jury duty last year."

Joe glanced at Sam, who raised an eyebrow. "You were on a jury last year?" asked Joe. Rosberg gave him a thumb-up. "Do you remember the case?"

Rosberg gave a thumb-up and then wrote, "MV homicide."

"Motor vehicle homicide?" asked Joe.

Rosberg gave him a thumb-up.

"Would you happen to remember the name of the defendant?"

Rosberg wrote, "Jeremy Moeller."

"Jeremy Moeller," repeated Joe.

Another thumb-up.

"You have a good memory."

"And what was the outcome of the case?" asked Sam, who was showing an interest in this new development.

Rosberg folded over the top sheet of his tablet and began writing on the next page. He held it up to reveal one word: "Guilty."

"Did he receive a prison sentence?"

Rosberg gave them a thumb-up.

"That's good to know," said Joe. "Thank you. We'll look into it."

"Let us know if you think of anything else," added Sam. "This has been helpful. Thanks."

Another thumb-up.

Joe and Sam left the hospital and returned to Area 3, where they went to work researching the motor vehicle homicide case against Jeremy Moeller. Moeller, a twenty-one-year-old Columbia College student, was driving at high speed late one night when he lost control of his car and hit a utility pole.

His female passenger was killed instantly. At the hospital, a blood alcohol test revealed a level of .15 %, nearly twice the legal limit of .08 %. He was subsequently charged with DUI and aggravated vehicular homicide, a Class 4 felony. His case went to court, and he was convicted on the aggravated vehicular homicide charge in a jury trial. The defense contended that if the victim had been wearing her seat belt, she would have survived the crash. The jury did not agree. Moeller was sentenced to three years in the Illinois Department of Corrections penal system.

While an inmate in the Central Illinois Correctional Center, a minimum-security prison downstate, Moeller was fatally attacked while working in the kitchen. His death occurred six months ago, and the inmate responsible for Moeller's death is presently facing trial on a first-degree murder charge.

As soon as Joe read this, he walked to Sam's desk. "Did you read about the murder of Jeremy Moeller while he was incarcerated downstate?"

"I just did."

"We need to find out who else sat on that jury."

"I agree," replied Sam. "I'll get on that first thing in the morning. There's not enough time to start the search today."

"Why is it so many clues come late in the day, and we have to put them off until tomorrow?" asked Joe.

"I don't know. Lucky, I guess."

Joe looked at Sam and asked, "Are you thinking what I'm thinking?"

"Yeah. But I'm not going to get my hopes up."

"Me either. These leads have petered out too damned many times."

Chapter Thirty-Four

When he got home that evening, Joe was feeling optimistic. He wanted to tell Destiny about the possibility of a new lead, but he chose against mentioning it, thinking it might jinx the case. Still, he was pumped about what they had found, and Destiny picked up on it.

"What are you so upbeat about?" she asked.

"Oh…it's just that we had a good day at work for a change, that's all," replied Joe.

Sitting down next to him, she asked, "You make progress on the decapitation case?"

"Maybe. I can't call it a lead right now. At least, not yet. We'll know more tomorrow."

"So, no celebrating tonight?"

"No celebrating. We've been hopeful before, but when we followed up, it turned out to be a nothing burger. I don't know how many times we've had to refocus our efforts and start this investigation over again. So frustrating."

"I understand how you feel. You know the latest FBI stats for Chicago say that the percentage of murders solved has dropped to thirty percent."

"Thirty percent?"

"It was closer to fifty percent a few years ago, but since then, it's dropped.

"Did they give a reason?"

"No, but there are a number of factors that have caused it. And it doesn't mean the police aren't doing their jobs."

"So, statistically, you're saying we have about a one in three chance of making an arrest."

"Statistically speaking."

"And a two in three chance we'll never solve it."

"Statistically speaking, yes."

"Wonderful. That makes me feel a lot better," said Joe, his response dripping with sarcasm.

"Don't despair…your offender has attacked three people. With each attack, you've gained more information. The odds are better at catching a repeat offender."

"Yeah, but how many attacks is it going to take before we can make an arrest?"

Destiny leaned over and kissed him. "Don't worry about it. You'll get him. You and Sam have one of the department's best closure rates. Far better than thirty percent."

"That may be, but it's getting harder," said Joe. "I only hope we can find this guy before he kills someone else."

Destiny knew it wasn't good for Joe to bring work home with him, even though she appreciated his trust in her opinions. She was well aware of his frustration with this case, so she decided to change the subject and get his mind off of work.

"You haven't told me what you're doing next on the car," she asked. "When do you think you may need my help again?"

"Once I run the wiring for the ignition and the fuel injection, I'll need you to key the switch while I check for fuel and spark."

"When will that be?"

"Maybe in another week or so. There's a lot of wiring to do with electronic fuel injection."

"When do you think you'll be able to have it painted?"

"Next spring. It'll give me time to have everything together before they blow it apart for paint. I've already contacted one of the best custom shops around, and their painter has me on his list for March. I've chosen the color. I told you about that already, right?"

"You did. 'Triple black,' as I recall. The blackest black there is."

"That's right. I've seen this guy's work. He's really good, <u>and</u> he's fast, too. It won't sit in his shop for months waiting for him to get around to it. Some shops are notorious for that. When it's done, that black finish will look two feet deep. You'll see."

"Why do you like black so much? Your daily driver's black, you wear black clothes, and now this Camaro is going to be black. What's with you and black, anyway?" she teased.

"Because I'm the prince of darkness. You haven't figured that out yet?"

Destiny laughed. "Oh, I figured that out a long time ago."

"Black's my favorite color. Always has been. I doubt if it has any deep, dark psychological meaning."

"Just asking. Inquisitive minds, you know."

Good question for a shrink," he said and took a sip of wine. After that, he looked at Destiny. "Oo. This is good."

"I think so, too."

Joe stared into his glass for a few moments before saying, "You know, Dr. Lemke never mentioned my thing for black during our sessions. Maybe she wasn't aware of it. She saw the clothes I wore but never asked me about it. To me, nothing is more beautiful than black. A black car, a black suit, a black dress. Of course, anything black requires a lot more work than other colors, but no other color is as deep and reflective as black. In my line of work, I can blend in or disappear more easily if necessary."

"Okay," said Destiny. "Now...what should we make for dinner? Blackened fish with black-eyed peas and blackberries?"

Joe laughed. "Why not?"

* * *

Joe got in to work a few minutes late the following day because he witnessed a car accident while jogging. A young woman, who admitted she was texting while driving, missed a stop sign and T-boned another car that was going through the intersection. Fortunately, neither vehicle was traveling at high speed, and the two drivers were simply shaken up. But the impact heavily damaged both vehicles. Being the first on the scene, Joe called 9-1-1 to report the accident and check on the drivers. He hung around long enough to give the investigating officers his contact information and explain what he saw. What a way to start the day.

When he got to work, Joe saw Sam seated at his desk, focusing on his computer screen. Sam looked up as Joe approached and said, "I came in a little early."

"You? In early?" asked Joe in mock surprise. "I'm shocked."

"I know, I know. But I wanted to start searching for the names of people who sat on the jury along with Quentin Rosberg."

"Found them yet?"

"I didn't come in that early."

"I'm going to the hospital to speak with him. I want to show him photos of Jennifer Logan and Leah Sarandon to see if he recognizes them."

"Good idea."

"Hopefully, he'll remember them as fellow jury members. He's still in pretty bad shape, so...who knows what he can recall."

"Okay. Talk to you later."

Joe drove to the hospital and took the elevator up to the floor where Rosberg was recovering. As he walked to the nurses' station with photos in hand, Nurse Woodward looked up, and her expression suddenly changed.

"Good morning," greeted Joe, wondering why her expression looked worrisome.

"Let me call Dr. Li. He'll want to speak with you."

Woodward picked up the phone and paged Dr. Li. A few moments later, Joe saw Dr. Li come out of a patient's room down the hall and walk toward him. Joe sensed something was wrong.

"You're here to see Mr. Rosberg?" asked Dr. Li.

"I am. Yes."

"I'm sorry to inform you that Mr. Rosberg passed away last evening."

Joe was shocked. "What? I thought he was recovering. Did something happen?"

"Mr. Rosberg went into cardiac arrest last evening. Doctors worked on him for over twenty minutes, but they couldn't restart his heart."

"How could this happen?" asked Joe.

"He had a history of cardiac issues. Given the severity of his injuries and weakened state, the strain on his heart must have been too much. Unfortunately, this can occur sometimes. But it's not something we can predict."

God dammit! thought Joe. After a moment, he looked at Dr. Li and said, "I'm sorry to hear that."

"Yes. We are sorry, too. It was an unexpected death."

Joe thanked him, and, as he was passing the nurses' station, Nurse Woodward said, "Detective?"

Joe stopped and turned. "Yes."

"I'm sorry you had to find out about Mr. Rosberg this way. We were going to call you this morning, but things got busy."

Joe saw the regret on her face and said, "Sometimes we get busy, too."

Once back in his car, Joe drove to the nearest coffee shop and bought two large, dark roast coffees. Back at the office, he saw Sam still glued to his computer screen. Joe walked over and set a coffee on his desk.

"Thanks. What did you find out?"

There was no sense beating around the bush. "Rosberg's dead."

"What?" exclaimed an astonished Sam.

"Last night. He went into cardiac arrest, and they couldn't revive him.

"That's a hell of a thing," grumbled Sam.

"Yeah. What else is going to kick our ass on this case?"

"Well, there is some good news to report. While you were gone, I found something."

"Yeah?"

The names of the jurors in the Moeller case."

"And?"

Sam smiled, "All three of our victims sat on that jury."

"No kidding. That's our link!"

"Appears so."

Joe returned to his desk and began doing deeper research on Jeremy

Moeller. As it turned out, Jeremy had a twin brother named Jesse. Joe looked them both up in the Illinois Driver's License database. They were clearly identical twins. Jesse Moeller was a student at DePaul University. Their parents, James and Janelle Moeller, live in Evanson along with their fifteen-year-old daughter, Jerilyn. *What is it with these J-names, anyway?* thought Joe. James Moeller is a design engineer for Stratford, Inc., an engineering and construction firm, while his wife is the sole proprietor of J&J Investments, a wealth management company. *Hm. I smell money.*

A wrongful death lawsuit was filed by the parents of Alicia Hartley, the young woman who was the passenger in Jeremy Moeller's Dodge Challenger. An out-of-court settlement had been reached, but the details were not disclosed.

The Moellers hired Victor McBride, one of Chicago's high-powered criminal defense attorneys, to represent their son at trial, but despite McBride's past successes and courtroom savvy, the jury found Jeremy Moeller guilty of vehicular homicide. The judge sentenced Jeremy to three years in prison. An attempt to appeal the verdict failed, and Jeremy was remanded to the Illinois Department of Corrections, where he would have to serve a minimum of one year before he was eligible for parole. Joe thought it was fairly lenient, given he was responsible for a young woman's death.

Jeremy was housed in the Central Illinois Correctional Center, a minimum-security facility, to serve his sentence. While inmates in such prisons are determined to be of minimal risk to the public and are often non-violent offenders, violence has been known to occur.

Jeremy's work assignment was in the kitchen, and while there, he was stabbed and decapitated by another inmate. There was no mention of a motive for the attack.

Joe abruptly sat back in his chair and took a breath. *Decapitated? Holy shit!*

He read on. Following Jeremy's death, his father filed suit against the Illinois Department of Corrections. The case has yet to go to trial or be resolved.

After a few moments of reflection, Joe took out a pad and began writing questions. Could this be the actual link to the person who killed two people and indirectly caused the death of one more? A revenge motive? And was serving on a jury what brought three people from disparate backgrounds together? After writing a page of questions, he looked at his watch and saw it was time for lunch.

Deciding to treat himself to a good lunch, he drove to an Italian restaurant he enjoyed and ordered pasta with sausage and arrabbiata sauce, one of his favorites. Eating the meal lifted his spirits, and when he returned to his desk, his head was in a better place. Good food can do that for a person.

Chapter Thirty-Five

Later that afternoon, Sam jumped up from his chair and nearly ran to Joe's desk. "Got it!" he said in an excited voice.

Joe turned in his chair and saw the smile on Sam's face. "You strike paydirt?" he asked.

"Sure did. I got the contact information for the remaining jurors."

"Good work, man. It's about time we find out who they are."

Joe looked at his watch and said, "We need to start looking into other people who were associated with the trial, like the prosecutor and the judge. They could be at risk, too."

"Good idea."

"Maybe a visit with the defense attorney would be a good place to start, you think?"

Sam nodded. "But I think there's something more crucial. We need to alert the remaining jurors they could be in danger. Whoever the offender is, I'd be willing to bet he's already picked out his next victim."

"Okay," said Joe. "You do that, and I'll make an appointment with Victor McBride, Jeremy Moeller's defense attorney. Then, I can help you track down the jurors, judge, and prosecutor. Hopefully, the jurors haven't changed phone numbers and addresses since they last served."

Sam returned to his desk, and Joe looked up Victor McBride's office phone number. It turned out that he worked at McBride, Wayne, Benson & Tyler, Attorneys at Law. It wasn't surprising McBride's name was first, given his notoriety.

Joe called the general office number, and a woman answered. "McBride,

Wayne, Benson, and Tyler. How may I help you?" she said in a cheery voice. *Do all receptionists use the line 'How may I help you?'* wondered Joe. He heard it constantly from receptionists. *Oh, well, I guess it's preferable to 'What do you want?'* "This is Detective Joe Erickson with Chicago PD. I need to make an appointment to speak with Mr. McBride."

"Is this personal or professional?"

"I'm afraid it's police business."

"Ah. Well, let me see what times he has open."

He was put on hold, and Joe recognized Beethoven's Moonlight Sonata, playing as he waited. A few moments later, she came back on the line and said, "He has tomorrow morning at 10:15 open. Would that time work for you?"

"It would. Thank you."

"I'm sorry, but could you tell me your name again, please? Just to make sure I have it right."

"It's Erickson. Detective Joe Erickson. E-R-I-C-K-S-O-N."

"Thank you," she said cheerfully. "We'll see you tomorrow at 10:15."

After hanging up, Joe stepped to Sam, who was just hanging up his phone. He looked up at Joe and said, "One juror down. Elizabeth Petrenko."

"What did you say to her?"

"I told her that three fellow jurors have been the victims of homicide, and we feel someone could be targeting members of the jury that she served on. She was quite disturbed by that, so I suggested if she avoided activities where she'd be alone, she wouldn't be a likely target. I explained the three victims were jogging and bicycling alone when the attacks occurred."

"What did she say?"

"She said she didn't go anywhere without her husband. But they would be careful when they went shopping."

"Okay. How do you want to split up the list?"

"I'll email you the link for their contact information. There are eight juror names left. I'll take the judge and the top four, and you take the bottom four and the prosecutor."

Joe returned to his desk and clicked on the link Sam sent him. He began with the fifth name on the list, Lamont Johnson. When he called, he got an answering machine. He began leaving a message with his name and phone number, saying it was very important for him to call back. Just as he was about to end the call, a deep voice interrupted saying, "Hello. This is Lamont Johnson. You said jer with da police?"

"That's right," replied Joe. "I'm calling because you served on a jury for a vehicular homicide case almost a year ago. Is that correct?"

"Yeah, I did."

"Are you aware that three of your fellow jury members have been attacked and killed within the last couple of months?"

"Uh…no, I…dint know that."

"We're calling all the remaining members of the jury to caution them because there's reason to believe someone could be targeting you. So, to be safe, we suggest you avoid situations where you'll be alone. Jogging, walking, sitting in a park, things like that."

"Damn, man! I live alone. And I walk ever day fer exercise."

"Do you walk with anyone else?"

"A friend o' mine, most a time."

"That's good. So far, the offender hasn't attacked anyone who was with other people. Only those who were alone. Make sure you always walk with someone else. It's critical you are diligent and avoid making yourself vulnerable to an attack."

"What kind of attack?"

"A knife attack."

"Man…when you gonna 'rest this muthafucka?"

"Soon, we hope. We'll let you know when we make an arrest."

"Okay. I 'preciate cha lettin' me know."

Joe looked at the list and called the next person. Once again, his call was picked up by an answering machine. He left a message, hoping the person would call him back. He then called the third person, Clare Bickford, and got an automated message saying the number was no longer in service. Wonderful. Out of curiosity, he looked up Clare Bickford in the Illinois Driver's License database. She was a forty-seven-year-old woman with an address in Old Town. He noted her address so he could check it out tomorrow. Then he searched the obituaries just to make sure, but nothing for anyone named Clare Bickford pulled up. That's a relief. Either she changed her phone number or moved out of the city and didn't bother to change her address.

Looking at the clock, Joe had only half an hour until Miller time. He tried calling the remaining name on the list, but his phone rang and rang with no answering machine picking up. Unable to leave a message, he would have to try again tomorrow. He didn't try to call the prosecutor's office since it was late in the afternoon. That would also have to be done tomorrow.

In the time he had left, Joe looked up James Moeller, Jeremy's father. He found Moeller and his wife lived on Sheridan Road in Evanston. He figured Victor McBride could give him Moeller's phone number.

When Joe arrived home, Autumn greeted him. A scribbled note from Destiny that was stuck to the refrigerator stated, "Went to the store—back soon."

He looked down at Autumn and said, "Go for a walk?" Autumn barked and began dancing around, excited she was going to go for a jaunt around the block. Joe put her collar on and carried her out the door to begin their walk. Autumn took off, walking so fast that Joe could hardly keep up. Then she stopped abruptly to smell some mystery scent on a tree trunk. "It's probably pee, Autumn," said Joe, as if she could understand him. He let her finish her investigating, and soon, they were on their way down the sidewalk again.

When they returned to the house, they went in, and Joe saw Destiny had returned. She was busy at the island, slicing some vegetables. He spotted the wok on the stove.

"I found a recipe I wanted to try tonight, but I didn't have any scallions, and I was almost out of sesame oil. Had to make a trip to the store."

"What are you making?" asked Joe.

"Mushroom and scallion stir-fry. And I'm baking salmon to go along with it."

"Sounds good."

"Hope so. How was your walk?"

"Autumn was her usual exuberant self. She was particularly interested in smelling tree trunks tonight."

"Someone else's dog, probably."

"That or some wild creature." Autumn looked up at him with her beautiful brown eyes. Then saw her, he realized, "Oh, Autumn. You've been waiting for your T-R-E-A-T, haven't you?"

Autumn replied with a little bark. Destiny smiled and said, "You know she can spell now."

"Treat!" said Joe, and Autumn barked an affirmative and jumped up on his leg. He walked over to the counter, shook a treat out of the package, and gave it to her. She practically swallowed it without chewing. She looked up at him as if she were Oliver Twist, asking, "Please, sir, I want some more."

"Beggar," said Joe. And he tossed her a small Milk Bone, which she caught, took over to her bed, and began crunching.

"You're such a soft touch," said Destiny. "She has you wrapped around her little paw."

Joe walked over to Destiny and kissed her. "She's not the only one who has me wrapped around something."

"You think so?" replied Destiny.

"I know so."

Destiny chuckled.

"Can I do something?" asked Joe. "I feel funny just sitting here watching you work."

"Keep feeling funny. Everything will be done in fifteen minutes. How are things going at work?"

"They're going. Nothing to report yet."

Joe poured himself a glass of water and sat at the island.

"Have you talked to your mom lately?" he asked.

"This morning, as a matter of fact."

"How's she doing?"

"She must be feeling pretty good. She's planning a river cruise down the Danube next month."

"By herself?"

"I didn't ask. It might be a Marathon thing."

Chapter Thirty-Six

As Joe was jogging the next morning, he could tell the day would be a scorcher. The sign on the First National Bank confirmed it was eighty-eight degrees already.

He began to think about the lead they would be following up on later today. What kind of man was James Moeller? Would a wealthy man of forty-seven dress up in a black sweat suit and ski mask and execute people he held responsible for his son's death? And why did he decapitate them? Revenge for what happened to his son? But accounting for rage and a powerful desire for retribution, anything would be possible. He had encountered stranger, more horrific things during his years on the force.

Joe and Sam drove to Victor McBride's office the following day for their 10:15 appointment. Located on West Wacker Drive, the 31-story light gray tower was in the West Loop area, just steps away from the Riverwalk.

As they entered, they saw a sign indicating McBride's office was located on the 16th floor. They rode the elevator along with six other people who got off on various floors. Finally, the doors opened onto Floor 16, revealing a posh office suite dominated by walnut wood features and light gray walls. The middle-aged woman seated behind a large wooden desk looked up and rose from her chair when Joe and Sam stepped through the doors onto the polished marble floor.

As they approached the desk, she said, "Detectives Erickson and—"

"Renaldo," said Sam, completing the sentence for her.

"Welcome. Mr. McBride is ready for you. I'll take you to his office."

They followed her to the end of the hall to a pair of walnut double doors.

The receptionist, who did not reveal her name, knocked on the door and opened it a crack, saying, "Your appointment is here."

"Send them in, Jan," came a voice from inside.

She opened the door for Joe and Sam to enter. They saw a large office with a wide window overlooking the Chicago River and skyline. The room was decorated with photos of exotic sports cars, including Ferraris and Lamborghinis. Joe spotted one with a man standing next to a red Ferrari 488 Spider. McBride came around the side of his desk with his hand out to shake hands. "Vic McBride," he said as he shook Joe's hand. Joe recognized him as the man in the photo.

"I'm Detective Joe Erickson, and this is my partner, Detective Sam Renaldo," said Joe as McBride shook hands with Sam. McBride was impeccably dressed in a blue pinstripe suit, a Stefano Ricci necktie, and what looked like Gucci shoes. He was in his early fifties and sported what Joe suspected to be a hairpiece. A very good one. And his smile revealed perfect, very white teeth.

"Why don't we sit down over here?" said McBride, pointing to three leather chairs surrounding a round table. After being seated, McBride asked, "What can I do for you?"

For a defense attorney, McBride seemed quite friendly, and Joe suspected it could be an act for their benefit. His experience with defense attorneys ranged from aloof to hostile, but he would give McBride the benefit of the doubt, at least for the time being.

Joe began, "Are you aware that three of the jurors in the trial of Jeremy Moeller have been brutally killed in the last two months?"

"I am. It was brought to my attention by one of my colleagues. Quite troubling," said McBride, shaking his head. "Am I to assume you're in charge of investigating the case?"

"We are. We're working on the premise these are revenge killings associated with the guilty verdict and the subsequent death of Jeremy Moeller."

"Well...I can understand how it may look that way, given they were on the jury," said McBride.

"I'm sure the verdict was a huge disappointment to Jeremy's family and friends. His tragic murder while incarcerated must have been devastating."

"Indeed. It was horrific."

"Were you in contact with the family following his death?" asked Sam.

"Yes. It was a very sad situation that should never have happened. As you suggested, his family was utterly devastated."

"How well do you know the family—the father, the brother?"

"I know Jim, Jeremy's father, fairly well. I don't know his son, Jess. I met him, but that's all. He was in college at the time, and it was difficult for him to attend the trial due to his class schedule. His father was adamant he should not skip any classes."

"I see. What's Jim like?"

"Driven, astute. Highly intelligent and capable. And he's a dedicated family man."

"What about his temperament?"

"He could be emotionally charged when it came to Jeremy."

"Angry?" asked Joe.

"I saw him angry a few times. Especially when the verdict was read and after the sentencing. The idea of Jeremy going to prison infuriated him."

"Do you think Jim's anger could have festered and motivated him to begin killing members of the jury? As a way to get revenge for his son's death?"

McBride thought for a moment and then said, "I don't feel comfortable answering your question. Sorry. I mean, Jim could be volatile at times, but would he go off the deep end and begin killing people? I doubt it, but…we both know seemingly normal people are capable of crazy things."

"What's Jeremy's mother like?" asked Sam.

"Very bright. She developed her own company, which has become quite successful. From what I observed, she seemed to respond intellectually to the trial rather than showing any emotion."

"How did she respond when the verdict was read?"

"She remained stoic after the verdict. Ice, really.

"And at the sentencing?"

"She rose from her chair and left. She didn't show much, but by the way she walked out, I could tell she was upset."

"Not heartbroken?"

"I'm sure she was, but she appeared to be suppressing it. No tears. Not at that moment, anyway. I was a little surprised she didn't hug her son or even speak to him before he was led out of the room. From what I saw, she simply turned and left, maintaining her dignity as she walked to the door."

"Strange reaction."

"Did you speak with her afterward?"

"No."

"What about the interim when you were seeking an appeal?"

"Not then, either. The appeal was actually Jim's idea. We didn't have a chance in hell, to be honest. Everything about the trial was on the up and up, but Jim insisted. Our appeal was shot down immediately, just like I knew it would be."

"What was their reaction to the appeal being denied?"

"They were both disappointed. Angry about it. They didn't want to hear it, but I told them they needed to resign themselves to the fact that Jeremy would have to spend a minimum of twelve months in prison. After that, he could probably get out on parole. I encouraged Jeremy to think of it as an extended vacation. Read. Take an online class. Minimum security has a lot of privileges."

"But it got him killed," added Sam.

"Tragically, it did. I was told Jeremy lipped off to another inmate, and the guy went ballistic and stabbed him. The inmate told authorities he didn't intend to kill Jeremy, just teach him a lesson. But that made no sense since he'd beheaded him. Like I said, it should never have happened in a facility like that."

"You wouldn't have a phone number for James Moeller, would you? We need to speak with him."

"I do," said McBride, rising from his chair. "Let me get it for you."

Joe and Sam followed him as he walked to his desk and pulled up the phone number on his computer. "It's 312-555-8899. I assume it's still current. It's been a while since we last spoke."

After writing down the number, Joe looked at Sam, who gave him a nod. "Well," said Joe, "I think we have everything we came for. We appreciate your cooperation."

"Thanks for your time," said Sam.

"Glad I was able to help," replied McBride as he stood, hitching up his pants.

"Is that you with the Magnum P.I. Ferrari in that photo?" asked Joe.

"It's the same model they used on the reboot of the show, but that one happens to be mine."

"Nice," said Sam.

"Beautiful," added Joe.

"It's my way of indulging myself a little. Getting away from work. You're in another world when you're behind the wheel of that car."

"I know what you mean."

After leaving McBride's office, Joe and Sam got on the elevator. When the door closed, Sam asked, "What's a car like that cost, anyway?"

"You could probably pick one up for around two hundred grand," replied Joe. "You could pretend to be Magnum P.I."

"Yeah. I look so much like him." He looked at Joe and said, "You know, we don't live right."

"Chuckling, Joe said, "Yeah, I guess we don't."

That afternoon, Joe tried to call James Moeller, but his call went to voicemail. He left a message stating who he was and that it was important for him to return his call. No return call came in the rest of the day. A few minutes before leaving work, Joe called Moeller's place of business. He was told that Moeller works from home most days and only comes to the office one day a week. *Hm*, Joe thought, *Means, opportunity, and motive.* He asked to speak with someone who worked closely with Moeller, and he was given Bruce Chaplin's name. He asked to be transferred, but the receptionist stated Chaplin had already left for the day, but would be in again tomorrow.

Another job for tomorrow, thought Joe.

Chapter Thirty-Seven

The following day, Joe called Bruce Chaplin at work and made an appointment to speak with him at eleven o'clock. Joe and Sam drove to Stratford, Inc., located on South Wabash Avenue, and arrived fifteen minutes early. Stratford, Inc. occupied a section of the nineteenth floor of a forty-five-story rectangular tower in the Loop.

They took the elevator to the nineteenth floor and found Suite 1910. Upon entering the office complex, they saw a counter with Stratford, Inc., in large letters above it. A smartly dressed young woman in a dark blue business suit greeted them.

"Good morning, gentlemen. Welcome to Stratford Inc."

"Good morning," said Joe. "We have an appointment with Bruce Chaplin at eleven o'clock. We're a few minutes early."

"And you are…?"

"Detective Joe Erickson and Detective Sam Renaldo," replied Joe, holding up his ID.

"I see. Let me buzz him and tell him you're here," she said, as if it was inconvenient for her to make the call.

Picking up her phone, she dialed a number. A moment later, she said, "Mr. Chaplin, your eleven o'clock is here…Detectives Erickson and Ricardo."

"That's 'Renaldo,'" corrected Sam, annoyed by her mistake. "I'm not married to Lucy."

Her eyes darted from Sam to the phone. A moment later, she nodded and said, "I'll let them know." Looking at Sam, she gave him a cold smile and said, "My apologies for getting your name wrong." Looking at Joe, she said,

"He'll be with you in a second." Returning to her chair, she sat down and ignored them, apparently miffed by Sam's snappish correction.

It wasn't long before a man approached. He was around fifty years of age, well-dressed in a gray pinstriped suit and red tie. Glancing back and forth at Joe and Sam, he said, "I'm Bruce Chaplin." Looking at Joe, he said, "Am I to assume you're Detective Erickson?"

"Yes," said Joe as he shook his outstretched hand. And this is my partner, Detective Sam Renaldo."

Looking at Sam, Chaplin extended his hand, saying, "Pleased to meet you, detective." Following the handshake, he said, "Why don't we talk in my office? If you'll follow me."

Joe glanced at the young woman behind the counter. Her eyes could have burned holes in them. *A bit touchy today, aren't we?* thought Joe. As they followed Chaplin a short distance to his office, they saw the door had been left open. It was furnished with Chicago Bears sports memorabilia. After closing the door, he said, "Why don't you have a seat?" He indicated two black leather guest chairs in front of his desk.

After sitting behind his desk, Chaplin asked, "What can I do for you?"

Joe took the lead as he usually did during these interviews. "You work with James Moeller, is that correct?"

"Yes. We're both design engineers. We've collaborated on many projects over the years. Robotics, primarily."

"How well do you know him?"

"Oh...Pretty well, I guess. What's this about?"

"His name came up during one of our investigations," said Sam.

"Right," said Joe. "Are you familiar with his son Jeremy's story?"

"Yes. That was a tragedy," replied Chaplin, his expression revealing sadness and regret. "Terrible thing."

"So, he spoke with you about it?"

Nodding, Chaplin said, "He did. I'm a good listener. He found the sentencing devastating. If that wasn't bad enough...he just fell apart when Jeremy was killed."

"What do you mean by 'fell apart'?"

"Well…after the shock and the grieving were over, he seemed to clam up. I could tell he was angry—the look in his eyes, his demeanor. He wasn't the guy he used to be."

"Did he say anything about his anger?"

"Said he was angry with his lawyer, the judge, the jury, everyone associated with Jeremy's arrest and trial. In a way, I can't blame him. I don't know how I'd react if something like that happened to one of my kids. I suggested he get some help, you know—talk to a clergyman or a counselor or someone."

"And what did he say to that?"

"He'd say, 'It's nothing. I'll get over it in time.' But I think he really needed to talk with a shrink."

"And did he?"

"Not that he told me. Of course, one usually doesn't reveal that sort of thing to others."

"Did it affect his work?" asked Sam.

"Not with me. He seemed to be okay when he was involved with a project. Maybe his focus on work was helping him cope."

"And what about now?"

"Same. He used to be openly friendly. Now, he doesn't say much unless it has to do with the project. He doesn't laugh and socialize with others like he used to. It's strictly business now."

"Do you know his wife?" asked Joe.

"No. I mean, I know who she is. We attended the same company functions. But I don't think we ever said anything other than 'hello' to her. At least, not that I can recall. My wife might know more."

"So, they know each other?"

"Not well. They aren't what I would call friends."

"What about his family?"

"He used to mention his family once in a while, but not very often. He was rather private about that."

"Did he ever say anything about his boys?"

"Not after what happened to Jeremy."

"What about his wife?"

CHAPTER THIRTY-SEVEN

"Not that I recall. Like I said, he's been strictly business."

"Let me ask this," said Sam. "Do you think Jim Moeller is the kind of man who would take revenge on those responsible for sending Jeremy to prison? Like the judge, jury, attorneys?"

"Is that what this is about?"

"Just answer the question."

"Honestly, I don't know. He's wrapped pretty tight, so I wouldn't be surprised if he exploded at somebody. He seems like a bomb ready to go off sometimes."

"So, he only comes into the office once a week?" asked Joe.

"Yeah. He prefers to work from his home office these days. He says it's easier for him to concentrate. And the company allows it, given the amount of work he gets done."

"Is he an athletic person? Is he in good physical shape?"

"Uh, well…yeah. He's always worked out and remained trim. I should have taken his example long ago and kept in shape myself. I guess I'm too comfortable being a couch potato," joked Chaplin.

"There's still time," said Joe. "I was like that once, but I got a physical trainer, and she whipped me into shape. It made me feel a lot better."

"I should probably do that."

"You should. For your family's sake."

"One thing," said Sam. "You might want to keep our conversation to yourself. Moeller doesn't need to know about this interview, and he might not appreciate you answering questions about him."

"Oh, I intend to. Given his temperament, I don't want him going off on me. I have to work with the guy."

"So, you think he'd go off on you?"

"Possibly. You never know."

Joe and Sam thanked Chaplin for his time. They didn't talk on the elevator ride down to the lobby since two other people were riding with them. Once out on the street, Sam asked, "So, what do you think?"

"I think we have a new person of interest, don't you?" said Joe.

"Yeah," replied Sam. "We'll see if he graduates to suspect status."

"You were a little hard on that receptionist.

"Maybe. It pisses me off when people get my name wrong. Ricky Ricardo, I'm not."

"Oh, Loo-oo-oo-cy!" kidded Joe.

"And I was going to bring you coffee tomorrow morning," said Sam.

Chapter Thirty-Eight

After lunch, Joe and Sam drove to James Moeller's residence on Sheridan Road in Evanston, a city north of Chicago. Joe stopped the car in front of the large brick landmark house that was meticulously landscaped.

"I think this is a little above my pay grade," observed Sam.

"Yeah," replied Joe. "I'd say James Moeller has done well."

They walked onto the spacious front porch and rang the bell. A few seconds later, a surprised middle-aged woman answered the door. Displaying their IDs, Joe said, "Chicago PD. We're here to see James Moeller. Is he home?"

"He is. Hold on, and I'll get him," she said, closing the door.

"Didn't invite us in," said Sam. "That was accommodating."

"This could be difficult," replied Joe.

A minute or so later, a middle-aged man dressed in a maroon shirt and khakis opened the door. "I'm Jim Moeller. Can I help you?" His thin face looked drawn and tired.

Displaying their IDs once again, Joe repeated, "I'm Detective Joe Erickson. My partner, Detective Sam Renaldo. We need to speak with you."

"About what?"

"An investigation we're conducting."

"What kind of investigation?" asked Moeller, displaying some annoyance.

Joe glanced quickly at Sam and then at Moeller. "Like I said, we need to speak with you. We can do it here, or we can take you downtown. Your choice," added Sam.

"All right. Come on in," said Moeller, reluctantly opening the door for them. Moeller looked fit and tanned, like someone who played golf or tennis a lot. His movement appeared effortless, something uncommon given his age.

They followed him through a grand foyer to a formal dining room, where sunlight shone through the windows. Moeller sat at the table. He did not invite Joe and Sam to sit, but they did anyway.

"What's this about? I'm very busy at the moment."

"We are investigating a series of murders," said Joe.

"So, what's that got to do with me?" His belligerence was beginning to irk Joe, so he looked at Sam, who picked up his cue to take over.

"We're investigating three murders. All three victims were people who sat on your son's jury."

"That's why we're here," added Joe.

Joe observed the subtle expression on Moeller's face change from belligerence to surprise. Then the realization set in, and Moeller's hostility returned.

"So, you think I did it?"

"We have to investigate all possibilities. Right now, you appear to have the strongest motive."

"This is bullshit!" said Moeller, rising from his chair. "I'm going to call my attorney."

Joe and Sam both rose from their chairs.

"You can do it from our office," said Sam. Pulling his handcuffs. "Now, turn around and put your hands behind your back."

"You're handcuffing me?" protested Moeller.

"I have to, if you're going to ride in a police vehicle. It's the law."

"Or..." said Joe. "You can choose to answer our questions. If you haven't done anything wrong, you shouldn't need an attorney present. But that's your prerogative, of course."

"Do you wish to have an attorney present or not?" asked Sam.

Moeller thought for a few seconds before saying, "Let's just get this over with. I'm working on a project, and it's time-sensitive." Moeller returned to his chair, as did Joe and Sam.

"I understand your grief and anger over your son's tragic death," said Joe. "But I'm sure you can understand that we have to look at anyone who may have had a motive to seek retribution on members of the jury. After all, they convicted your son. And it was his conviction that placed him in that prison."

Moeller took it all in, and his belligerence diminished. "Look," he said. "I had nothing to do with what happened to those people. I work from home most days, and so does my wife. I'm sure she can corroborate my presence here on whatever dates those crimes were committed."

"Using one's spouse as an alibi is pretty weak," said Sam. "Spouses are notorious for providing false alibis."

Moeller's lips pressed tightly together, and his eyebrows furled, reflecting his annoyance. After a sigh, he said, "Alright. What dates are we talking about?"

Joe looked in his notebook and said, "The early morning hours of June 9th, June 20th, and July 14th."

"Let me get my phone." Moeller rose from his chair and walked into another room. While he was gone, they heard another person enter from the front door. Joe glanced out into the foyer and glimpsed a college-age young man who stopped when he realized there were people in the dining room.

"Sorry, Dad. Didn't know you had company," he said.

Moeller replied, "It's okay. They won't be much longer." Then Moeller came back into the dining room and sat down. "My son, Jess. He probably came home to get food."

"College student?" asked Joe, even though he knew he was.

"Uh-huh," Moeller nodded. "What were those dates again?"

"June 9th," began Joe.

Looking into his phone, Moeller said, "I was here all day."

"June 20th."

Moeller pressed buttons on his phone. "Looks like I was here all day."

"July 14th."

After inputting the date, Moeller's expression brightened. "Ah. I was in Washington, D.C., speaking with Senator Marx about a proposed project we're seeking federal funding for."

"We'll need you to document that," stated Sam.

"You can speak to our CEO, Rohan Kumari. We traveled there together."

After asking for the correct spelling of the CEO's name and his contact information, Joe pushed his notebook and pen to Moeller and asked, "Could I have your cell number? In case I need to contact you? That way, we won't have to disturb you by showing up on your doorstep."

"Fine," said Moeller, who wrote down his cell number, holding the pen in his left hand. Joe looked at Sam, who returned his look. *Left-handed, just like the offender.*

Moeller passed back the notebook and pen. As Joe picked it up, he rose from his chair, saying, "I think our interview is over."

"Thanks for your time," said Sam.

Moeller followed them to the door and closed it behind them.

"You think the CEO will confirm his travel to D.C.?" asked Sam.

"If he spoke to our two senators, I think we need to confirm it with one of them. He could be calling the CEO right now, asking him to lie for him."

When Joe was back in his office, he called the U.S. Capital switchboard. After identifying himself, he asked to be transferred to the office of Illinois Senator Justin Marx. A moment later, a man's voice answered, "Senator Marx's office. Could you state your business, please?"

Joe identified himself and said, "I need to confirm a meeting took place with the senator and two people from Stratford, Inc., on July 14th."

"Let me transfer you to the senator's aide, Mr. Francisco. Hold on, please."

After one ring, his call was picked up, and a voice answered, "Tom Francisco."

Once again, Joe identified himself before saying, "I'm calling to confirm that a meeting took place with the senator and two people from Stratford, Inc., on July 14th. It's part of an ongoing homicide investigation here in Chicago."

"Homicide, huh?"

"Afraid so."

Joe was expecting some pushback about accessing the senator's appointment schedule, but Francisco seemed cooperative. "All right. Let me pull up Senator Marx's schedule for July 14th."

Joe waited for a minute or so, and then Francisco said, "I see a meeting scheduled at 11:15 a.m. on the date in question. It was with James Moeller and Rohan Kumari of Stratford, Incorporated from Chicago."

"You said it was scheduled. Did the meeting actually take place?" asked Joe.

"I can confirm that," said Francisco. "I happened to be in attendance."

"That's what I needed to know," said Joe. "Thank you. I appreciate your time."

The call ended, and once again, Joe felt dejected. Their investigation just hit another bump in the road.

He stepped to Sam's desk. Sam looked up and said, "I have a call into Rohan Kumari's office. His secretary said he wasn't in today."

"Well," said Joe. "I just got off the phone with Senator Marx's office in D.C. His administrative assistant confirmed a meeting took place between the senator and Moeller and Kumari on July 14th at 11:15. We're screwed again."

"Shit!" reacted Sam. "Now what?"

Chapter Thirty-Nine

Destiny saw the expression on Joe's face when he got home, and she could tell he was not happy. He walked past Autumn without petting her and plopped down on a stool at the island.

"What happened?" she asked.

"Well…we thought we had a suspect in the decapitation case. He looked good for it in so many ways. Means, opportunity, motive. He was even left-handed, like our offender. Everything seemed to be there."

"Who was it?"

"The father of the young man who was sent to prison for vehicular homicide and was then killed by another inmate. During our investigation, the father was described as distraught, angry, and vengeful. He was the best lead we've had so far."

"But…?"

"He had no alibi for the first two murders. He works from home and only goes into the office once a week. But he claimed he was in D.C. with his boss for a meeting with Senator Marx on the day of the third attack. I called the senator's office, and their meeting was confirmed by his assistant, who attended the meeting. Poof! Another lead gone. Again."

"You want a glass of wine or something?"

"No. It would just depress me more."

"Well, I need to put the lasagna in the oven. Excuse me a second."

Joe nodded. He looked down and saw Autumn sitting at his feet. She pawed his leg, and he said, "Hi, Autumn. Have you had your T-R-E-A-T yet?" She gave a barely audible cry.

"No, she hasn't," answered Destiny. "But I walked her half an hour ago."

"We need to fix this, don't we, Autumn?" said Joe in response to her plaintive look. He got up, triggering Autumn's excitement. She turned a circle and ran to the counter where her treats were kept. Joe reached into the cupboard and opened a sealed package containing her treats. The sound of the package being opened excited Autumn even more.

Holding up the treat, Joe said, "Speak." Autumn barked, and he handed her the treat. She practically inhaled it. Looking up at him, she begged for another. "Sorry. You only get one. We don't want you to get roly-poly, do we?"

"You're so cruel," teased Destiny.

"I know. I'm a b-a-a-d dad."

Rather than a second treat, Joe picked up one of Autumn's toys, rattled it, and then tossed it into the living room. Autumn chased after it lickety-split and brought it back to him. He tossed the toy again and again. The last time, rather than bringing it to Joe, she took it over to her bed and began gnawing on it. Playtime was over. Joe's mood had improved as a result, and he returned to sit on his stool.

Destiny set a glass of water down in front of him. "She waits for you every night, you know. She senses what time you get home and gets excited when she hears your car. She recognizes the sound it makes."

"She wants her daddy," he smiled.

Joe could be a pretty tough customer when it came to doing his job. He had faced down dangerous suspects and exchanged gunfire with offenders intent on killing him. But Autumn had a calming, mood-altering effect on him that ultimately benefited his mental health.

Destiny wasn't sure she should bring up work again, but she thought maybe talking about it could get Joe's creative juices flowing. Sometimes, she felt a little like Myrna Loy, who was William Powell's wife and crime-solving partner in *The Thin Man*.

"It'll be another twenty minutes before the lasagna is done. You want to talk about your investigation?"

Setting his glass down after taking a drink, Joe said, "Sure. Why not?"

"You said the father was a potential suspect in the crimes, but he was eliminated due to his alibi. Do you think the third attack could have been committed by someone else?"

"No. All three victims served on the jury that convicted Jeremy Moeller. We're certain one offender is responsible, given the matching descriptions by witnesses."

"You said the father had means, motive, and opportunity. If the motive is revenge, it almost has to be someone linked to Jeremy Moeller, doesn't it?"

"That makes the most sense. Yeah."

"Then, what about the rest of the Moeller family?"

"Well, besides the father, there's a mother. And there's a brother and a sister…" Then a sudden realization popped into Joe's mind. He considered it for a minute and then looked at Destiny.

Seeing the expression on his face, she asked, "What is it?"

"The brother. Jeremy's twin brother, Jesse, or Jess as he's known. I didn't think of him."

"What about the sister?"

"Too young and not strong enough to overpower someone. But Jess…"

"How old is he?"

"He'd be about twenty-two, twenty-three. I caught a glimpse of him when we were interviewing his father today. Looked like he was pretty athletic."

"Does he work somewhere?"

"He's a college student."

"He could have had opportunity at the time of the attacks if he doesn't have early classes. If he's a junior or senior, he probably would've opted for classes later in the morning and early afternoon like I did."

"I did that, too," said Joe.

"Unless he has a job that has an early start."

"I doubt it. Not with his parents' money. And he doesn't live at home, based on something his father said. Probably has an apartment where he can come and go as he pleases."

"Losing a brother is one thing," said Destiny. "But losing your twin…that would be especially traumatic for the surviving twin. Twins have a unique bond that goes beyond being just siblings. He would feel as though he'd lost his other half, a piece of himself. Grief hits them especially hard."

Joe considered what Destiny said. A moment later, he leaned over and kissed her, saying, "You're the best."

"Mm. That was nice," she said, smiling. "Glad I could help."

"Sam and I'll pursue that angle tomorrow. The way this investigation has gone so far, I'm not getting my hopes up. But it sounds like our next best path."

Chapter Forty

When Joe saw Sam arrive at work the next day, he walked to his desk and said, "When I was with Destiny last night, I had an epiphany."

Sam turned in his chair and replied, "I don't want to hear about your sex life."

"Very funny."

"So, what mysterious vision appeared to you?"

"Well, we had to eliminate James Moeller from our persons of interest list. But…what about his son?"

"The college kid, you mean? The twin brother?"

"Yeah."

"So, what makes you suspect him?"

Joe pulled up an empty chair next to Sam and sat down. "A college kid has a flexible schedule. And he's old enough to register early and select classes that meet later in the morning, rather than sign up for those early eight o'clock classes. I used to hate those."

"Because you wanted to sleep in, and you were hungover."

"Among other things. But I liked to study in the morning."

"Okay," said Sam, taking it all in. "Go on."

"He could easily find out the address of a particular member of the jury and spy on their movements. He found three people who would prove vulnerable because they were physically active first thing in the morning. A bicyclist and two joggers. And if they were creatures of habit and used the same routes each day, he could plan his attacks knowing where they'd be. It would be easy for him to lie in wait, kill them, and use a preplanned escape route."

"Okay, I'm following you so far."

"He doesn't live with his parents, so he must have an apartment where he could come and go at any time without suspicion. And he could drop his bloody clothing in the washer after returning home."

"All right," said Sam. "You sold me. I could see him so upset about his twin brother's death that he wants to focus his rage on members of the jury."

"Yeah. Maybe he sees the jury as the instrument that led to his brother's death. If he does, that's one helluva motive."

"Then, let's check him out."

Joe returned to his desk and began researching Jess Moeller. He was presently a senior at DePaul University, a highly respected private institution in the city. His Facebook page showed he did not post often, but some of what he did post included dark images and disturbing references to violent graphic novels and horror films.

Exploring his posts around the time his brother was killed, Joe found he responded to a friend that there were "people who have it coming" and "karma can be a bitch." But those were months before the killings started. He received many messages of condolence from friends, but as time went on, his posts and associated emails became fewer but darker.

Joe thought this kid needed to see a counselor, and he wondered if he had actually seen one. Even if they could get a counselor's name, he wouldn't be able to reveal much, if anything, given the confidentiality between doctor and patient. He felt certain the university would be unwilling to share Moeller's class schedule without a warrant. And the reasons for a warrant were flimsy at best right now.

Checking the Illinois Driver's License database, he found a current license for Jesse James Moeller. It listed his parents' address as his own rather than his off-campus residence. The license stated his height as six feet one inch and his weight as 185 pounds. What Joe briefly saw of him at his parents' home, coupled with his height and weight, suggested he could have a strong, muscular physique—strong enough to overpower his victims and plunge a knife into them.

He searched for Jess Moeller in Illinois' Vehicle Registration database. It showed Jess Moeller had a three-year-old blue BMW 5 Series registered in both his and his father's names. He noted the license plate number and looked up the car's year and model to see what it looked like. Typical BMW front and profile.

Next, Joe found Moeller's high school yearbook online and discovered Jess and his brother, Jeremy, were members of the swim team during their senior year. The team photo showed they had lean, well-muscled bodies. Jess would certainly be strong and athletic enough to quickly attack and stab a victim to death and dash away after decapitating them. But why decapitate his victims? Is he paying them back with the same kind of death experienced by his brother?

Joe checked the jury list again and discovered Jennifer Logan acted as the jury's foreman. He tried to think it out. *The "head" of the jury had her "head" cut off. Symbolic or coincidental? If it was symbolic, why was the second victim, Leah Sarandon, decapitated as well? Guilt by association, maybe? Did he like it? Did it satisfy his rage? Or was it a way to humiliate them?*

What Joe needed to find was Jess Moeller's address and determine whether he had a roommate or lived alone. After several searches, he came up empty-handed. He decided to call the law office of McBride, Wayne, Benson & Tyler to see if he could talk Victor McBride's secretary into sharing Jess Moeller's address. However, before making the call, he thought it best to ask Sam first.

"Have you found Jess Moeller's address?"

"I have," replied Sam. "McBride's secretary gave it to me."

"Good thinking. I was set to call McBride's office but didn't want to duplicate what you'd already done."

"I had to sweet-talk her. She wasn't going to give it to me, but I used my suave and debonair charm, and she became putty in my hand."

"It's getting deep in here."

"Hey. I got it, didn't I?"

"You did. Let's meet over lunch and discuss what we've found."

"You buying?" asked Sam.

"I guess so," smiled Joe, knowing that Sam probably owed him for a dozen such lunches in the last couple of years.

Over lunch at an Irish Pub that Sam picked out, they discussed what each of them had found. After sharing their findings, they began discussing how to move forward.

"You think we should start surveilling him?" asked Sam.

"I do. If he's the offender, he's not going to stop killing jury members until we stop him," replied Joe. "I'd be willing to bet he's already selected his next victim."

"He's had plenty of time. Probably stalking the person already."

"Maybe we can find out who it is if we can follow him and catch him observing someone."

"Hopefully, he isn't ready to make his move yet."

"Right."

"You know this means we'll have to start work earlier in the morning," said Sam. "I'm not crazy about getting up two hours early without being compensated for it."

"Yeah," replied Joe. "We'll need to run this past Lieutenant Bellamy. See if he'll agree to some overtime."

When they returned to their Area 3 office, they checked in with the sergeant sitting outside Lieutenant Bellamy's office. He told them to go in since Bellamy was not meeting with anyone at the moment.

After listening to their plan to surveil Jess Moeller, Bellamy said, "I don't have any money for overtime right now. But I can approve one of you coming in early and then leaving early. I can't do it for both of you at the same time since I need one of you here to cover your normal shift hours."

"We can switch off every other day," suggested Joe. "That way it won't fall on one of us to get up early every day."

"That okay with you?" asked Bellamy, looking at Sam.

"Yeah. Fine with me."

"Okay, then. I'll let the desk sergeant know what's going on. Good luck."

They left Bellamy's office, and Joe volunteered to come in early tomorrow morning and observe Jess Moeller's movements. Sam didn't argue.

"You know," said Sam. "It may be harder for Moeller to single out his victim now that the jury members have all been told to avoid making themselves vulnerable to an attack."

"Agreed," replied Joe. "But he's driven by his rage. I think he's smart enough to figure out a way. And, of course, not everyone will heed our advice. You know how people are—'It could never happen to me.'"

That evening, Joe explained the plan to Destiny.

She understood and approved the idea of surveilling Jess Moeller, saying, "Are you going to use one of your disguises again?"

"At some point, I might have to. I still have my wino clothing around somewhere."

"If it hasn't rotted away."

"I washed it before packing it up, you know."

"Still. I think it's in a storage container in the garage if I remember correctly."

"Moeller hasn't seen me. He walked in while Sam and I were sitting at the dining room table, where we were interviewing his father. But he didn't really look at us when he passed the doorway. I doubt he'll recognize either one of us if he happens to look our way."

"So, when do you start?"

"Tomorrow morning."

Chapter Forty-One

Joe woke up to his alarm, which he had set for four o'clock. He quietly slipped out of bed to avoid disturbing Destiny, who was sleeping beside him. Since he would not have time to jog on his surveillance days, he quickly showered and dressed in his usual clothing for his first day of surveilling Jess Moeller. Skipping breakfast, he picked up coffee and a breakfast croissant at a 24/7 mini-mart and drove to Moeller's apartment building on East Washington Street. He parked his Camaro half a block away.

Getting out of his car, Joe walked into the building's parking lot and located a blue BMW. He checked the license plate and confirmed it was the one listed for Moeller's vehicle. He re-parked his Camaro on an adjacent street so he would have a better view. The entrance to the building faced the parking lot, and he was now in a position to keep an eye on those coming and going.

Joe sat for hours watching the door but failed to see Moeller exit the building until after 10:30 a.m., when he saw him walking to his car. He followed Moeller's BMW to the DePaul University campus. Nothing suspicious happening this morning.

Joe drove to his office. Getting a much-needed coffee refill, he walked to Sam's desk. Sam noticed him approaching and looked up.

"Well?" said Sam.

"Nothing until around 10:30. Then Moeller drove to the DePaul campus. Going to class, I assume."

"What time did you start surveilling him?" asked Sam.

"Five o'clock. I figured since the earliest of the three attacks came at around

6:30, it would give me time to catch him coming out of the building early if he was going to stalk someone."

Nodding his head, Sam said, "Then, I'll do the same. I live about the same distance from Moeller's apartment as you do. I told Carolyn about it, and she said she'd get up and make me coffee to go."

"Wow! Lucky guy."

"I hope this early morning stuff doesn't go on for a month or more. She may change her mind."

"If you park on the side street north of the apartment building, you'll have a good view of the apartment's entrance door and the parking lot. Moeller's car was the only blue BMW in the lot when I checked."

Joe arrived home three hours early. It caught Destiny by surprise, even though he had told her he would be getting off early on the days he surveilled Jess Moeller.

"I kind of like you home early like this," she said.

"Getting up at four o'clock isn't much fun, though," replied Joe. "I hope this doesn't drag on too long."

"Aw," she teased.

* * *

While Joe was jogging the next morning, he received a phone call from Sam. That was unusual, so he assumed Sam's surveillance had proven fruitful. It was shortly after six o'clock.

"Hey, " Joe answered. "What's up?"

"Moeller left his apartment and drove to West Blackhawk Avenue. He parked there."

"What's he doing?"

"Sitting in his car. He's not doing anything but sitting there."

"He wasn't dressed in a black hoodie and sweatpants, was he?"

"No. A DePaul T-shirt and jeans."

"Okay. Wait a minute," said Sam. "He's getting out of his car. I'll need to call you back."

The call was abruptly ended, and Joe hoped Sam could determine what Moeller was doing so early in the morning. Forty minutes later, Sam called back.

"Well, he appeared to be observing someone."

"Could you tell who it was?" asked Joe.

"It was a woman. She walked from her apartment building to North Halsted, where she turned and walked to another building on West North Avenue. After she went inside, Moeller crossed the street and returned to his car. I ducked into an alley so he wouldn't see me. After he drove away, I checked out the building the woman entered. I looked around, but I couldn't find her. I got some photos of her walking down the street. Not very good ones, unfortunately."

"When you get back here," said Joe, "let's compare the addresses of the other jury members to the building this woman came out of. Maybe we can figure out who he was watching."

Sam came into the office forty minutes later. He gave Joe the address of the apartment building, and they began trying to determine which jury member lived there. Fifteen minutes later, Sam turned in his chair and said in a loud voice, "Joe! I got it."

Stepping to Sam's desk, Joe asked, "Who is it?"

"Judith Hazelton."

Joe was elated they had found out who she was. "Good work, Sam."

"We need to talk with her."

"And tell her what?" asked Joe.

"She could be in danger."

"We already did that. We don't want to freak her out and ruin Moeller's plans."

"Whoa!" Sam looked at Joe skeptically. "You're not thinking of keeping her in the dark so you can intercept the attack on her, are you?"

"Of course not," said Joe. "But I think we need to see if she'll cooperate with us first."

"What do you have in mind?"

"I agree that we need to talk with her and emphasize the fact that she's in danger. But what if we get an undercover policewoman who looks like her? Who can pass for her? She can walk the same route each morning, so if Moeller springs his attack, she'll be ready and able to defend herself. Then we can grab him."

"Okay. We'll have to put this together right away. We don't know when he'll make his move. Could be tomorrow for all we know."

"Right."

"We'd better run this past Lieutenant Bellamy ASAP.

Chapter Forty-Two

When Joe sat in his Camaro watching Jess Moeller's apartment complex the next day, he didn't have to wait long. After observing the building for twenty minutes, he saw Moeller come out the door carrying a small white trash bag filled with something. Instead of dropping the bag in the nearby dumpster, Moeller placed it on the passenger seat of his car when he got inside. *Strange. What's in the bag?*

Given the smooth look of the bag, Joe thought it might contain clothing, like the black sweats the offender dressed in when he attacked his victims. *Omigod,* wondered Joe. *Is today the day?*

He followed Moeller's BMW to a parking garage three blocks from West Blackhawk Avenue. Joe entered the same parking garage, driving past the blue BMW before locating an open parking space. Getting out of his Camaro, Joe left the parking garage carrying a briefcase so he would look less like a cop on surveillance if Moeller happened to see him.

As he stepped out onto the sidewalk, Joe spotted Moeller walking toward West Blackhawk Avenue carrying the trash bag under his arm. He crossed the street and walked parallel with Moeller, who was half a block ahead. Moeller turned the corner onto West Blackhawk Avenue, and after Joe crossed the street to follow him, Moeller was no longer in sight. *Shit! Where did he go? Did I get made?* He didn't think so. He looked innocent enough with his briefcase in hand. And Moeller never really saw him while he and Sam were at his parents' home. But where did he go?

Joe crossed the street to be on the same sidewalk where Moeller was walking. Not wanting to be seen, he ducked into a small alcove leading to the entrance of the first building. It kept him out of sight while he considered what to do next. Looking across the street, he saw an alley in the middle of the block. Was there a corresponding alley between buildings on this side of the street as well? If so, Moeller could be lurking there, waiting for Judith Hazelton to pass by. From there, he could jump out, attack her, pull her into the alley, and decapitate her. Then, he could escape through the alley to the next street. While deep in the alley, he would have a chance to change out of his bloody sweats and mask, stuff them in the garbage bag, and make his way back to the parking garage.

If Sam was here, he could have waited by Moeller's car to apprehend him with the bag of sweat clothes after Joe had surprised him and started chasing him down. But since he was alone, he wanted to catch Moeller stepping out of the alley to attack Hazelton. It was a dangerous idea, maybe even reckless, using Hazelton as bait like this. His timing had to be just right to ensure she would not be injured. He would have felt more confident if a policewoman was taking Hazelton's place, but that was not an option at this point. He was forced to improvise.

If his plan was going to work, Joe needed to be closer to the alley and in a position where Moeller could not see him. However, Hazelton would need to be visible to him as she walked past the mouth of the alley. He decided to stroll down the sidewalk carrying his briefcase, moving past the alley and hoping there would be a doorway he could use to conceal himself. Moeller would certainly check in each direction for possible witnesses before launching his attack.

Joe stepped out and began walking nonchalantly down the sidewalk past an alley. Out of the corner of his eye, he noticed a dumpster inside the alley. As he walked by, he realized it could be used to conceal an attacker. Should he flush Moeller out now to keep Hazelton safe? Or should he wait for him to attack so he could arrest him for attempted murder?

As luck would have it, the first building past the alley had a small alcove with one step up to the entry door. It provided a good vantage point.

About ten minutes later, Joe spotted Hazelton walking down the sidewalk and crossing the street to the block he was on. As she did, he briefly saw a hood peek out from the alley. Quickly, Joe pulled his head back so Moeller would not see him.

Pulling his Glock, Joe watched in anticipation. He could feel drops of sweat running down his neck as he watched Hazelton getting closer and closer. As Hazelton stepped into the mouth of the alley, Joe stepped out just as a black-masked figure burst from the alley with a knife held high in his left hand.

Hazelton became aware of Moeller when she saw Joe step out with his weapon raised. "POLICE! FREEZE!" yelled Joe as he prepared to shoot. Hazelton screamed and ducked down and away, falling onto the sidewalk. At the same time, the ninja-like attacker leaped away and dashed into the alley with Joe in hot pursuit. He wished he could have stayed to help Hazelton, but he could see she was probably more frightened than injured, and it was wiser for him to pursue and apprehend her assailant.

As he chased the attacker, Joe was yelling, "STOP! POLICE!" But the attacker kept running. And he was fast. Joe figured he could catch him if they were running a long distance since he had the endurance from jogging three miles a day. But the attacker's youth gave him an advantage, and he was sprinting away faster than Joe could run.

As he pursued, Joe called in his situation to the police and gave his location. Running at full speed out of the alley and across the next street, Joe narrowly missed getting hit by a passing car. Into the next alley, Joe was still in hot pursuit, but as the assailant fled across another street, Joe stopped, knowing he was not fast enough to catch him.

Rather than continue his pursuit, Joe decided to run to the parking garage and wait by Moeller's car. When he reached the blue BMW, he dropped to his hands and knees and concealed himself next to the car parked beside it. He refrained from calling in his location because he didn't want to risk police cruisers scaring Moeller off.

Twenty minutes later, Joe saw the reflection of a person in Moeller's car window. When he heard the BMW's door lock click and the driver's side door start to open, Joe jumped up with his Glock drawn.

"POLICE! FREEZE!" A startled Jess Moeller dropped the white garbage bag and froze in place.

"You try to run, and I'll shoot your ass! Now, put both hands on top of the car and spread 'em!"

Moeller hesitated.

"DO IT!" yelled Joe. A moment later, Moeller turned toward the car and put his hands on the roof.

Joe slid over the hood of the car he was hiding behind and cuffed him. Then he laid him over the hood and patted him down. No knife. He read him his rights from a card he carried and continued to hold him down over the hood.

"What the fuck? I didn't do anything," protested Moeller.

"That's what they all say," replied Joe as he gave him a jerk. "Now, don't you so much as twitch!"

With one hand on Moeller to keep him pinned to the hood, Joe called in his location for uniformed officers to transport the suspect. While waiting, several people passed by on the way to their cars and gave them curious or fearful looks. Holding up his ID, Joe repeated, "Chicago PD. Go about your business."

No more than five minutes later, a police cruiser from the 18th District pulled up, and a uniformed officer stepped out. Holding up his ID, Joe said, "This man is under arrest for attempted murder. He's been read his rights, so he needs to be transported."

"Got it," replied the officer, who grabbed Moeller by the collar and upper arm, placing him in the back seat of his cruiser.

Another cruiser pulled up, and Joe explained what had taken place to both uniformed officers. Then, he called for Evidence Technicians to evaluate the contents of the white garbage bag as well as the interior of the BMW. He hoped they would find blood evidence from the three previous attacks. Moeller was driven to District 18 Headquarters and placed in a holding cell.

Next, Joe called Sam to tell him about the arrest. Forty-five minutes later, Evidence Techs Art Casey and Jerry Bristow arrived. They worked for two hours taking samples and vacuuming the BMW's interior. They would examine the contents of the garbage bag, which included a black hoodie, sweatpants, and a ski mask, back in the lab, where they could be checked for blood. Joe believed Moeller must have disposed of the knife somewhere before returning to his car, since it was not on him or in the bag. After Casey and Bristow completed their work, uniformed officers oversaw the BMW being towed to the impound lot.

Uniformed officers searched for the missing knife and, after an extensive search, found a discarded knife with a seven-inch blade in a dumpster three blocks from the attack. It was sent to the crime lab, where it would be tested for fingerprints and DNA evidence.

That afternoon, Joe and Sam drove to District 18 Headquarters to interview Jess Moeller. His father, James, had already arrived, and he was speaking with Victor McBride, his attorney. They eyed Joe and Sam as they entered, but said nothing. Joe asked for Jess Moeller to be placed in an interrogation room so they could interview him. Jess was accompanied by McBride, who advised him not to answer any questions. That was that.

Outside the interrogation room, James Moeller accosted Joe and Sam about his son's arrest, his outburst drawing the attention of several officers. Joe looked at McBride, who had just come out of the interrogation room. "You need to control your client, Mr. McBride, because I'm about to arrest him for obstruction."

McBride pulled the elder Moeller aside and began trying to calm him down. Joe and Sam returned to Area 3 and asked the sergeant if they could see Lieutenant Bellamy. He happened to be available, and they entered his office with a sense of accomplishment, having made an arrest in the ongoing decapitation case.

"What's going on?" asked Bellamy. "I just got hold of a policewoman for your investigation."

"We made an arrest in the decapitation killings a short time ago," said Joe. "I caught our suspect in the act of attacking another member of the jury. Turns out it was Jess Moeller, the twin brother of Jeremy Moeller."

"So, we don't need the undercover policewoman, after all," said Sam.

"That's good news," said Bellamy. "Solid arrest?"

"In addition to catching him in the act, I think we could have DNA evidence that confirms he's the killer," said Joe.

"Good work, guys," smiled Bellamy. "Good work."

Jess Moeller was arraigned on a charge of attempted murder. Given he was a suspect in two murders and an additional attack, his request for bail was denied.

When Joe arrived home that day, he was anxious to share the good news with Destiny. He entered the kitchen from the garage and found her on the phone with her mother. To celebrate, he poured himself a glass of Pinot Noir and sat down at the island with Autumn in his lap. Several minutes later, Destiny finished her call and came in.

"Well, look at you two," she said. "I have good news about Mom. She went in for a scan a couple of days ago, and she got word today that there was no sign of cancer. Of course, she'll need to be monitored for the next several years just to make sure."

"That's wonderful," said Joe. "I'll bet she's breathing easier about it now."

"Oh. She is. And so am I."

"Well, I have good news, too," he smiled.

"And what's that?"

"I apprehended the decapitation killer this morning."

"Wow. That's great," said Destiny. She stepped to where he was sitting and gave him a big kiss. "I knew you would. You and Sam are the best. Who was it?"

"Jess Moeller, the twin brother of Jeremy Moeller."

"Really. Well…"

"I appreciate your help."

"I didn't do anything."

"Oh, yeah, you did."

"Well, this calls for a celebration, don't you think?"

Destiny called in a reservation at their favorite Russian restaurant, and after a wonderful meal, they held hands as they walked around the area, looking in store windows and talking about taking a vacation.

"A vacation, huh? Where would you like to go?" asked Joe.

"Italy."

"Italy?" he asked, surprised she was thinking of a foreign country.

"Yeah. I've always wanted to see Rome, Florence, Venice. Haven't you? See the Coliseum, Michelangelo's David, ride down a Venetian canal in a gondola."

"Yeah, but I never thought of it as a vacation. I didn't think I would have the chance to travel abroad until I retired and had the time."

"We need to make the time. There's no time like the present, as they say. And there's no one else I'd rather see it with than you."

"Well then, I'll tell you what," said Joe. "Why don't you plan it? Fall would be a nice time to go, don't you think?"

Chapter Forty-Three

Evidently, Jess Moeller did not realize that DNA does not disappear entirely by simply running blood-stained clothing through a washing machine or a knife under a faucet. The police lab was able to recover DNA evidence from his hoodie, gloves, sweatpants, and the knife, which was traced to an online purchase he had made. Once the DNA results came in, it proved Jess Moeller was connected to the attacks on Jennifer Logan, Leah Sarandon, and Quentin Rosberg.

While Jess' father urged Victor McBride to plead his son innocent and go to trial, McBride convinced him that the best course of action was to seek a plea deal since the evidence against Jess was overwhelming.

Given the heinous nature of the killings, the District Attorney refused to downgrade the murder charges, but he was willing to drop the two attempted murder charges for a plea of guilty in the deaths of Jennifer Logan and Leah Sarandon.

Jess Moeller pleaded guilty to two counts of first-degree murder. The judge referred to the heinous nature of his crimes before imposing two life sentences without the possibility of parole. Moeller was transferred to the Illinois Department of Corrections, where he is currently incarcerated at the Dixon Correctional Center in Dixon, Illinois. He will spend the rest of his life there and never taste freedom again.

Acknowledgments

Joyce Johanson; Detective Timothy O'Brien, Chicago PD; Shawn Reilly Simmons; Verena Rose; Deb Well; and the staff of Level Best Books.

About the Author

Lynn-Steven Johanson is an award-winning playwright and novelist. Reviewers and readers alike have praised his Joe Erickson Mystery novels. His plays have earned numerous awards and have been staged across the United States, the U.K., India, Australia, New Zealand, and the Kingdom of Bahrain. Johanson holds a Master of Fine Arts degree from the University of Nebraska-Lincoln and is retired from Western Illinois University. He and his wife live in downstate Illinois and have three adult children.

AUTHOR WEBSITE:
  https://LSJohanson.com

SOCIAL MEDIA HANDLES:
  Facebook: https://facebook.com/streetsofmarathon
  Twitter: https://twitter.com/JohansonLS
  Instagram: https://instagram.com/lsjohanson
  LinkedIn: https://www.linkedin.com/in/lynn-steven-johanson
  Bluesky: https://ajoeericksonmystery.social

Also by Lynn-Steven Johanson

Rose's Thorn

Havana Brown

Corrupted Souls

One of Ours

Sins Revealed

Reprisal Road